Beckside Lights

John Ackworth

BECKSIDE LIGHTS

BY

JOHN ACKWORTH,

1897

TO MY WIFE

INTRODUCTION

THIS volume is in reality a continuation of *Clog Shop Chronicles*, and a few words of explanation are here inserted for the assistance of those who may not have read the former book.

At the time of which we write, Beckside was a small Lancashire mill-village, situated on the south side of Brogden Clough, an irregular sort of glen running almost due east and west. The only public buildings in the place were the schoolhouse and the little Methodist Chapel. The latter stood on the right, just as you came down the hill along the highroad from Duxbury. A little farther down, on the left, stood the Clog Shop, the little irregular row of cottages at the eastern end of which it stood forming the top or south side of a triangle, made by the abrupt turning of the highway down towards the Beck, and by Mill Lane, which led through the mill-yard on to Beckbottom and Clough End.

The Clogger was the chief official at the chapel, and, being of a somewhat self-assertive disposition, he had become in course of time the ruling spirit of the village. Long Ben, a tall, bony, mild-tempered carpenter, was his lieutenant. And Sam Speck, a small-featured man living on a small annuity, acted as henchman to both. Besides these there were Lige the road-mender, Jonas Tatlock the choirmaster, Nathan the Smith, and Jethro the knocker-up. These worthies resorted to the Clog Shop at all convenient times, and there discussed such topics as the life of the village provided. And it is these conversations and the circumstances connected with them which are here detailed. The dialect is that spoken in the neighbourhood of Bolton.

CONTENTS

THE STUDENT.

SQUIRE'S lat ta-neet," said Sam Speck, turning the palms of his hands to the Clog Shop fire and looking towards the window with a vain assumption of indifference; "bud he allis is when yo' wanten him."

"'Specially upo' th' plan neet," added Lige the road-mender. "Aw've noaticed it naa fur mony a ye'r."

"He does it o' pupuss," snapped Sam irritably; and then, after a pause, he added, "He keeps a horse as is a disgrace to th' village. As owd as Mathusalam an' as booany as a herrin'."

Now, Squire Taylor, the unlucky object of this abuse, was the village greengrocer, who on Fridays became the village carrier, and brought from Duxbury the various consignments of goods sent out to Beckside. He was the usual medium of communication between Beckside Methodism and its ecclesiastical chief, bringing the book parcel once a month, and the new plans every quarter. These plans were of course objects of great interest to the frequenters of the Clog Shop, and so the night on which they arrived was always one of great importance; and to sit waiting for Squire's arrival, and to unite in denouncing his dilatory ways, became a regular part of the quarterly programme.

On this occasion, however, the interest was greater than usual, for it was the first plan after the reopening of the chapel, and several times lately the "super" had dropped mysterious but eagerly accepted hints about the new importance of Beckside, and his intention to improve its pulpit supply.

Hitherto the position of the village amongst the other places in the circuit had been a somewhat lowly one. It ranked amongst the smallest, was supplied chiefly by the less distinguished of the local preachers, and had for years been a sort of starting-place for young aspirants to pulpit fame. In fact, the "exhorters" so inevitably opened their commissions' at Beckside, and received their first heckling in the Clog Shop parlour afterwards, that the village had acquired amongst the preachers the title of the "College," and many a luckless wight remembered it as the scene of his first and *last* appearance in the pulpit.

Our Beckside friends were quite aware of their dubious distinction, and whilst grimly satisfied to be "a terror to evil doers," or those who couldn't do at all, they had long protested against being practised upon by "ivvery Jack-i'-th'-box as thinks he can preich." But now, of course, in the enlarged chapel, things would be different, and the expected new plan would show them in their true position.

"Plans," cried a stentorian voice outside, and the door was burst hastily open. A small roll of papers came flying into the shop, striking Isaac, the apprentice, on the head, and rebounding, extinguished his candle, whilst a volley of more or less uncomplimentary expletives was fired at the invisible and retreating carrier by those around the Clog Shop fire.

"If Aw thowt he'd done that o' pupuss"—began the injured Isaac, as he rose from his seat and commenced to relight his candle. But Sam Speck had stepped across the shop, and, pushing the apprentice on one side, he grabbed at the roll of plans, and returned hastily to his seat.

Sam appeared to be about to open the roll himself, and, in fact, had already commenced to do so, knowing only too well that if it passed into Jabe's hands they would be some time before they got any information, as the Clogger always held the parcel tight, and would neither distribute the plans nor even read out the appointments until he had carefully examined things for himself. But as Sam hesitated, the Clogger reached out his hand with a significant gesture.

"When thaa gets my shop [appointment] tha'st dew my wark," he said sternly, and Sam was constrained to surrender the parcel, whilst the rest resigned themselves to wait as patiently as possible until

Jabe should have got through his characteristically deliberate preliminaries and be ready to give them information.

A minute or two elapsed, during which Jabe was untying the string round the plans, refilling his pipe, and searching for and carefully cleaning his best spectacles. Then, adjusting the glasses upon his nose with extraordinary care, he slowly opened the crackling paper, and with a grossly overdone appearance of indifference glanced all round the floral-border of the plan, ran his eye leisurely down the column of the preachers' names, scanned the notices, and even scrutinised the printer's name, just as if the word Beckside did not appear on the sheet at all, and just as if five intensely curious men were not waiting "on tenter-books" to have the Beckside appointments read out to them.

At length the Clogger's eye wandered to that place low down on the plan where he knew by long experience he would find the most important of all place-names. And as he struck Beckside and began to run his eye along the plan, he suddenly started to his feet, crying, in tones of intensest amazement—

"Well, Aw'll be bothert!"

"Whey? Whey? Wot's up, Jabe?" cried one or two, whilst Sam Speck tried to dodge round behind the Clogger, and look over his shoulder. But the wiser ones sat still and said nothing.

"Wot's up?" shouted Jabe, swinging round out of Sam's reach, and holding the plans high up. "Didn't Aw tell yo' as Beckside wur summat naa? We'en getten a sthudent planned fuss Sunday."

Every man in the company seemed suddenly to become taller, their faces assumed expressions of grave dignity, and every man became clamorous for his own copy of the plan. Then Jabe fetched Isaac's candle, and, curtly bidding that worthy to "Ger off whoam," he brought it and fixed it in an old mill bobbin, to afford extra light for the important business in hand. Returning to their seats, and using, those in the chimney-nook the fire, and the rest the lamp and candle, they were soon eagerly and silently scrutinising the all-absorbing sheet.

"Ther's noabry else hez a sthudent bur uz and Duxbury," said Long Ben, with his shaggy black beard nearly singeing in the fire.

"Neaw, that's it," replied Jabe; "they'n ne'er been planned noawheer bud Duxbury afoor."

The rest lifted their heads and looked steadily at each other to assist themselves in comprehending the full significance of this great fact, and then Lige added emphatically—

"Wee'st ha' noa mooar hupstart exhausters here, yo'll see."

Then the other appointments were examined, and a somewhat lengthy discussion arose as to whether Billy Fatcake, who had been certainly quite welcome in former days, and Hallelujah Tommy, who had the fatal misfortune to be a Clough Ender, were quite up to the newly-acquired importance of Beckside. But the debate lost much of its heat and asperity from the fact that the first appointment had given a satisfaction which no ordinary matter could disturb.

Next day was Saturday, and by Sunday the Clog Shop magnates had schooled themselves into a becoming modesty on the subject of the new plan. The preacher for the day was a brother from an adjoining circuit, a great crony of Jabe's, and consequently a person of interest and influence to all the rest of the village.

"Dun yo' iver hev' ony sthudents at yore chapil?" asked Jabe, as the pipes were being lighted after supper.

"Neaw; an' we dooan't want," was the answer, in sharp, raspy tones, as if the question had touched a sore place.

All the Becksiders exchanged glances of surprise and concern.

"Whey not?" asked Jabe, in a slightly resentful tone.

"Whey not? When we goon ta th' chapil i' Sharpley we goon fur t' yer th' gospil, and no' Greek and grammar and shirt-neck."

There was a long pause, during which every man present stared at the speaker with wide-opened eyes, and Sam and Lige turned and nodded at each other in a manner expressive of unutterable things. But the preacher broke in again—

"Them colleges 'ull be th' ruin o' Methodism, yo'll see. They goon theer dacent, modest lads, an' afoor they'n bin theer mony wik they're aw cooat and collar and white neck-clout. Thank goodness! noabry ne'er shoved a grammar daan my throttle."

Now, it would have been impossible for the speaker to have found better soil into which to drop his seeds of prejudice than that provided in the minds of those to whom he was talking. For if there was one thing upon which they were more completely agreed than another, it was that pride was the blackest of all sins, and especially so when it appeared in the pulpit, and they shared to the full the common suspicion of their class against all unsanctified learning. The speaker's words, therefore, came like a heavy wet blanket upon the hopes and self-gratulations they had indulged concerning the coming student, and when the preacher departed he left behind him six depressed and sulky men.

When he had gone, and a gloomy quiet had settled on the company, Long Ben broke silence for the first time that night by staring hard at the oatcake-rack over his head and reciting as if he had been saying a lesson—

"'Wrath is cruel and anger is outrageous, but who shall stand before envy?'"

Nobody seemed to understand what Ben's quotation had reference to, but, as he was much given to such mysterious allusiveness, nobody was greatly disturbed. Jabe, indeed, looked for a moment as though he were going to ask a question, but repenting suddenly, he also lapsed into despondent silence.

Several times that evening, and in the early days of the week following, Ben tried to raise discussion on the subject of the coming representative of the "Hinstitewshon," but without success. Towards the end of the week certain mysterious hints began to be dropped as to what would happen if the student turned out to be of the character hinted at by last Sunday's preacher, and when it was found that in consequence of an interesting domestic event at the Fold Farm, and the absence of the doctor in London, the student would have to be entertained somehow at the Clog Shop, every man who was present when the arrangement was concluded looked at Jabe with such expressive commiseration in his eyes that the old Clogger began to feel something of the hallowed delights of minor martyrdom.

All day on Saturday Aunt Judy was busy "fettlin' up" at the Cloggery in preparation for the advent of the stranger. Jabe was manifestly depressed. He was also strangely uneasy. He kept coming out of the shop into the parlour where Judy was busy, without any visible reason for so doing; and at last, when his sister began to tell him where he would find various eatables she had provided for the week-end, he turned round as he was leaving the parlour and snapped out with quite unaccountable temper—

"Dust think Aw'm gooin' to molly-coddle fur yond' chap fur tew days? Aw'll ler him clem fust! Tha mun come an' feed him thisel', if tha wants him feedin'."

Now Judy quite understood what was the matter with her irascible brother, had been, in fact, expecting some such demand, and had come prepared to stay. She knew that Jabe was secretly in great fear of being left alone with the student. So she hung her shawl behind the parlour door, and settled down as the temporary mistress of the Clog Shop.

Meanwhile Jabe, though evidently relieved, was still very uneasy. The statement of his friend from Sharpley as to students in general had grievously disappointed him, but it was so entirely in harmony with his own suspicions as to the ungodly character of learning and

6

its disastrous effects on religious life, and so fully confirmed his opinions as to the "forradness" and "pompiousness" of the rising generation, that he greatly feared it would turn out to be only too true. If it did turn out so, he was morally certain he would not be able to restrain himself all the time from Saturday to Monday, but would be sure to explode upon the student. And if he kept down his own chagrin, he would not be able to restrain his friends, for they were already charged to the full with anticipatory resentment, and were so well primed as to require very little indeed to set them off.

But then the student was to be his guest, and a Lancashire villager's ideas of hospitality are as high as those of the Arabs, and it would be a most shocking thing to be entertaining a man and "basting" him at the same time. The dilemma worried him, and the whole thing created in his mind an impression distinctly unfavourable to the coming visitor.

A little later, Sam Speck arrived, and was ordered, in tones he knew better than to resist, to meet the coach and bring the student home.

As the time of arrival drew near, Jabe seated himself in an arm-chair, and in his shirt-sleeves and his best clothes waited the great arrival, pulling nervously the while at a clean churchwarden.

"Aw reacon it 'ull be a mee-mawin' donned-up, grammarified young sprig o' some sooart!" he said to Judy in tones of depreciation, but before she could express her evidently different opinion the front door opened and Sam Speck stepped over the sanded floor, ushering in the student.

Jabe's fears were abundantly confirmed.

A tall, smart, well-dressed young cleric, with kid gloves, a silk hat, irreproachable linen, and—saddest sign of ministerial worldliness— a hair watch-chain with gold mountings, and a gold locket that dangled itself aggressively before jabe's very eyes.

Jewellery in the pulpit was the most unendurable of all things in Beckside, as more than one preacher had found to his cost, and Jabe was telling himself that it was no use resisting the inevitable, and that, guest or no guest, he would have to deliver his soul, when the stranger stepped up to him with easy confidence and shook him heartily by the hand, which still further confirmed Jabe's conviction that he would have to do some painful taking down.

Then the student greeted Aunt Judy as Mrs. Longworth, and thereby discovered Jabe's peculiar opinion of women, on which he took Mrs. Judy's part, and became quite animated in his defence of the gentler sex. Jabe had the utmost difficulty in preventing himself from reminding this assured young man of his age, and by way of avoiding it, pointed to the table, and invited his guest to "Reich tew an' get yore baggin'."

Whilst the student ate, talking chiefly to Aunt Judy, and getting thereby on most excellent terms with her, Jabe was quietly taking stock of him—examining him slowly from head to foot a dozen times, and coming back after each scrutiny to that ungodly gold locket. Sam Speck, too, seemed in a meditative frame of mind, and sat looking into the fire with a company smirk on his small face.

Then Long Ben came in, followed by Jethro and Lige, each man nodding with a stiff "How do?" to the stranger, and then sidling off into a chair, which was gradually turned round to an angle from which the visitor could be furtively examined.

Somehow it was difficult to get a conversation started; and though the student, having finished tea and declined an invitation to "smook," drew briskly up to the fire and plunged at once into the most popular Methodist topics of the hour, he was unable to get on, his companions sitting there in impenetrable silence, and answering—when they answered at all—in freezing monosyllables.

At length, after a depressing pause, Long Ben asked a question which set the student off describing the "institution" and its ways. He waxed eloquent on the learning and ability of the tutors, told stories of the college prayer-meeting, and gave several instances of success achieved by his fellow-students on their preaching excursions.

Every man in the company was listening intently, expecting every next word to contain some allusion to the student's own oratorical triumphs. But though they waited with studiously stolid faces, the expected reference never came, and they were not able to detect the note of conceit they were all confidently anticipating.

"An' dun *yo'* ne'er ha' noa convarsions?" asked Long Ben at last.

"Y-e-s," said the student, suddenly very sober; "but not so many as I should like." And he flushed slightly and coughed apologetically, whilst every man in the company seemed lost in far-off contemplation. But the student had scored his first point.

"Tell uz abaat some of yore good toimes," said Aunt Judy, coming forth from the scullery, where it was not supposed she had been listening.

"Well, I haven't had many conversions, I'm sorry to say," was the answer, with a shadow on the speaker's face, and a little sigh, "but I had one little bit of encouragement about two months ago. I was out from college, and had to walk in the afternoon to a place across some fields. As I went along with a friend we overtook a poor woman who looked very wretched. I got into conversation with her about good things, and when we parted I invited her to come to the evening service. She did so, to my surprise, and, ah—well, she was converted that night, and then she told me she had been a bad woman, and was on her way to drown herself when I spoke to her,"

The tale was rather lamely told, but to those listening to it, its halting style greatly enhanced its value.

"Han yo' yerd owt o' th' woman sin'?" asked Ben, with shining eyes.

"Yes," said the student hesitatingly; "she sent me a chain made out of her own hair, and with a locket on it containing a little copy of my text on that evening."

"An' is that it yo' han on?" asked Jabe.

"Yes," said the student; and the Clogger began to vow vengeance on his friend from Sharpley.

When they left that night every man in the company shook hands with the stranger, and the good man did not know how great a compliment they were paying him by so doing. His appearance certainly had prejudiced them to begin with, but his frank, hearty, unassuming manner had severely shaken those prejudices.

Jabe had already thawed considerably, and before they retired he had waxed quite confidential, as the young preacher listened with evident appreciation to all the details of the rebuilding of their beloved sanctuary.

Next morning, however, the Clogger's hopes were somewhat dashed when he found his guest carefully conning a manuscript as he waited for breakfast. A more disturbing sign could not well have appeared, for Beckside could not away with "parrotty papper" in the pulpit. The consequence was, therefore, that Jabe drew into his shell again, and the student was chilled.

And the morning's sermon, though it was far from the least suspicion of paraded learning, deepened the Clogger's discontent. It was far too pat and glib for so young a man. Hesitancy and confusion would have been more becoming, and Lige expressed the opinions of most of the recognised sermon testers when he shook the preacher by the hand at the bottom of the pulpit stairs, and said, loud enough for all to hear—

"If tha'll put a bit mooar ginger into that sarmon, it 'ull be a fizzer."

But, then, as he saw Long Ben nodding emphatic endorsement from the side pew, and Nathan and Sam grinning approvingly from behind the choir curtains, Lige lost his head and added the reckless and dangerously compromising statement—

"Tha'll be fit fur t' preich aar Sarmons some day if tha goes on."

That was the worst of Lige, he never knew when to stop. What was the use of putting such an utterly unlikely idea into the young man's head. Only very great men indeed preached the Sermons, and even they felt it to be a great honour. Besides, wasn't pride the one deadly danger of the class to which the student belonged, and wasn't it the sacred duty of all experienced Christians to do their very utmost to keep it out of the hearts of those so tempted?

So Lige was in disgrace all day, and Jabe felt it to be his bounden duty to remove any vain hope which might have sprung up in the young man's heart by telling him of all the illustrious stars who had officiated at those memorable annual celebrations.

The evening sermon tasted better. It was freer, warmer, simpler,—a plain gospel appeal in fact; and when the preacher in the after-meeting told, in husky tones, the story of his own conversion, the character of students had been redeemed in Beckside, and the anxious responsibles who gathered in Jabe's parlour felt as nearly contented as it was possible to do under the circumstances.

Just as they were drawing up to the table for supper, a timid knock was heard at the front door, and Judy hastened to open it. After a minute or two's earnest whispering, she came hurrying back, crying, "Howd on a minute," and turning to the student, she continued—

"Ther's a wench here wants her babby kessening. Yo'd better dew it afoor yo' begin."

"Oh, but I can't! I daren't!" cried the student in alarm. "I'm not ordained, you know; I really cannot."

"Of course he conna," said Jabe oracularly, and rising from his seat, he limped to the door to inspect the applicant. Aunt Judy tried to intercept him, but he dodged her, and was soon heard speaking in stern, hard words to the invisible mother.

"Whether yo' con kessen gradely childer or not, yo' conna kessen yond'," he said to the student as he resumed his seat a moment later at the table, flashing at the same time a look of peculiar significance at Long Ben, who hung his head.

The student blushed as the meaning of the Clogger's words dawned upon him, and a very awkward pause ensued.

Anxious to find a topic on which conversation could be safely started again, the young preacher glanced up towards the joists, and noticing an odd-shaped green baize bag hanging there, he asked—

"That isn't a bass viol, is it?"

"If yo' guessen ageean yo'll guess wrung," answered Jabe, following the direction of the student's eyes.

"Then I suppose you play it, do you, Mr. Longworth? "

Every mouth stopped eating, and every eye was turned upon Jabe as he answered with an elaborate affectation of indifference—

"Ther's noabry else played on't for this last thurty ye'r, at ony rate."

The student expressed his delight, acknowledged he could fiddle a bit himself, and Jethro, Nathan, and Sam Speck hastily finished their supper, and went off to fetch their instruments, so that in a few moments the preacher had his choice of three.

The student certainly could fiddle, and he knew all the good tunes,— i.e. the old tunes, "tunes as wur tunes," as Jethro, the greatest of the Beckside musical authorities, declared. Then he played one or two new tunes, which were received with carefully-guarded approval.

And then Jethro and Sam Speck gave their visitor a sample of Beckside "Sarmons" music, and then another and another, until the evening seemed gone in no time, and it became unmistakably evident, by the way she poked at the fire, and ostentatiously brought clog-chips from the workshop and piled them on the parlour hob, that Aunt Judy thought it was time for them to be gone.

But again that timid knock came at the front door, and Judy, with a startled exclamation, hurried, as fast as her bulky form would allow her, to open it. Then an excited but whispered conversation was heard going on outside, and presently Judy came back with desperate resolution written on her face. She hastened across the parlour into the scullery, and in a moment came out with a white china basin filled with water, which she placed on a table before the student.

"Mestur" she cried in agitated tones, "that poor wench at th' dur has a babby as hoo shouldn't have. Bud hoo were browt up i' aar schoo', and her muther lies i' th' chapil yard. Hoo knows hoo's dun wrung, bud hoo doesn't want fur t' dew wrung to her babby. An' hoo's bin to th' Brogden vicar, and he winna kessen it; and hoo's tramped aw th' way to th' Hawpenny Gate, an' he winna; bud, Mestur, Aw think Him as yo' bin preichin' abaat ta-neet 'ud dew it if He wur here, an' wot He could dew yo' con dew, and chonce it."

There was a sob and a rustle at the door, and a pale, shamefaced factory girl stepped forward, unwrapping as she did so a bundle containing a five-weeks-old baby, and sobbing audibly the while.

"Look at it, Mestur," she cried, holding out her little one. "It's as bonny as ony o' them 'at Jesus tewk in His arms," and then, pressing closer and almost forcing the baby upon him, she pleaded—

"Tak' it, Mestur, tak' it. Aw know *Aw'm* aat o' th' kingdom o' God, but Aw dunnot want mi babby to be."

In a moment the student, with face all awork, had snatched the wee thing from its pleading mother, and was offering a simple prayer for it as he held it in his arms. Then he sprinkled it in the "Blessed Names," and, still holding it, prayed again,—prayed for babe and mother too,—and then, as he handed the infant back, his eyes wet with tears, he stooped down and tenderly kissed it.

"God bless yo' fur that" cried the agitated mother; "an' ha'iver lung yo' live, an' wheriver yo' goa, yo' con remember as there's wun poor woman as 'ull allis be prayin' for yo', if hoo is nowt but a nowty factory wench an' a woman as is a sinner."

And then she hugged her little one to her breast, and again blessing the student, departed; and Jabe, with face struggling between embarrassment and joy, and tears that wouldn't keep back, seized the student by the hand, and, wringing it until he winced again, he cried—

"If we liven till next Wis-sunday, yo'st preich th' Sarmons!"

LEAH'S LOVER.

I.

THE BLACK SHEEP.

SUNDAY SCHOOL was being held in the new schoolroom one hot Sunday afternoon some months after the reopening of the chapel.

The superintendent was temporarily absent, and Lige, who was taking his place, though he frowned dreadfully in rather grotesque imitation of his great model, had none of the terrors for juvenile minds with which Jabe inspired them, and so the order of the school was scarcely what it ought to have been.

The boys in the Testament classes were pitching their voices high, and fiercely competing as to who should read loudest, the work being done with a peculiar intonation supposed to be the correct thing by all Beckside juveniles.

In the mixed and rather crowded infant class, whilst a few were giving the teacher languid attention and some were fast asleep, two were standing behind the teacher and helping each other to drink out of a small bottle containing that best wine of Beckside childhood—Spanish juice water. Three more were trying to get sound out of a wicken whistle they had made by a peculiar method of treating the bark of a certain soft wood, and started guiltily when the desired sound unexpectedly came.

The top classes of youths and maidens, though removed from each other by the width of the school, were contriving to hold such communications as only the mystic telegraphy of youth admits, and the little girls were making pocket-handkerchief rabbits, retrimming each other's hats, and glancing longingly every now and again towards the desk, impatient for the moment of release.

15

Presently a little door leading out of the chapel vestry opened, and in walked Jabe, Ben, and Nathan the smith. None of these gentlemen could ever be charged with lack of seriousness in facial expression, but now, as they appeared, their countenances were positively alarming in owlish portentousness. Jabe limped to the desk, with slow, impressive manner; and after heaving a deep sigh and glancing nervously towards the young men's class, he rang the bell and cried—

"Silence, childer! Put th' beuks away;" and the sad sternness of his tone caused several of the teachers and most of the elder scholars to glance up inquiringly at him.

When the box-seats had all been filled with books, and two small boys had been "seaused" on the ears for banging the lids, Jabe rang the bell again. He really seemed very uncomfortable, and mopped his face and nearly bald head with a great red cotton handkerchief, whilst Ben and Nathan, seated behind him, held down their heads with a fidgety, apprehensive look.

"Aw ne'er thowt Aw should iver see this day," began the Clogger, shaking his head and looking round on the upturned faces; and Ben and Nathan groaned sympathetically.

"Aw've bin th' shuper o' this schoo' for welly thirty ye'r, bud Aw ne'er thowt we should come to this."

By this time every eye in the school was upon him; even the infants, who understood little of what was being said, realised that there was a new and significant tone in Jabe's voice, and stopped their pranks to listen.

After another pause and another laborious employment of his handkerchief,—for heat and excitement were both telling upon him,—he seemed to get the better of his feelings, and changing his voice to sudden sternness, he demanded—

"Whoa wur it as blacked his face an' went a pace-eggin' [mumming] last Yester [Easter], and welly feart owd Nanny aat of her wits?"

Some dozen small boys immediately answered, "Luke Yates"; and there were signs of unwonted excitement in the young men's class.

"An' whoa wur it as went riding th' Stang up Slakey Broo just afoor last Wis-Sunday?"

Again came the answer from at least twice as many juveniles as before—

"Luke Yates."

Then Jabe, raising his voice, and almost shouting in angry sternness, continued—

"An' whoa wur it as ran a race fur brass yesterday amung bettors an' gamblers an' pidgin-flyers?"

Grand unanimous chorus of small boys "Luke Yates."

And then Jabe raised his eyes from the scholars and looked round at the windows and walls, and apostrophising them, cried, with a break in his voice—

"An' his fayther wur a local preicher!"

A young fellow in the first class, with short red hair, brown laughing eyes, and a mischievous mouth, suddenly dropped his head, and all his classmates glanced at him with painful interest.

After another pause of most uncomfortable stillness, Jabe went on—

"We'en done aw as we con fur him. We'en talked to him, an' we'en prayed wi' him. Bud we conna goa on no longer o' thisunce. Aw ne'er thowt Aw should live to see a scholar o' this schoo' turnt aat.

Bud Aw have. An' Aw feel that ill abaat it Aw could start o' skriking."

Jabe's quivering chin fell on his breast for a moment, and then raising his head and looking at the red-haired youth, he said in a husky, tremulous voice—

"Tak' thi cap, an' away wi' thi."

Luke sat perfectly still, and his generally merry, impudent face became suddenly white and drawn.

"Dust yer me? Away wi' thi," shouted Jabe more sternly, stretching out his hand and pointing towards the door.

Long Ben, from behind, gasped, "Lord, help him," and Nathan was rubbing one side of his head, as he generally did under unusual mental disturbance.

Jabe's own face was a struggle between stern resolution and something very close to tears, whilst the youth addressed, after hesitating a moment, slowly rose to his feet, and, with a sickly attempt at a laugh, reached his cap from the peg over his head and strode towards the door.

As he was turning round the corner of the last form, however, an irresistible fit of his old mischievousness seemed to seize him suddenly, and turning defiantly round, and facing the whole school, he made a grotesquely elaborate bow and cried, "Gooid-day, and gooid shuttance," and then shooting a quick, stealthy glance at the teacher of the lowest girls' class, who was, perhaps, the only person in the school who was not watching his departure, and whose fine little head was bowed, whilst two round spots of flaming feeling glowed on cheeks of marble, he hastily opened the door and disappeared.

Now, nobody noticed Luke's quick glance, neither did anybody notice the white flame-spotted cheeks of the young person towards whom he threw it. And if they had noticed it, nobody, in Beckside at any rate, would have been surprised; for Leah Barber, Ben's eldest daughter, was the one person in the school who would be certain to endorse the superintendent's action.

Leah was a quiet, staid little Puritan, almost prudish in her manner, but with an intense attachment to the chapel, and a whole-hearted interest in its affairs. She had little in common with the girls of her age, and her name was generally omitted from the flirtation gossip so popular with her sex.

When Billy Botch began to "shape" for the ministry, one or two had suggested the suitability of a match between Leah and the young preacher; but Billy went away without giving any sign, and everybody knew without being told that, whatever she felt, nobody was ever likely to get anything out of Leah. The Beckside youths stood in awe of her; the one or two rash spirits who had ventured to approach her with amatory intentions suddenly repented of their attempts; and Jack Westhead, the latest of her wouldbe lovers, declared, after the second experiment, "Hoo isna a flesh an' blooid wench at aw, hoo's a lump o' icet."

Besides, she was so mature and serious in all her deportment, and seemed so entirely given up to chapel and school affairs, that she appeared to have neither time nor inclination for the ordinary interests of maidenhood.

The peculiar expression on her face, therefore, as the disgraced Luke disappeared through the school door, was just such as everyone would expect; and those who retained any lingering sympathy for the banished scholar, knew perfectly well that it was useless to go to her for support.

It was a pity she was so cold, and that her standard of conduct was so exacting, for outwardly she was very attractive. The smooth roundness of youth softened a face that would otherwise have been almost severe. She had features of faultless regularity, was a trifle above medium height, and had limbs that were nearly perfect in their modelling. Every movement was graceful, and would have been more so but for that restrainedness which ruled the spirit that governed them. Her skin was marble white, and her full, dark eyes, screened by long eyelashes, would have been dangerous gifts indeed to a girl of a different spirit. She dressed with almost Quaker-like plainness, but had her full share of that air of superiority which such plainness sometimes gives to those who practise it. Nobody could have passed her as she walked home from school that hot afternoon without noticing her, but he who looked twice would also think twice before needlessly accosting her.

In Long Ben's parlour, where tea was always laid on Sundays in honour of the day, nothing was talked about but the event which had taken place at school. Ben himself, divided between a judgment which endorsed Jabe's action and a tender heart which regretted it, said little. Mrs. Ben held forth very earnestly on the subject, holding up the abandoned Luke as a terrible warning to Ben, junior, and his twin-brother Andrew; whilst the two younger girls raked their memories for bygone transgressions of the wretched Luke, which they retailed with unconscious but impressive embellishments.

But Leah said not a word, although, as she never said much, nobody noticed the omission.

Ben's workshop stood end on to Sally's Entry, a short cut to the mill, and faced the road. Next to the shop came the woodyard, which was separated from the house and garden by a flag fence, backed up by a row of shrubs. The house stood back from the workshop, having a small garden in front and a larger one behind.

The front garden was given up to flowers, and as Leah was chief gardener, and had a weakness for old-fashioned flowers, the whole patch was on this particular Sunday one mass of bloom.

Just after sunset, and whilst long red rays were contending for mastery with the encroaching twilight, Leah sauntered aimlessly out of the front door, and began to pick here and there a faded leaf, and now an over-spent bloom, from her beloved flowers. Presently she got down to within a yard or so of the gate, and stood in the soft twilight with her back to the woodyard, looking pensively down on a bed of snapdragon. She was just stooping down to examine them more closely, when there came from somewhere behind her a loud, but slightly hesitant, whisper—

"Leah!"

But she did not move, and, but for the sudden setting of her face, it might have been concluded that she had not heard. She stooped a little lower, until her face nearly touched the taller of the flowers, and seemed to be absorbed in studying them.

"Leah! "—clearer this time, and yet it had a penitent, coaxing sound in it.

Still she kept her face over the flowers, and only a slight quiver in her lissom fingers showed that she knew she was being called.

"L-e-a-h!" — this time drawn out with most plaintive anxiety.

Leah paused a moment, raised herself, glanced cautiously at the house windows, hesitated for a while, and then stooped down again over the flowers as though she had heard nothing. Again came the thick loud whisper

"Leah! come i' the' yard! If thaa doesn't, Aw'll come ta thee."

The stooping maiden's face flushed a little. Then she raised herself, turned round, and, moving slightly nearer to a sweetbriar bush against the flag fence, said, in cold, severe tones, looking across the woodyard, and speaking apparently into vacancy—

"Tha's dun me a gooid turn fur wunce, Luke."

A red head and a pair of roguish brown eyes shot up from behind the flags, and Luke Yates asked dubiously —

"Wot wi?"

"Aw've bin forgettin' mysel', an' desavin' my payrunts, an' hurtin' my sowl, an' tha's cur't me."

"Well, bud come i' the' yard a minute. Aw want t' tell thin summat."

"Thaa towd me aw as Aw want ta know when thaa went aat o' th' schoo' ta-day."

"Well, it's thy fawt."

Leah frowned, but avoiding the eyes gleaming so eagerly at her from behind the briar bush branches, she asked, with both surprise and resentment in her tone—

"My fawt? Wot dust meean?"

"Aw meean Aw could be a saint if tha'd ha' me, bud Aw'st goa ta Owd Harry if thaa winna."

"If thaa winna be a Christian ta get me, tha winna be wun when thaa hes getten me."

"Thaa wants me ta be a hypocryte then?"

But Leah had already repented of going so far. She had meant to be both cold and brief with Luke, and he was already getting the better of her, as he always did in argument. She felt also that he had caught her, and placed her at a disadvantage, and so, drawing herself up and making an effort, which even her self-restraint could not conceal, she said—

"Luke, tha's disgraced thisel'; tha's disgraced th' schoo', but tha shall never disgrace me."

And then, after a moment's pause—"Aw wuish thi weel"—and here her voice became just the least bit unsteady—"an' Aw've tried ta think weel on thi, bud they mun be noa mooar on it. Gooid-neet, an'—an' God save thi soul."

And as tears were rushing into her eyes she turned hurriedly away, and in a moment more was indoors.

Half an hour later Leah stood in the darkness, looking out through the bedroom window with a far-off wistful look. Presently she lighted a candle, took a little key from her pocket, and opening a small rosewood box which she reached down from the drawer top, took out a little paper parcel containing a small box made of sea-shells, such as can now be bought at any watering-place for a few coppers, but then somewhat of a rarity in a place like Beckside.

It was only a cheap little toy which a rough lad had bought some four years before on his first and only trip to the "sayside," and which he had kept until it was sadly tarnished before he mustered courage to give it to her. She was in short frocks then, and very shy, but she had kept it all this time as her one earthly treasure, and had lately had many "fightings within" about the possible sinfulness of keeping it, especially as story after story of Luke's pranks came to her.

But now she stood looking at it with unwonted softness in her beautiful eyes. Suddenly she made a sort of grab at it as if intending to destroy it, but she only took it in her hands and turned it over and over. Then with a quick start she threw it on the bed, and stood back as if it had suddenly become a venomous reptile seeking to wound her.

After standing there and looking at it, half in fear and half in covetous desire, she took it up again, kissed it hastily, as if afraid of being caught in the act, hurriedly dropped it into their rosewood case, and then turned abruptly to the window and stood looking long and silently out, heaving many long soft sighs as she did so.

Then she backed away from the window, and sat down on the bed; and presently sliding softly to her knees, and burying her beautiful face in her hands, she cried—

"O Lord, Aw darr na loike him, but it conna be wrung to pray fur him. If Tha'll save his soul Thaa can give him to onybody Thaa loikes. O Lord, save him."

Meanwhile the event of the day was being discussed in all its bearings at the Clog Shop, or, rather, in the Clog Shop garden, for the heat was so stifling that the chairs had been taken to the back door, where, in the long Sabbath evening, Luke and his transgressions were comprehensively considered.

Sam Speck, in his shirt-sleeves, emphatically approved of Jabe's action in the matter. Nathan and Jonas talked more mildly, but, nevertheless, heartily supported him. Long Ben said little. He never could be relied upon where firmness was required; but as he was not quite so mysterious and circuitous in his conversation as he generally became when in reluctant dissent, it was concluded that he agreed as much as he could be expected to do.

Jabe, so far from being elated by the commendations he received, accepted them somewhat restively, and it was clear that he was far from being at ease with himself. He was constantly bringing the conversation back to the subject of Luke, and though nobody questioned what he had done, his every word had a defensive and almost apologetic tone about it.

All this time Lige the road-mender had been sitting with his back against the rain-tub, puffing out volumes of smoke at express rate, whilst he was evidently giving more than usual attention to the conversation.

The fact that he had never spoken was not noticed, especially as his opinions, loudly and frequently repeated though they were, were not generally regarded as of much importance, being almost always feeble reflections of Sam Speck's or Jabe's.

Great, therefore, was the amazement of all when, just at the close of one of Jabe's most successful efforts at self-justification, Lige suddenly rose to his feet. Standing before the Clogger, and stretching forth his hand in emphatic gesticulation, whilst his face looked fierce and excited, he cried, glaring almost savagely at Jabe—

"It's th' biggest blunder tha's iver made."

The whole thing was so sudden, and the source from whence it came was so unusual, that all eyes were suddenly turned on Lige in astonishment, and Jabe's jaw dropped with significant bewilderment.

"Naa, Aw meean it," shouted the excited Lige. "If some o' yo' owd bachelors hed a lad or tew o' yur own, yo' wouldna be sa keen at bullocking other foakses."

Then everybody suddenly remembered that Lige's only child was a long-absent prodigal, wandering nobody knew where, and there was a rapid softening of scowling faces and a nervous clearing of throats.

But Jabe, with much more inward agitation than he cared to show, and most unusually sensitive to criticism, replied—

"Whey, he wur feightin' nobbut last neet; feightin' wi' Bob Tommy as is big eneugh ta eight [eat] him."

This seemed to incense Lige more than ever, and, almost flying at Jabe, he cried—

"An' dost know wot he wur feightin' abaat?"

"Neaw."

"He wur feightin' th' biggest bully i' Brogden Clough 'cause he caw'd thee a limping Methody."

There was a hasty dropping of heads, partly in startled self-consciousness, and partly in sympathy with the badly hit Clogger.

Lige glared round upon the company, as if challenging the next to come on, and as nobody responded, he cried—

"Which o' yo' wur browt up wi' a druffen [drunken] step-fayther? Which o' yo' hed ta feight his fayther ta save his muther fro' brokken boanes afore he wur fifteen ye'r owd? Aw'd ha' sum sense if Aw wur yo'!"

And then, exhausted by his very unusual effort, and alarmed all at once at his own temerity, Lige sank back against the rain-tub, with a look in which defiance and apology were curiously blended.

It was some time before the conversation flowed freely again. Lige's outburst not only let loose feelings which had been resolutely held back in Jabe's mind ever since Luke's expulsion, but it greatly disturbed the rest, and Jabe noticed with a pang that Long Ben seemed to want to get away, and, in fact, did depart as soon as he could. When he had gone the Clogger became morose and raspy, and though Lige made several overtures for reconciliation, Jabe maintained an air of injured dignity towards him. This sent poor Lige home also; and very soon the party melted away, and Jabe was left alone to torment himself with reproaches.

On his way home Long Ben was full of commiseration for the disgraced Luke, and began to accuse himself of helping to drive him to the bad.

There was no half-way house in the Beckside system of ethics, and the boys of the school who showed no inclination to profit by their religious privileges were all described as being on their way "ta th' gallus"; and so by the time Ben reached home he could already see the unhappy Luke sitting in a condemned cell, and accusing him of driving him to his doom. It was a relief, therefore, to get indoors, for his wife, though given to gentle raillery, was clearheaded and safe in her judgments, and would be almost certain to give him her opinion before she retired to rest.

But he found Mrs. Ben in a brown study, from which she awoke and glanced at him with a discontented and troubled look as he spoke to her.

Without replying to an unimportant remark, she arose, and going into the cellar, drew him a pot of foaming dandelion beer. After taking a long swig at it, Ben held the half-empty pot at arm's-length, and making circles with it in the air to rouse its life, he remarked—

"Aw wunder wot yond' wastril thinks of hissel' ta-neet?"

There was no answer, but Mrs. Ben's round face, although almost invisible in the shade, was puckered into ominous frowns.

Ben waited a while, but as his wife did not respond, he continued—

"Aw'm feart he'll come ta sum lumber afoor lung."

"It'll be woss fur thee if he does," jerked out Mrs. Ben sourly.

Ben caught his breath. He had expected that his wife would relieve the pressure of the anxiety he was beginning to feel, and lo! here she was adding heavily to it.

But surely she was only trying to frighten him; and so, with an awkward attempt at indignation, to conceal his uneasiness, he asked—

"Wot'll it be woss fur me fur? Wot have Aw ta dew wi' it?"

Mrs. Ben bent forward and looked dreely at the long-cased clock against the opposite wall, and said very quietly—

"'Cause aar Leah loikes him."

II.

THE COURSE OF TRUE LOVE.

NOW the word "loike" has undergone a curious reversal or intensification of meaning in its use amongst Lancashire villagers, especially compared with the stronger word "love."

The natural reticence of the North-countryman leads him to avoid the use of "love" whenever possible; and in Lancashire, "loike," the weaker word, has come to be most commonly used about amatory matters, and expresses the strongest possible affection.

When, therefore, Mrs. Barber employed this term about her daughter's sentiments towards Luke Yates, there was no room for doubt as to what she meant by it. And if there had been, Mrs. Ben's manner as she made the statement with which the last chapter closed removed any such possibility.

Poor Ben was simply overwhelmed. Amazement, alarm, and profound perplexity took possession of him, and he sat upright in his chair and stared blankly before him in the uttermost consternation.

It was the last thing in the world he would have expected—so wildly improbable, in fact, that if even his wife had stated it to him under any other circumstances he would have laughed at its utter absurdity.

He reflected also, when he recovered a little from his first amazement, on what he knew of the quiet intensity underlying the surface stillness of his eldest daughter's nature, and did not need to be told that, if such an affection had really taken possession of her, neither her own judgment nor any other influences in the world whatsoever would upset it.

But a union between Leah and Luke was an utter impossibility. They had not a single thing in common,—were, in fact, at extreme opposites in almost all their tastes and sympathies; and how Leah had ever brought herself to give a second thought to such a wild scapegrace he could not imagine.

Besides, what would people think? The utter incongruity of the thing would only make it the more exciting and interesting as a subject of gossip; and Ben already heard the rasping voice of Jabe uttering choice pieces of crabbed, sententious philosophy on his favourite subject—the ways and wiles of women.

These and many other like thoughts rushed through the slow-moving mind of the carpenter with most unwonted rapidity, and the more he thought the more entangled and terrible did the dilemma appear; and at length he turned his eyes back upon his wife and gazed at her with helpless stupidity.

But Mrs. Ben was almost as dumbfounded as her husband, and returned his stare with her round face longer than Ben had ever seen it, and a look of appealing helplessness in her eyes that went to his very heart.

At length, to break a silence which was fast becoming unbearable, he stammered out "Tha'rt dreamin', woman."

"Aw wish to God Aw wur," was the reply, in a wailing tone that drove the iron deeper into Ben's soul.

"Haa hast fun it aat?"

"Aw wur gooin' past her chamber dur an' Aw yerd her prayin'. An', oh! if thaa 'ad yerd her, Ben" —and the distressed mother broke into sobs that nearly drove Ben wild.

The parents sat up long that night, talking in fitful snatches of their trouble, and at length Ben took off his Sunday coat, and dropping down in front of his arm-chair, began the usual evening prayer. Like many other such petitions, it had become of late years almost entirely an intercession for the children, who were named to God in turn, but to-night, when Ben came to his firstborn and had stammered out, "An', Heavenly Fayther, bless Le——," he broke down, and the two knelt sobbing together on the hearthstone with their newest sorrow weighing heavily on their hearts.

It goes without saying that neither the carpenter nor his wife slept much that night, for added to all the other difficulties of the case was the fact that they were both somewhat afraid of their quiet daughter, and neither could see how they were going to approach her on the subject.

"Well, ther's wun consolation," said Mrs. Ben, as they were dressing in the morning.

"Wot's that?"

"Hoo may breik her hert abaat it, bud hoo'll ne'er merry him if he isn't religious."

But Ben, though not so quick and observant as his wife, had a deeper knowledge of his daughter's nature, and remarked—

"Aar Leah's th' sooart as 'ull merry a chap to save him—ay, if hoo deed fur it."

The sigh with which Mrs. Ben responded spoke more eloquently than words could do of her entire endorsement of Ben's opinion now that it had been placed before her, and the two left their bedroom to face the battle of life encumbered by a very heavy anxiety.

They struggled hard to keep up appearances, especially before Leah, and she, going about her duties as usual, though they watched her with love's keen closeness, gave not the slightest sign that anything was the matter.

But the shock of the discovery and the suspense together were telling very heavily on both the carpenter and his wife, so much so that Ben's looks and manner awakened the curiosity and concern of the

Clogger, and placed Ben in an awkward dilemma. If he went to the Clog Shop he was in momentary dread of a straight question which he could not evade, and if he stayed away it was absolutely certain that Jabe would come in search of him and institute rigorous inquisition. The Clogger was already in a state of most restless curiosity, though there was no evidence that he had any suspicion of the cause. Any hour, however, he might take it into his knotty old head to put Ben through a searching cross-examination, or to sound Mrs. Ben on the cause of her husband's depressed and sickly look. To add to Ben's distress, his wife began to press him to speak to Leah about the matter; and though at first he nearly lost his temper, and utterly refused to do anything of the kind, yet the growing restlessness of the mother and his own anxieties compelled him to admit that the thing must be done somehow.

Then he delayed and postponed the terrible task on the ground of lack of proper opportunity, every time being the wrong time; and once, when a chance of unusual favourableness presented itself, he got so very flurried and hastened from Leah's presence so abruptly as to make the quiet maiden open her eyes in momentary surprise.

But Leah was too much occupied with her own affairs to give much thought to her father. Her heart was fighting a severe battle with her principles, and giving her an altogether uncomfortable time. Ever since that sad Sunday she had been reproaching herself, not for dismissing her clandestine lover, but for not giving him his *congé* [Ed.—*Formal or authoritative permission to depart*] more kindly.

She could never admit in her most secret heart that there was any excuse for Luke's conduct, but she began to remind herself that he had had a harsh stepfather, and a sickly mother, who had now been dead for some two years, and that since then he had lived in lodgings. It had only been by a doggèd pertinacity which would not be rebuffed that her lover had got on even speaking terms with her since they had been grown up. And then Luke, though disreputable, was very popular somehow with the young women of the village, and might have had many a girl whom she knew. Besides, there must be some good somewhere in a lad who gave such a decided preference to a quiet, religious girl like herself.

Altogether Leah's mind was greatly disturbed, and to make matters worse, Luke, the irrepressible, who could not be snubbed or shaken off either by coldness or ill-treatment, had taken her at her word for the first time and was keeping carefully out of the way. And worst of all, he had never been to chapel since the day he was expelled from the school. Twice indeed she had seen him pass the house, but he never even turned his head that way.

One evening, about this time, she was sitting in the parlour skinning rhubarb for rhubarb wine, and meditating abstractedly on her peculiar situation, when the front door opened and in stepped her father.

Now, Ben had told himself twenty times that all he needed was a proper opportunity of speaking with his daughter, and that the fates were most strangely against him; nevertheless, when he thus came suddenly upon a chance that was unexceptionable, his heart dropped into his clogs, and he would doubtless have retreated but for the fact that it seemed difficult to do so without appearing remarkable, and so, after a guilty start and a moment of hesitation, he sauntered awkwardly into his chair and took refuge in his pipe.

It was Providence. There was nothing for it but to have it out with Leah; but when—whilst he was still meditating how to begin—Sally Meadows, one of Leah's fellow Sunday-school teachers, opened the front door and asked Leah to go for a walk, Ben became quite earnest in urging her to accept. Leah quietly excused herself, however; and Ben sank back into his chair with a faint look of disappointment and even irritation on his face.

A minute or two later Leah opened the front door to relieve the air of the room; and Ben got up a little debate with himself as to whether it would be proper to discuss such delicate matters as were in his mind with an open door, but he could not quite convince himself that the interview ought to be postponed, and so, after fidgeting in his chair and furtively eyeing Leah over until he had taken a complete inventory of her garments, he finally coughed, cleared his throat, turned his head round and glanced uneasily through the window, and then commenced—

"Thaa leuks badly, wench. Artna weel?"

"Yi, Aw'm reet enuff," answered Leah, composedly, but with an alert little glance at her father out of the corner of her eye.

"Then thaa must be i' luv. Hast started o' cooartin'?"

Ben said this with an attempt at jocularity, but a slight choking sound in his throat betrayed him to Leah's anxious ears, and in a moment her white face had become a rich crimson. She felt she was blushing, and betraying herself, which only made the colour deepen on her face and neck, and she made a feeble little effort to save herself.

"Eh, fayther, haa yo' talk. Yo' mak' me goa red."

"Wheer ther's smook ther's feire," said Ben, still keeping up a show of fun, but with strange nippings about the heart.

Leah started to her feet with confusion and fear. Another moment and she would have to choose between an impossible falsehood and an equally impossible confession. The picture she had conjured up in her mind of her father's horror, if ever he discovered to whom she had given her heart, filled her with dismay. There was nothing for it but to flee. In another moment she would have been safe in her bedroom, but Ben suddenly crossed the floor, dropped heavily into the mother's chair by her side, and faltered out—

"Leah, my hert tells me as ther's summat wrung. Naa, wot is it, wench, wot is it?"

Leah worshipped her father, and this unwonted tenderness in his tone moved her profoundly. She went white to the lips, gasped a little for breath, her head fell on her heaving bosom, she began to pick nervously at the hem of her apron, but never a word could she get out.

Ben, with shaking hand, laid down his pipe, drew his chair nearer to hers, and Leah trembled to feel her father's arm slowly stealing round her slim waist. Lancashire folk are always very sparing of caresses and tender words, and Leah never remembered her father treating her like this before. She struggled feebly to escape, but he held her tight, drew her still closer to him, and then murmured —

"Aw dunna want to meddle, thaa knows, bud tha'rt t' leet o' my een, wench. Wot's up wi' thee?"

A convulsive shudder went through Leah's frame; she made a supreme effort, turned her face, white but resolute, to her father, and looking him full in the face, said —

"Fayther, Aw'm niver goin' fur t' merry. Niver! soa dunna fret abaat me," and then with a sudden wrench she tore herself from her father's grasp and fled to her own little bedroom.

Ben heaved a great sigh, fell back into his chair, and groaning, "Lord, help us," closed his eyes in troubled reflection.

He had got more out of his daughter than he expected, and what he had learnt confirmed his worst apprehensions.

Just at that moment he heard the garden gate click and a limping footstep come up the garden. Then the door opened, and Jabe, looking very resolute and aggressive, stepped across the threshold.

"Oh, tha'rt theer arta? Wot art mopesin' i' th' haase fur?" he demanded, glaring fiercely at his friend, but Ben only handed the tobacco-box and sat staring before him.

Jabe suspected that Ben's continued depression had a financial origin, and he glanced round the room and through the door into the kitchen in search of Mrs. Ben, who was always his chief supporter in his periodical attacks upon the carpenter for allowing people to get into his debt. But his ally was nowhere to be seen, and Jabe was constrained to go to the battle alone. After puffing away in grim silence for a few moments, staring hard the while at a fancy shoehorn hanging at the side of the mantelpiece, he demanded, without deigning to turn his head—

"Haa lung is it sin' Jerry Mopper paid thee owt?"

"Setterday," was all the response Ben gave.

"Haa mitch does that leave?"

"Nowt."

Jabe turned his head half round for a moment, and an expression of surprise escaped him, and then he relapsed once more into an earnest contemplation of the shoe-horn. If Jerry Mopper had at last paid off his long-standing account, Ben could not be troubled about finances. But Ben had never before even attempted to conceal any other of his troubles from him. His curiosity increased, and with it came a feeling of resentment softened by a vague apprehension of some unknown calamity impending over the Barbers. And so the two sat in silence, each apparently oblivious of the other's presence, Ben longing to unbosom himself, and yet terrified at the thought of such a thing, and Jabe piqued, puzzled, and increasingly uneasy at his friend's most unusual manner.

The silence continued, and the shoe-horn would have blushed if it could under the fierce, annihilating stare of the Clogger. At last, however, Jabe could hold no longer, and rising to his feet, still glaring at the shoe-horn, he cried, with scornful sarcasm—

"Ther's ta mitch neyse here fur me. Aw'll goa wheer it's quieter," and with his nose very high in the air he stalked stiffly out of the house.

Left to himself, Ben was more miserable than ever. And though he followed the Clogger after awhile to the shop, and tried to atone for his conduct by taking some interest in the conversation, yet being compelled to leave early lest Jabe should reopen the inquisition, he went away, feeling that for the first time for nearly thirty years a shadow had come between him and his old friend.

Several weeks passed after this, and still there was no change in the situation, except that Luke, the cause of all the trouble, had removed to Clough End to lodge, although he still worked at the mill. Meanwhile Leah went about her work just as usual, but although Ben noticed it, and took it as a hopeful sign, Mrs. Ben's sharper eyes showed her that her daughter was still feeling her trouble.

She grew paler still, and very nervous. Her mother would come upon her gazing out of the window with a painfully abstracted look, and once she caught her hurriedly wiping her eyes. Anxious for her daughter's health, Mrs. Barber now began to invent errands for Leah which would take her into the open air, and comforted herself with the thought that it seemed like doing Leah good.

One evening later in the summer Leah had been sent to Lamb Fold with a basket of fruit and eggs for her grandmother. Lamb Fold was on the hill on the other side of the Beck, and the road to it ran along Shaving Lane, and over a plank bridge a quarter of a mile higher up the Clough than the village.

The evening was soft and calm, and Leah, as she returned, was beginning to forget herself in the sweet stillness about her. Just as she had reached the home side of the plank a stick snapped just before her, and lifting her head quickly, she found herself face to face with Luke, who had evidently been crouched behind a gate-post and perhaps waiting for her.

Leah started with a bitter cry, and looked hastily about for a way of escape, but Luke was too quick for her, and stepping between her and the little bridge, effectually barred the passage in that direction.

A flash of haughtiness came into the girl's eyes, and she lifted them to Luke's face as if to annihilate him.

But Luke's face was such a roguish, laughing, irresistible one, and withal had at any an rate such an appearance of open frankness, that the moment her eyes and his met, her anger began to fade, and a helpless, almost foolish feeling took possession of her.

"Wot dust want?" she asked faintly, as if out of breath.

"Want, wench? Aw want thee," and then suddenly seeming to see more in his own words than he had intended, he went on. "Ay, that's just wot Aw dew want, ta mak' me a gradely mon. If Aw hed thee, Aw could be a dacent chap. Aw could be a Methody; ay, if tha'd a moind thaa could mak' me into a, a—cherubim," and Luke laughed at the unexpected brilliance of his own fancy.

There was a momentary pause, and then Leah said—

"Aw yer tha's started o' drinkin'."

Luke seemed to be about to deny this, but a second thought striking him, he said—

"An' wot if Aw hev? Aw've nowt else ta dew wi' my brass. Aw've noa whoam ta goa tew an' noa muther and noa sister nor noabry."

Quick stabs of pity and self-reproach pricked at Leah's tender heart. She paused a moment to obtain control of herself, and then she said as calmly as she was able—

"If thaa wants me, whey dust keep gettin' i' sich lumber?"

"Lumber? it's nowt but marlockin'. Thaa talks as if it wur lyin' or thievin', or summat," and Luke put on an excellent imitation of injured innocence. Leah felt herself giving way, and taking alarm thereat, she said—

"Aw've towd thi mony a toime as Aw shanna merry onybody as isn't a Christian. Aw darna if Aw wanted."

And now Luke seemed to be really annoyed.

"Ay," he cried, "if Aw'd start o' sniggering, an' pooin' a fiddle face, an' gooin' up to th' penitent form, tha'd ha' me. Bud, Leah," he cried, flaming up and looking really handsome, Leah thought, in his indignation,—"Aw'd dew fur thee wot Aw wouldna dew fur aw th' wold beside. Aw'd work fur thee, Aw'd slave fur thee, Aw'd *dee* fur thee, bud Aw winna be a hypocryte even fur thee. If Aw'm iver convarted it ull be a gradely convarsion, wun as Aw should be satisfied wi' mysel', an' not a woman-catching dodge."

But Leah scarcely heard the last sentences. Her woman's pride was touched, and so, drawing herself up with a look of proud disdain, she asked in cold surprise—

"Wot art botherin' abaat, then?"

But Luke's excitement had vanished as quickly as it came, and dropping once more into his old wheedling tones,—the most dangerous of all his moods to Leah,—he said earnestly—

"Leah! Aw loike thi that weel, Aw'm feart o' mysel'. When Aw see thi Aw want ta goa reet off to th' penitent form to get thi. An' that ud be wuss nor aw. Leah, little, bonny, breet-eed Leah, tak' me as Aw am."

As Luke spoke, and his passion increased, he drew gradually nearer to her, and as he finished he suddenly raised his arms, and in another moment would have had her in his embrace, but just then a couple of strollers came round the top corner of the lane, and Leah, seeing them, stepped back just in time, as she thought, to save appearances, whilst Luke, suddenly checking himself, and realising that he must not compromise his sweetheart in the eyes of the villagers, jumped the hedge, scudded off into the fields behind, and was gone.

III.

A NEW FINGER IN THE PIE.

NOW the couple whose sudden appearance round the corner of Shaving Lane had brought Luke and Leah's interview to such an abrupt termination, happened to be Johnty Harrop and his wide-awake little wife, whom our readers have met before in these chronicles. Johnty, of course, saw nothing, and was not even aware of Leah's presence in the lane until they actually met her on the way home, when the unsuspecting "Minder" glanced at her and remarked, when she had passed, that Leah was losing her good looks.

But Mrs. Johnty had seen, trust her for that, and was so absorbed in what she had observed, that she did not seem to hear what her husband was saying. She was amazed. The little scene was a revelation to her. As the next-door neighbour of the Barbers, she saw a good deal of them, and, being a kind little soul, had got of late somewhat deep into Mrs. Ben's confidence. They had talked over the flag fence of the front garden, and over the low wall at the back, and once or twice of late Mrs. Ben had dropped hints about being worried about Leah; and Susy, whilst very sympathetic, had felt that her friend's anxiety was oddly out of proportion to any change she could perceive in Leah. And the thing, though she had not dwelt much upon it, had puzzled her.

Now it was clear as noonday. She only knew Luke by sight, but she was well aware of his reputation, and realised what an inappropriate match it would be, and what scandal would be caused in the village if it ever came to anything.

And with Susy to think was to act. Her sympathies went out strongly towards Mrs. Ben and her husband, though she was young enough to feel very tenderly towards Leah. She wondered how much Mrs. Ben knew. Had she any idea that her daughter was thus entangled? And especially did she know to whom Leah had given her heart? Or was she only uneasy about Leah's manner and sickly looks? She must be careful if she tried to help them lest she did more harm than good; and having not so very long since had secrets of her own, she felt she must be as kind and helpful as possible to such a "noice quiet wench" as Leah. At anyrate she would keep the secret, unless she found she could use it to good purpose, and in the meantime she would get all the information she could.

It seemed difficult to do anything with the Barbers at present, so she would begin on the easier task of getting to know something definite about Luke. Her unsuspicious husband was, of course, easily drawn, and before she got home from their little stroll she had ascertained his view of the case as far as Luke was concerned.

Johnty commenced by calling Luke a "gallus young wastril," at which, of course, Susy was not surprised, though she affected to be. On being deftly led out into particulars, however, the Minder became very hazy, and, after contradicting himself several times, he explained—

"He's nor a gradely bad un, thaa knows; nowt o' th' sooart. Bud he's that *mischeevious.*"

"Wot's he dew at th' shop [mill]? " asked Susy.

"He's a mechanic."

"Then he'll mak' good wages, winnot he?"

"Oh ay, an' he owt dew. He's nobbut twenty-one, but he's th' best mechanic abaat th' place."

"It's a pity he wur turnt aat o' th' schoo'; he'll happen goa wrung."

"Nay, nor him. He's plenty o' sense, Luke has, on'y he's so gammy wi' it. As for them owd jockeys at th' Clog Shop, they durn't know ivverything by a foine soight. But," he went on, suddenly remembering himself, "what dust want to know fur?"

But Susy very easily put Johnty off, and went to bed to make plans for extending the range of her inquiries.

During the next few days she gathered a great deal of information. By assuming tentatively a censorious tone towards Luke, and commending the action of the Sunday-school authorities, she drew out of her unsuspecting neighbours many interesting particulars. Luke was, a "wik un if iver ther' war wun," "a marlockin', pace-eggin' young imp," and so on. Some of the victims of Luke's mischievous pranks used language that ought not to have been employed to a lady, and which of course cannot be written down here. It was clear that Luke was the ringleader of all the mischief and practical joking in the neighbourhood, and a very sad character altogether. When questioned, however, on the more strictly moral aspects of Luke's character, her informants showed considerable hesitation and difference of opinion, and most agreed that the expulsion from the school was an extreme step.

Now Mrs. Johnty had more than her share of woman's secret admiration for a young fellow who was "lively," and had herself suffered much by misrepresentation. She really could get at nothing very wicked in Luke's character, and so before long she had conceived quite a prejudice in his favour, and was beginning to range herself on his side.

At last she found herself in conversation with old Mary Jane, with whom Luke had lodged previous to his recent removal to Clough End. She overtook the old woman coming from the mangle, and carried her basket for her. As they approached Susy's house she invited her in to rest and have "a sooap o' tay," which invitation Mary Jane promptly accepted.

"Yo'll ha' some peace naa yond' wild good-fur-nowt's left, Aw reacon, Murry Jane," Susy began, watching her visitor as she did so.

"Peace! wot dust meean? Whoa art talkin' abaat?"

"Whey, that Luke. He led yo' a bonny life Aw reacon."

Mary Jane's mouth had opened in astonishment and perplexity at Susy's words, but it suddenly closed like a trap, her lips tightened, and pausing with the teacup in one hand and the saucer in the other, she said slowly—

"If them as runs him daan and turns him aat wur hawf as gooid, they'd be a foine soight better 'an they are."

"Hay, Murry Jane, has yo' talken. Whey, they aw say as he's a hard-herted young wastril."

"Hard-herted! Sithee, wench, his hert's as sawft as a woman's. When Aw wur badly with pains Aw've seen him stop' o'er me, an' skrike loike a chilt. He's bowt me mony an' mony a bottle o' Eli's drops."

"Aw reacon he paid yo' weel," said Mrs. Johnty, suspecting a possible mercenary motive for the old woman's praises and regrets.

"Paid me! Ay, he did that! Bud Aw'd ha' kept him fur nowt if he'd ha' stopped. He wur a foine soight better tew me nor me own, Aw con tell thi."

"Bud wot did he leeave th' village fur?" asked Susy.

Mary Jane paused a moment, dropped into a low, confidential tone, and proceeded—

"Aw'll tell thi, wench. He ne'er thowt they'd a turnt him aat o' th' schoo'. An' when they did, he wur that takken to, he wur fair shawmed of hissel'. He wur that ill off abaat it, he couldn't abide. It mak's me badly to think has he leuked when he thowt Aw wurn't watching him."

"It's a wunder he's ne'er started o' cooartin'—bud whoa'd hev him?" remarked Susy.

"Hev him? Bless thi, they wur niver off th' dur-step, if they thowt he wur abaat. An' Aw' durn't wonder, if they know'd him as weel as Aw dew, they'd ha' bin feightin' fur him."

Much more to the same purpose was said, and when Mary Jane resumed her journey home, with two of Susy's hot tea-cakes in her clothes-basket, she left behind her a little woman who was almost as stout a supporter of Luke as she was herself. Still, in such a case, in which there was so pronounced a difference of opinion in the village, it was necessary to be very careful, and to get all the light possible, and so she decided that she must get acquainted somehow with Luke himself, and make a personal study of him. But how? She did not see her way at all at first, and it was a day or two before she could decide what to do.

One evening, however, when Johnty came home from his work, he found his little wife in a state of impatience and distress. Her sewing machine had broken down. Such implements were comparatively rare at that time, and there was no person in Beckside or the neighbourhood who could be called in to do repairs. Hitherto Johnty, who, as a minder, had considerable knowledge of machinery, had served his wife's purpose, and of course, as soon as he had had his "baggin'," he had to set to work on the broken sewing machine. In a few minutes all was apparently right again, and Susy set to work afresh. Most provokingly the machine went wrong again, and as often as Johnty repaired it, so often did it break down again after a minute or two's working.

"Is they' noabry else abaat as understands sewing machines?" asked Susy at last in a well-dissembled tone of despair. Johnty could think of nobody, and laughed when Susy suggested Nathan the smith.

"Is ther' noabry at th' shop [mill] as is handy an' cliver?" she asked, with a show of great impatience.

"Neaw," answered her husband, —considering slowly as he spoke, — "noabry bud Luke Yates."

"Him!" cried Susy, with apparently most genuine scorn. But presently, after suggesting two or three improbable persons, she said, with a clever simulation of reluctance—

"Well, Aw mun hev it done, chuse haa. Bring him tew his baggin' ta-morra neet. He winna eight [eat] us, Aw reacon."

Johnty promised to do so. Next night Luke was brought, and though shy and awkward at first, the beguiling chatter of the Minder's wife soon set him at his ease, and he laughed and joked and told stories until the disabled machine seemed in danger of being entirely forgotten.

Presently, however, Johnty suggested an examination, and Luke brought all his mechanical resources to bear on the matter. Now, Johnty could not for the life of him see that the young mechanic had done anything to the machine but what he had already done himself. But, strange to say, it worked without the slightest inclination to relapse, and the audacious Susy actually chaffed her husband on his deplorable lack of skill. This, of course, had its effect on Luke, who stayed on and chatted, and still stayed, until Susy really couldn't send him away without supper. And as the meal was a very tasty one and very much to Johnty's tooth, he ate it and joked about it, and then actually went and saw Luke part of the way home to Clough End without even the glimmer of an idea that his wife had been, as he would have termed it, "bamboozling" him.

Susy's mind was now made up. She had taken her measure of Luke, and honestly liked him. If possible, he should have his rights in popular esteem at any rate. The Barbers should know what he was like.

"My machine's aw reet naa," she said to Leah's mother over the flag fence the following night. "Aar Johnty browt Luke Yates tew it, an' he put it reet in a jiffy,—hay, but he's a cliver lad wi' his fingers."

Mrs. Ben gave a slight start, and glanced suspiciously at Susy, whose face at that moment would have disarmed a detective.

44

"He's cliver at aw mak' o' mischief, Aw know that," was the sharp answer.

"Ay! Aw reacon soa," sighed Mrs. Johnty in affected sympathy with her neighbour. "Bud yo'd ne'er think soa. A dacenter behaved lad Aw wouldna wish to see i' my haase."

Mrs. Ben was listening with an almost painful interest, and the crafty Susy continued with studious deliberateness—

"Ther's wun thing abaat him; he burs na malice. He spak' weel o' booath Jabe an' yore Ben last neet. Them's foine dahlias o' yo'rs, Ellen."

"Ay," sighed Mrs. Ben, glancing indifferently at the flowers; "bud they say as he's a weary bad un."

"He's nobbut a bit gallus, full o' gam an' sich loike," replied Susy, tossing her head with careless impatience. "Aw wouldna give a bodle fur a young felley as hadn't a bit in him; but Aw mun be goin' i' th' haase."

"Aw'm feart he'll turn aat badly," replied Mrs. Barber anxiously, and stepping nearer to the fence, as if by that means to detain her neighbour.

"Well, *Aw* dur tak' him; so theer," rejoined Susy with sudden energy. "He's gooid wages, an' aar Johnty says as he'll be th' yed mechanic afoor lung, and owd Murry Jane says as he's better tew her nor her own. An' that's gooid enuff fur me. Gooid-neet, wench," and, with this last heavy shot, Susan retreated indoors, with a conviction that she had not entirely laboured in vain.

And she was right, for Mrs. Ben, ready to do anything to relieve the tension of anxiety, soon instituted inquiries on her own account, and told all she discovered to her husband, only to find out, from a slip in Ben's speech, that he had been at the same employment, and was well up in all the details of Luke's character and career.

45

As the carpenter sat thinking by the fireside, just before retiring to rest one night, Mrs. Ben came and sat opposite to him, and, whilst darning away at a heap of stockings, began to collect her thoughts, with a view of coming to some understanding, if possible.

"Ben, dust think aar Leah's getten th' decline?" she said, looking up at him anxiously.

Ben winced, for this was the very question he was trying to settle for himself at the moment his wife spoke. But now he belied his own apprehensions by answering shortly—

"Neaw."

"Hoo will be afoor lung if things doesn't awter;" and there was a moan in Mrs. Ben's usually cheery tones.

But Ben saw no way out of the difficulty, so he sat in silence and stared sadly before him.

They sat in the candle-light for a long time without speaking, and then Ben said—

"If hoo has him wee'st lose her, and if hoo doesn't have him wee'st lose her. Hay, dear, my hert's welly brokken!"

The mother began to sob quietly, and Ben looked at her with a strong inclination to do the same.

The difficulty to them was very real. They could have brought themselves, and in fact had brought themselves, to accept Luke as a member of their own family, but when all personal likes and dislikes had been got over there remained still the religious aspect of the case. The command was to them clear and unalterable that neither they nor theirs were to be unequally joked together with unbelievers. How could they fly in the face of a plain Divine precept, and how could they expect to prosper if they did? They could retire from the case, of course, and leave Leah to bear the onus of it herself, but that would be exposing her to a great temptation, and laying upon her a grave responsibility. As it was, they did share her burden, and were resolved to do so to the end. Ben, indeed, thought desperately more than once of breaking away from all religious scruples and commanding his daughter to marry Luke, thus taking the whole responsibility on himself, and saving Leah's soul at the expense of his own. But this mood passed also, and after another long silence Mrs. Ben said—

"Young wenches allis feels as they wanten ta dew wot they're towd they manna dew. It's happen o' thatunce wi' aar Leah. When hoo knows hoo can pleease hersel' hoo'll happen nor be so keen on it."

"Ellen," replied Ben, "tha knows aar Leah better tin that. If hoo geet wed an' lost her soul, Aw should feel as if Aw'd scrambled inta heaven o'er her distruction. Tha can pleease thisel', but moind thi, if owt comes on it, Aw want th' blame ta faw on uz an' nor on her."

And so the conversation ended, but next day, as Leah seemed rather paler than usual, her mother resolved that she should know their minds on the subject whatever the consequences. But humble people have often to resort to strange awkward ways of expressing themselves when the matter is one on which they feel deeply, and so as she was sending Leah out on a few errands, she said

"An' caw at Jabe's an' see if aar Simeon's clogs is done; an', fur goodness sake, wench, donna leuk sa mitch loike a lump o' stoan! Thaa mak's me fair miserable. If thaa wants Luke, tak' him, and ha' done wi' it," and before the startled girl could answer she had pushed her out of the door into the front garden that she might not see her mother's painful breakdown.

Now, this was perhaps the most important communication that Ellen Barber had ever made to her daughter, and it may seem that she did it in a very clumsy way. But it was her way. Awkward and bungling it may have been, but its awkwardness was the measure of its eloquence, and to Leah it spoke of a great effort, and a great sacrifice, which were the expressions of a wonderful love.

Leah was profoundly moved, and had to linger in the garden with her head down among the flowers for some time before she dared to go forth on her business. She put a severe restraint upon herself as she went about the village, and it was quite necessary, for rumours that she was "in decline" had been commonly circulated, and gave her acquaintances a painful sort of interest in looking at her.

When her errands were done and she was approaching home, she turned in at the end of Shaving Lane nearly opposite her father's workshop, and in a few minutes was standing near the autumn-tinted hedge, on the very spot where she had had her last interview with Luke. With her back to the lane, and her face looking up the Clough, she gave full play to her thoughts.

The law as to marriage with unbelievers, which, according to Beckside canons of interpretation, meant all non-church members, was clear and uncompromising, and the more she thought of it the clearer and more inexorable it became, and never in the whole of the terrible struggle through which she was now passing did she allow that to be obscured for so much as a moment. That by accepting Luke she would be breaking this law, was distinctly recognised.

On the other hand, her heart was as full as ever of a deep and quenchless love for Luke. How it came there she could not imagine. It had been a constant amazement to herself, and more than once she had tried to convince herself that it was Providence. Then she realised that the thought was a snare of the devil, and resolutely repressed it and cast it out of her heart. For some time after their last interview she did not admit to herself even the possibility of renewing the intercourse. Her remembrance of how soon she might have yielded to the impassioned Luke frightened her.

But she had scarcely seen Luke since that last struggle. Oh, where was he! And then she was startled to discover that the suggestion that he did not care a great deal for her gave her much strange pain. And then, though she had not seen much of her lover, she had heard, and what she had heard deepened her distress. She could not forget the rumour about Luke beginning to drink, and she recalled with fresh pain the remembrance that when she charged him with it he had not denied it. More recently she had been told that there had been an atheist lecturer at Clough End, and that conspicuous amongst the little handful who went to hear him was Luke. He had several times, in pleading with her, threatened to "run th' country," and only yesterday she had heard that he was preparing to emigrate to America. What if she had driven him to this? And what if he went away from Beckside and got amongst wild, lawless people at the ends of the earth?

Oh, if only they had never turned him out of the school! Surely, with all his associations and attachments to the chapel and chapel folk, it might not have been difficult to draw him in. But she knew by this time that Luke, under all his frolicsomeness, had a proud heart, and a strong, masterful will, and that he would probably never come back to the chapel unless she took him. She was perfectly certain he had a good heart, and good principles, as far as mere morality went, though morality apart from grace was of little account in Beckside theology. In fact it was generally regarded as a dangerous form of worldly pride and hypocrisy.

By this time her agitation became so uncontrollable that she feared to be suddenly discovered by a passer-by, and so, yielding to her own restlessness, she crossed the plank bridge, and walked slowly up the field walk to Lamb Fold. There she turned back, and as the body turned the mind did the same, and she went once more over all the arguments for and against accepting Luke.

As she returned to the place she had left half an hour before, she began to recall stories of female self-sacrifice of which she had read in the books of the Sunday-school library, but could not remember a case in the least like her own. Once more Luke's spiritual condition came before her, and the terrible risk of sending him adrift on the world in his present reckless and unregenerate mood.

Then the thought of self-sacrifice for a beloved one, the sweetest thought that ever touches the deep heart of woman, came once more into her mind, and seemed sweeter and more beautiful than ever.

And at last, leaning heavily against the stone gate-post near her, and, dropping her head on the crossbar of the gate, she cried—

"Is it my soul fur his, Lord? Then let it be his. If Tha'll let me bring him safe to heaven, Thaa can shut th' dur ageean me—if—if—if Thaa *con*."

And then the passion subsided. A calm almost more terrifying to Leah than her former agitation took possession of her, and she went home convinced that she was going to commit the unpardonable sin, but that she was going to save Luke.

Two days later she had consented to marry him.

IV.

BETTER THAN HER FEARS.

BUT Leah's battle was not over when she had given her consent to marry. The stony calm which existed within her from the time she decided to accept Luke until the moment when she told him so, or, perhaps, more exactly, the moment she was alone after she had told him so, vanished as quickly as it came, and for the next day or two she would have given worlds to recall her consent.

But Luke evidently knew with whom he had to deal, and for a lovesick swain showed a most singular reluctance to see his sweetheart. He was "ter'ble busy," he explained hurriedly, when Leah, four or five days after her consent, sought him out. He had been "puttin' th' axins in" for the marriage, and would be compelled to be absent a good deal just now in order to conform to the law with regard to the question of residence. It was only years later that Leah learned that they had been married by special licence.

Besides, Luke urged, he was "up to th' een i' furnishing, an' hadn't toime for nowt."

Then he took to sending little notes to her, using Johnty Harrop the "minder" as his messenger, and Leah, remembering his schoolboy handwriting, was astonished at the bold, dashing caligraphy of the missives, and half suspected him of employing an amanuensis. And yet she didn't see how he could.

The marriage was, of course, a profound secret, and Luke seemed to take a most characteristic pleasure in the fact that the affair was to be, in appearance at any rate, an elopement. On the few occasions when they did get conversation together, Leah was so preoccupied with desire to draw back from her promise that she never thought of inquiring what arrangements Luke was making as to house, furniture, etc., and Luke, as she pressed him for release, generally sought safety in flight, and brought the interview to an abrupt termination.

Consequently, when they got into the week on the Saturday of which the wedding was to take place, Leah literally knew nothing of what would be done when the ceremony was over, and was still so preoccupied with her own internal conflict that scarcely a thought of the future passed through her mind.

The Friday came, the last day of Leah's maidenhood. She was to meet her lover that night at the end of her father's woodshed, and all day long she was collecting her little personal possessions together one minute, and rehearsing the last passionate appeal she intended to make to Luke for release the next; and as evening drew near her agitation became almost painful, and the hour of tryst seemed as though it would never come.

Presently, however, she stole out of the back door, trying to nerve herself for what she knew would be a severe struggle, and was just stepping softly towards the yard through the darkness when she heard herself called. She stopped. It was not Luke's voice; it was a woman's. Before she could speak she heard a light footfall near her, and an instant later Mrs. Johnty Harrop's plump little arms were thrown around her, a letter was thrust into her hand, a hot little face, wet with sympathetic tears, was pressed against hers, and a caressing voice murmured, "God bless thi, wench! tha's nowt to fear," then the arms unentwined themselves, there was a flutter of receding skirts, and in a moment Leah was alone again.

A minute or two later she was up in her own little bedroom, reading Luke's letter with the aid of a candle.

The epistle was rather longer than usual. It stated that Luke found that it would be impossible to carry out their arrangements, except by going himself to Whipham on Thursday afternoon. He had therefore done so. She was to follow by Saturday morning's coach to Duxbury, and then by train to Whipham, where he would meet her. Some other directions were given, and then the letter concluded—

"Keep your heart up, my bonny wench. In a week's time you shall be prouder of being Leah Yates than ever you were of being Leah Barber."

Leah read this communication over and over again, and dwelt with a wistful, clinging feeling upon the closing sentences. She discovered now, for the first time, that she had never really believed that Luke would give her up, or even consent to a postponement, and she was alarmed to find also that there was something in her which would have made her feel disappointed if he had consented.

She felt, also, as if there was a sort of fate—she dared not call it Providence—in the affair, and that she was being swept on with the current of things in spite of herself, and it somehow relieved and comforted her to think so.

But why did she dwell so lovingly on the latter part of the letter? Somehow during all her struggles she had felt a strange faith in Luke in spite of all, and those last words of his seemed to promise that he was going to give her a sweet surprise. "God grant it might be so!"

And then she began to wonder where she was going to live. Probably not in Beckside, and under all the circumstances she felt it was better so, though it was an additional pang to be separated from her beloved ones.

This was her last night in the old home, the only home she had ever had, and she began to look round with a strange, softly sorrowful look. She stole into her father's bedroom, and stood long before an old daguerreotype portrait of him hanging over the drawers. Then she stole downstairs, and as the front room was empty, she took refuge in it, whilst her feelings rose and fell with the different articles that she looked so wistfully at. She found an old leather-bound Bible, familiar to her from earliest infancy, and kissed it again and again with choking sobs. Then she fell on her knees on the spot where her father always knelt at family prayer, and laying her cheek on the well-worn cushion of the arm-chair, she began to sob again with a violence that was almost hysterical. How long she knelt there, in the dim candle-light, she never knew, but presently a voice cried in tones of alarm

"Leah, what's to dew?"

And the portly form of her mother stood over her in distressful surprise.

Leah still hugged the cushion for a moment, and then, with a last impassioned kiss, she rose to her feet and faced her parent.

"Muther," she said, with grave, sad face, "Aw'm goin' t' leeave yo' aw i' th' morning. Aw'm goin' to save Luke, if Aw'm lost mysel' fur it. Aw conna help it, muther."

Mrs. Ben took her daughter quietly in her arms and held her there in a long, clinging embrace, and at length she murmured—

"Goa wheer thaa will, wench, an' dew wet thaa will, tha'll allis be aar Leah to uz, an' ther'll allis be a whoam fur thi here woll [whilst] thi fayther an' me lives."

And then Ben came in and had to be told. He dropped into his chair, and then down upon his knees, and— But there are some scenes even in Beckside history too sacred for strange eyes to look upon.

Next morning, Leah, dressed in her ordinary Sunday clothes, took her seat in the Duxbury coach. By her own choice she went alone, and sat as deep in the coach as she could get, trembling and quietly weeping, though her heart felt cold and hard as stone.

The train from Duxbury to Whipham was late that day, and it was half-past eleven before it pulled up at the station. Luke was there, dressed with a quiet, good taste, which even Leah, in her agitation, could not help noticing with a momentary pride. Then they hurried into a cab. Luke seemed sadly extravagant, she thought. This was the first cab she had ever ridden in, and as the parish church was close at hand, they could have walked in five minutes easily.

As she walked up the aisle, Leah thought she caught a glimpse of a bonnet she knew, but she had other things to think of.

The service was commencing. Dear! dear! was this the garrulous, graceless Luke. Even in the cab he had not been able to repress his overflowing fun, but here before this silver-haired old vicar he was sobriety itself. Yes, sober and something more, for if ever a man went with all his heart into the solemn covenant of matrimony that man was Luke Yates. Leah was puzzled, yet deeply gratified.

And then it was over, and almost before the minister had said "Amen!" this dreadful Luke threw his arm round her and actually broke out into a great sob; and whilst the first tears she had ever seen there stood brimming in his eyes, he cried, to the amazement of both Leah and the vicar, and the intense amusement of the old sexton—

"Aw've getten thi. Aw've getten thi. Thank God! Aw've getten thi!"

Then they adjourned to the vestry, and were preparing to sign the register when the door opened, and the best little bonnet in Beckside, surmounting the merry face of Mrs. Johnty Harrop, appeared in the aperture. The lively little woman seized Leah and kissed her as though she would never cease. Behind Susy came the "Minder" himself—sheepish and bashful. He was just beginning to wish Leah many happy re——" when Susy cried, "Johnty!" and the poor Minder broke down and stammered a sort of apology, but was afraid to attempt any further compliment.

The register got signed, the Minder and his wife witnessing, and then they went out, and that reckless Luke put them into a cab again, Johnty mounting the box-seat, and they were driven off to a quiet hotel, and there, behold! was a small but frighteningly elegant wedding-breakfast, which Leah felt almost afraid to taste as she thought of its probable cost.

Breakfast over, Johnty and his wife must go, and, of course, the bridal pair would see them off. Just as the train moved out, Susy leaned out of the window and cried to Leah—

"Aw winna say 'Gooid-day,' wench, Aw'st happen see thi ageean afoor lung."

And she looked so very arch and mysterious as she said it, that Leah was compelled to think that it was welcome news, and felt better after it.

Now all these things had been done so rapidly and in such a whirl of excitement that Leah had caught some of the infection of it, and felt somehow a most unusual elation, so much so, that when she began to rebuke Luke for his extravagance in cabs, etc., and that triumphant young man pulled a crooked penny out of his pocket, and wickedly declared that it was all he had in the world, Leah had a sudden rush of pride and trust in her new husband, snatched the penny from his hand, and threw it as far as ever she could over the railings, never even stopping to see it flop into the river.

Then they walked about the town viewing the places of interest, Leah trying to look as little like a bride as she could, and Luke doing his best to make everybody see that he was a happy bridegroom.

As the afternoon wore on and the excitement subsided somewhat, Leah's anxiety returned, and all the things that she wanted to know began to clamour in her mind.

"Luke," she said, stopping suddenly in a quiet walk on the edge of the public park and looking gravely at her husband, "tha's towd me nowt abaat nowt yet. Isn't it toime thaa oppened thi maath?"

"Hay! Aw'll tell thi owt as iver thaa wants to know. Naa, start off. Wot's th' fust thing?"

"Wheer are we going fur t' live?"

"Live? Whey, i' Beckside; wheer else?"

Leah was startled a little. In thinking of her future, so far as she had thought at all, she had somehow imagined herself living away from her native village, and thus escaping some of the consequences of her daring act. But to think she was going back to face it all out amongst those who knew her took her breath away, and so she faltered faintly—

"I' Beckside! Wheerabaats?"

"I' th' bonniest little haase i' th' Clough."

Luke spoke these words as though they were a quotation from somebody else, and Leah suddenly remembered that in the only lover's walk she had ever taken with Luke they had passed the cottage of Jimmy Juddy, then just emptied, and which had stood empty ever since, and so she said—

"No' Jimmy Juddy's owd haase, at th' Beckbottom?"

Beckside Lights

"Yi."

A rush of sweet feeling came upon Leah. Her face softened; gratification at discovering that a carelessly dropped word of hers had been treasured up by her lover, and woman's pride in the dear little house and garden, which everybody admired, struggled through the veil of her natural reserve, and the light in her eyes was abundant reward to the keenly observant man by her side.

By this time the early November day was closing in, and the bridal pair made their way to the station en route for Beckside. As they went along it began to rain and blow, and when they arrived at Duxbury it was as wild and dark a night as Leah had ever been out in.

However were they going to get home? The walk at any time would have been quite as much as she could manage, but after such a day, and in such a drenching rain, it seemed madness to attempt it.

Luke, however, seemed very cheerful about the matter, and laughed at her fears, and when the train stopped, he led the way to a side gate of the station, and before she had time to think, she was safe inside a covered conveyance, and bowling away through wind and rain towards Beckside.

How reckless Luke was with his money! He might have come into a fortune by the way he threw it about. This would be an additional task to the heavy one she had already undertaken, for unless she economised she could see they would soon be ruined. The wind still swirled and whistled about the coach, and the rain beat against the little window, but Luke and Leah sat in darkness and silence except for occasional laconic remarks about the storm.

They seemed to be going very slowly, and though they must be getting near their journey's end, and had already passed one or two lighted houses, even the reckless Luke dared not venture to look out.

A sudden drop made Leah aware that she was going down into Beckside and getting near her new home.

What sort of place would it be? She nearly smiled as she imagined her lively husband selecting and arranging furniture, and prepared herself for almost anything that might present itself in the way of ridiculous and even outrageous contrivances. But she would bear it all. Luke should see what religion could do for those who had it, and with a temperament such as his she was sure that submissive gentleness would be best. She was resolved that she would make the very best of what he had provided, and try to use this as one of the means of bringing him to God.

Just then the coach stopped, and in a moment the door was opened, and she was nearly lifted out by her excited and eager husband. The rain was still pouring down, and the cottage door, standing open a few yards down the garden, sent forth a most welcome and alluring light.

"Run, wench, run!" cried Luke. and Leah, in dread of the rain, made all the haste she could. As she stepped into the doorway, who should rush forward to meet her but Mrs. Johnty Harrop.

"Here thaa art, wench, at last! Come in wi' thi," she cried, with face abeam with gladness.

Leah stepped across the threshold, took a hasty glance round, and then stood stock-still in amazement and alarm,

Coming in thus from the rain and the inky darkness, with a mind prepared for almost anything except finery, the sight that met Leah's eyes quite overpowered her.

She took in the situation in a moment. Luke had evidently got acquainted somehow with the Harrops, and had taken Mrs. Johnty into his confidence, and the result was one of the bonniest and most cosy-looking little houses that Leah had ever seen.

Such a fire this wild night, and such resplendent fire-irons! And what armchairs and rockers and fancy cushions! And, oh, what drawers! And what a hearthrug! And of all the fancy clocks— But poor Leah could only stand and look round dumbfounded.

But at that moment Luke came in behind her, and drawing her forward and down into the rocking-chair, he cried, "Theer!" and stood back to watch her.

Leah glanced wonderingly round again, and was just about to speak, when she caught sight of a picture hanging over the mantelpiece. Something familiar about it arrested her eyes, and she rose out of her seat to examine it. What was it but a picture of the old Beckside Chapel before the alterations! It was framed in rosewood, and looked as if it had been drawn and coloured by someone whose heart was in his work. An artist would have seen many faults, doubtless, but to Leah it was just perfect, and great tears welled up into her eyes as she gazed at it.

Suddenly she wheeled round to speak to Luke, who was deep in whispered converse with Mrs. Johnty at the door going into the back kitchen, but as she did so, her eyes caught another picture on the wall opposite, and, stepping across to it, she discovered a representation in oil of her father's house and premises. It was a rude attempt, shockingly out of perspective, —the brickwork was very red, and the mortar lines were very white, whilst the garden was a most startling green,—but Leah saw no fault in it at all; and after gazing fondly up at it for a time, she sat quietly down again with a melting heart and pale but smiling lips.

Then Mrs. Johnty invited Leah upstairs, to take her things off, she said, but really that she might exhibit to her all the grandeur of her little home. Leah was quietly delighted, and grew softer and tenderer as she looked about. She had never seen anything like it; and when she had finished her tour of inspection, concluding with another loving look at the pictures, she turned to Luke, who had just come in from the back kitchen, and said, in her grave way—

"Luke, tha's capped me mony a toime, bud this beeats aw. Hast paid fur it?"

Luke's face lighted up with that roguish look, so frightening and still so fascinating to Leah, and he answered, reaching out his arm to snatch hold of her as he did so—

"Paid for it? Neaw. Aw've getten it aw on th' strap."

In another moment he would have had her in his arms, but she glided away, and Mrs. Johnty coming in, cried—

"Naa then! Noa clippin' afoor foak. Aw'm 'shawmed fur *thee*, Leah."

"It wurna me," cried Leah, and the rest laughed derisively; and then Johnty came in from the back kitchen hot and red with making toast, and they sat down to tea.

During the meal Mrs. Johnty gave Leah a full and particular account of the whole scheme of house furnishing, and wickedly pretended to be afraid to tell what it had cost. And when Leah in growing alarm pressed her, she presented the bills all duly and regularly receipted.

They sat for some time after that, until Johnty became quite sentimental, and told about his own wedding-day, and would have enlarged still more upon his domestic experiences, but that Susy, with the air of a woman of sixty, told her husband, "We'd better be piking off whoam; young foak are best by thersel's."

When the Harrops had gone, Luke and Leah went all over the house again, and Luke explained everything, and exhibited his various purchases, with all their marvels of contrivance and convenience, until Leah was quite overpowered, and her heart was full of the sweet music of the thought that this was Luke's mode of telling her how he loved her.

When they had gone through everything again, and were just about to sit down, she turned to Luke with a sweetly sad and yet earnest smile, and, touching him on his arm,—the first sign of a caress she had ever given him,—said, as she did so—

"Hay, lad! Aw should be th' praadest wench i' Lancashire toneet if on'y tha wur convarted."

Luke laughed an odd catchy sort of a laugh, and if Leah had been a little more observant she might have noticed a strange light in his brown eyes, but she did not, for the answer he made gave her room she thought for far more serious reflection.

"Convarted!" he cried. "Hay! Aw'st happen convart thee afoor Aw've done."

And Leah sent up a little prayer that she might be strengthened and saved from so great a fall.

Presently they began preparing for retiring, and Leah, after another proud yet somewhat pensive look round her little domestic palace, was making for the staircase, when Luke, who was looking very much at home in the easy-chair, called out—

"Leah!"

"Wot?"

"Aw thowt tha caw'd thisel' religious."

"Weel, Aw am, Aw whop" (hope), and she turned to look at him with a glance of inquiry.

"Religious foak han family prayers, hanna they?"

"A-y," said Leah faintly and with sudden loss of breath, and as she sank down on a chair wondering what was coming next, Luke got up and opened a drawer, brought out a new Family Bible, and handing it to her, said—

"Here! Tha'd ha' made a rare parson if tha'd bin a mon."

Leah took the book in a dazed sort of manner, and sat still with it on her lap with feelings too deep for utterance.

After a few moments' silence, however, she opened the book and began to read a psalm. Then she slid to her knees. Luke followed, and she began to pray.

Hesitantly, blunderingly, at first she spoke, but soon, as the thought of her husband's condition, and the responsibilities she had undertaken, filled her mind, she expressed her desires more freely; and if she had not been so fully occupied she might have observed that her young husband breathed out more than once sounds that were strangely like "Amens!"

Next morning, as she went about her new domestic duties, constantly discovering fresh evidences of the lavish manner in which Luke had provided for her, her mind was distracted by wondering how they would spend Sunday. She ought to go to chapel, but she dared not face it. She could go with Luke, but she had no hope that he would care to meet the people.

What was her duty? Ought she to take up her cross and go alone, whatever the consequences, and thus give her husband to see that she was beginning as she intended to go on; or ought she to stay at home with him, and try to restrain him from going off into bad company, as she felt sure she could do if she chose? Then she might gradually wean him from his dangerous associations, and some day, perhaps, she might coax him back to chapel.

A little before chapel time Luke came downstairs dressed in his Sunday best.

"Come, wench, artna gettin' ready?" he cried in mild surprise.

Beckside Lights

"Ready? Wot fur? Wheer are we goin'?"

"Goin'? Whey to th' chapil, arna we?"

And Leah sat down and cried, a soft sweet little cry it was in which her heart overflowed in thankful surprise and relief. She could face the chapel folk easily now; and in a few minutes they were crossing the fields in the shy November sunlight, Leah feeling as proud of her husband as he evidently was of her.

There was a buzz of sensation as they entered the little sanctuary, followed by much whispering, and when Long Ben, looking depressed and nervous, opened the vestry door for the preacher to pass into the pulpit, and caught sight of them, he stood for a moment transfixed, and then hastily closed the door, and it was far on in the service before he mustered courage to come into his own pew.

When the service was over, Ben came down the chapel and mutely shook hands with them; the juvenile Barbers somewhat shyly followed him, and gathering round Leah, asked all sorts of embarrassing questions, while Luke stood by with growing delight as he listened to his young wife's brave answers.

At the evening service Luke and Leah turned up again, and to everybody's astonishment, and most of all to Leah's, Luke insisted on staying to the prayer-meeting.

As the meeting proceeded there was a mysterious pantomimic display going on over the heads olf the kneeling worshippers. Jonas Tatlock and Sam Speck were standing up and nodding their heads to Lige the road-mender, who sat near the young couple, pointing significantly at them as they did so. But Lige shook his head and jerked his thumb behind him towards Jabe in the back pew. Presently Sam left his seat, and going on tiptoe to the Clogger's pew, he leaned over and whispered—

"Artna goin' ta speik ta yond' lad?"

"Goa thisel'," was the somewhat sulky rejoinder, for Jabe was suffering inward torment. "It 'ud leuk better if thaa went; thaa turnt him aat, thaa knows."

"Weel, Aw shanna;" and considering that they were in a prayer-meeting, the Clogger's tone was simply shocking.

After another unsuccessful attempt, Sam went back to his seat, and the meeting closed somewhat prematurely.

Meanwhile Long Ben, sitting in his pew, had made up his mind to a great deed. As soon as Leah had gone on Saturday morning, he went up to the Clog Shop and told his old friend what was taking place that day, and it was some time before he could make Jabe believe what he said. When he did realise it, however, all the stiffness which had come between them of late melted away in an instant, and though the fact was shown by neither word nor act, Ben knew that he had, if possible, a deeper place than ever in his old friend's love and care.

Ben, therefore, secure in the support of Jabe, hastened out of the chapel the back way as the meeting was dispersing, and stopping the young couple as they came out, he said—

"Yo' tew mun come daan ta aar haase."

To Leah's surprise, Luke seemed glad of the invitation, and his face did not change in its happy look even when Jabe and Sam Speck were invited.

Beyond a long careful look at her daughter as she shyly entered, Mrs. Ben gave no signs of any unusual feeling, and in a few minutes they were all seated comfortably round the supper-table. Comfortably, that is, as far as mere accommodation was concerned, for in every other respect the gathering was a failure, and everybody seemed awkward and taciturn.

The food was eaten almost in silence. A few words were said about the sermon and the weather, but nobody made even the faintest allusion to the great event that was uppermost in everybody's thoughts.

Luke, however, seemed to be eating rapidly, but it was more as a stimulating accompaniment to his own very active thoughts than because of any particular relish for the food.

Just as they were about to return thanks, Luke lifted his head, and looking towards the Clogger, said —

"Jabe, Aw want ta thank thi fur turnin' me aat o' th' schoo'."

Everybody looked up in astonishment, but as nobody spoke, Luke went on—

"Aw ne'er know'd haa mitch Aw loiked it till then, bud that made me think, Aw con tell yo'! Ay, an' feel tew! That schoo' and this wench" — laying his hand gently on Leah's shoulder—"has saved my soul."

Leah started up, with a glad, eager cry.

"Ay, wench!" Luke went on, looking down upon her with a burning glance, "tha's saved mi soul. Aw allis loiked thi, and the moor religious thaa wur, the moor Aw loiked thi. Aw dunno say as thaa did reet i' th' sight o' God wi' takkin' me, bud thaa did it. An' when Aw seed thi riskin' thi soul ta save me, it fairly knocked me o'er. Bud, wench, Aw'm converted. Aw've bin converted welly a fortnit, an' if God helps me, tha'st ha' the best husband i' Beckside. Bless thi! Bless thi!"

The scene that followed baffles description. Whether poor Ben, or his wife, or the still Leah, or Luke himself, was most excited, it would be difficult to say, but for the next two hours tongues were going and joys were being reciprocated until everybody felt young and bright again.

When at last the company began to break up, Jabe, who had been strangely silent all evening, drew Luke aside into a corner, and said in a subdued voice—

"Dost smook, lad?"

"Ay! A bit."

"Ther's a seeat fur thi at th' Clog Shop feire ony toime tha's a moind ta come."

And that being as near to an acknowledgment of mistake as Jabe could ever be expected to come, no more was ever said between them about Luke's expulsion.

SALLY'S REDEMPTION.

I.

UNRECIPROCATED ADVANCES.

"SAM."

"Wot."

"Yo' men's noa feelin's."

The speaker was Lottie Speck, Sam's long, angular, yellow-haired sister. She stood between the cupboard door and the edge of the table, and had been for some moments looking abstractedly through the front window.

"Wot's up wi' thi naa? " demanded Sam, who was busy mending a fiddle.

"Ther's poor Sniggy yond', goin' abaat loike sumbry dateliss sin' his muther deed, an' tha's niver bin th' mon az hes axed him ta hev' a sooap o' tay wi' thi'. Neaw, nor even of a Sunday. It wodna cap me if his trubbel druv him ta th' drink ageean; an' if it dooas, he'll be wur nor iver."

Sam lifted his head from his fiddle with a look of dull astonishment. This was never his hard, unsympathetic shrew of a sister! Ask anybody to tea! Why he hadn't dared to do such a thing for he couldn't tell how long. And the memory of the last occasion on which he did so was even yet a vision of terror to him. Whatever was coming over Lottie?

"Aw'll ax him ta-morn if thaa wants him," he said at length, gazing at his sister in puzzled surprise.

"Me? Aw dunna want him!" and Lottie tossed her head in lofty disdain. "Aw want noa felleys slotching abaat me, Aw con tell thi." And Lottie began to examine herself critically in the little looking-glass on the wall.

Sam said no more, but he resolved that if he had really caught his sister in an unusually amiable mood he would make the most of it whilst it lasted, and Sniggy should be invited on the very next day.

But whatever could it mean? Was this nipping, harsh sister of his, who ruled him with a rod of iron, and ordered him about as if he had been a slave, relenting? Had he been mistaken? Was there a soft place in that thin, bony body after all? Well, he would hope so; and in better spirits than he had felt for many a day, Sam hung his fiddle up and sauntered off to the Clog Shop.

But even in the short distance between that great establishment and his own cottage, Sam's surprise overcame him again, and he whistled a long, low whistle of wonderment, and stopped in the middle of the road to marvel.

Well, wonders never cease certainly, but this was the greatest surprise of all, and Sam jerked his head in amazement and resumed his journey.

But, somehow, he couldn't help having misgivings. He was anxious enough to believe that this was the sign of a change in Lottie, but it was really so entirely contradictory to her ordinary manner and spirit that he couldn't believe in it, do what he would. And as for lasting! Well, if Lottie held out for a week in her present state of mind he would give women up as insoluble riddles, as his great mentor declared they were.

Sam soon made it right with Sniggy. That worthy having lost Old Molly, his mother, a few weeks before, felt very "looansome" in his little cottage in the Brickcroft, and gratefully accepted any offers of hospitality that were made to him.

Sniggy regarded the Specks as somewhat above him in the social scale, and felt flattered by the invitation, but at the same time he knew enough of Lottie to be greatly surprised at it, and strolled down from the school on Sunday afternoon by Sam's side with somewhat apprehensive feelings lest he should find she was not of the same mind as her brother.

But Sam's sister received them with a manner as near to graciousness as Sniggy had ever known her to show, and set before them a tea which was in itself an additional welcome.

There was buttered toast and "pikelets," "pig-seause" (brawn), pickled onions, and a currant fatcake, to say nothing of such ordinary provisions as oatcake, white bread and butter, and tea-cakes, and Sam, as he glanced at the overcrowded little table, made up his mind that if Sniggy didn't come to tea pretty often in the future it shouldn't be his fault.

And Lottie was so amiable with it all. A thrill of horror went through Sam as Sniggy in his nervousness poured the tea over the saucer edge and stained their best tablecloth, but to his amazement Lottie treated it as of no moment whatever, and even pretended to blame the shape of the old-fashioned cups for the disaster.

Sniggy had a good healthy appetite, and Sam feared he might get into trouble about that, but his sister urged and better urged their guest to eat, declaring, with much apparent concern, that he must be badly, "peckin' at his meit loike a brid."

Sam was simply bewildered. What could it all mean? But just at this moment, as he was hastily and somewhat fearfully cramming the half of a pikelet into his mouth, his amazement was intensified by his sister saying—

"Thaa mun cum ageean, Sniggy lad. If Aw'da brother as wur woth owt, he'd a axed thi afoor naa, lung sin'."

Sniggy thanked her blunderingly, and seemed to think that a feast like this was not a thing he could expect every day. At last the tea was over, and they drew near to the fire.

Sniggy pulled out a short wood pipe and a steel tobacco-box, and was proceeding to charge.

"Sam, wot arta dooin'? Tha'rt no' lettin' Sniggy use his oan 'bacca, arta?" cried Lottie, as if that was a practice that might obtain with common people, but was not to be thought of at all in their house.

And Sam, wondering whether he were not dreaming, rose to get his tobacco-box, only to discover that someone had already filled it with a popular mixture just then coming into fashion.

But this was too much! Sam gave it up now, and simply sat and smoked, trying to resolve that after this nothing in the world should surprise him.

Presently he began to realise that he had never really heard Sniggy talk before. Under Lottie's dexterous manipulation the ex-pigeon-flyer was becoming quite a brilliant conversationalist, and supplied his lady listener with more details of his mother's last illness than had ever been given to the world before; and by the time they had to go to chapel, Lottie and Sniggy were quite "thick."

As for Sniggy himself, he was quite uplifted, and went to the chapel marvelling at the number of undiscovered saints there were in the world, and the blindness and prejudice of those who had so long and so persistently maligned Sam's sister.

And next Sunday the whole thing was repeated, only on an, if possible, ampler scale. And even in the week between, Lottie had been so unusually considerate, and spoken so often and so kindly of Sniggy, that Sam was simply dazed as he thought of it.

But on that second Sunday night, as Sam lay pondering these things in bed, a horrible idea all at once took possession of him. That was it! He saw it all at once now. Why had he been so "numb"? *His sister was setting her cap at poor Sniggy!* Of course she was! What a "cawf-yed" he'd been not to see that before. And as Sam tossed about in bed, and looked at this great matter, his astonishment gave way to shame and anxiety. What a terrible position it was for him!

No man who knew anything of Lottie would ever marry her. And though she was his sister, he could not allow his friend Sniggy to run his head into a noose without knowing what he was doing. If Lottie married him she would, by her naggling ways, drive the poor fellow to drink in no time, and in that case *he* would be, in at least some measure, responsible.

On the other hand, had he not for years been hoping against hope that his sister would marry, and thus set him free to do the same? He had not dared to think of it seriously whilst he had her to deal with, except on the solitary occasion when he had desperately risked everything and proposed to "Nancy o' th' Fowt," only to be rejected; and even though his former experience of married life had not been exactly encouraging, yet he would have experimented again long ago but for his sister, and indeed, in some sense, because of his sister, and in order to be rid of her.

It was a matter about which he could not very well consult his friends, and yet if he did not, and Lottie actually accomplished her purpose, they would never forgive him, especially if they discovered that he had known it, and, in a sense, aided and abetted it.

All night long poor Sam tossed about, wrestling with his great problem. Morning came, but no relief. For two or three days Sam dogged Sniggy's footsteps, and hovered about him in a most peculiar way, but could never make up his mind to speak.

On Friday night, however, as he returned from a little journey, and called at home for his fiddle on his way to the Clog Shop practice, he was surprised as he opened the door to find Sniggy and Lottie sitting on the long settle very close together, and evidently engaged in a very interesting confab. Sam uttered a sudden and astonished "Hello!"

Lottie hastily left the long settle, and began to lecture Sam in the old style about "comin' tumblin' inta th' haase loike a mad bull," and Sniggy, looking somewhat relieved, rose to his feet and announced that he must be going.

Sam was glad to go along with his friend, and when they were approaching the Clog Shop door, he took a sudden and daring resolution. Stepping into the Cloggery, and hastily putting his fiddle down upon the counter, he hurriedly rejoined his companion in the road, and took him into the fields, ostensibly for a walk, but really to unburden his mind to him.

"It's varry gooid on thi, Sam lad!" said Sniggy, when the great secret had been revealed, "bud tha's bin meytherin' thisel' fur nowt."

"Haa's that?"

"Ther's noa weddin' fur me, lad;" and Sniggy slowly and sorrowfully shook his head.

"Noa weddin'? Nowt o' t' sooart, mon. Thaa gets good wages, an' tha's a haase aw ready. Aw'd be wed in a jiffy if Aw wur i' thy place."

"Nay, thaa wodna."

"Haa's that?"

"Sam, afoor Aw was converted Aw did wrung."

"Well?"

"Aw uset marlock wi' Sally Shaw thaa knows."

"Well?"

"Aw'm feart Aw helped ta mak' her wot hoo is."

"Wot bi that?"

"Aw loike her yet, Sam," and Sniggy nearly broke down.

"Bud thaa conna merry her, hoo's a—a—a bad un!"

"Sam," and poor Sniggy set his teeth, and choked back a sob, "if iver Aw wed Aw'st wed Sally. Aw'd nowt ta dew wi'th' lumber hoo geet inta, bud it wur me as coaxed her away fro' th' schoo', an' it aw started theer. An' if hoo comes back Aw'st merry her, an' if hoo ne'er comes back Aw'st stop as Aw am."

Sam went away from that interview with a deeper and tenderer attachment to the reclaimed pigeon-flyer than he had ever had before, and it was as well he did, for the reception he met with at home tried his loyalty to his friend to its utmost; and when on the following Sunday he absolutely refused to bring Sniggy to tea any more, and then, in his fear and flurry, blurted out that Sniggy wouldn't come if he were asked, he was glad to get out of the house, and at any rate postpone the consequences of this unexpected rebellion.

Not to be baulked, however, of her purpose, on the following morning Lottie made one of her infrequent attendances at morning service, and managed to get hold of Sniggy as they were coming out of chapel.

But Sniggy almost curtly declined her very warm invitation to tea, and when Lottie, affecting great surprise, demanded to know the reason, he became even more taciturn.

"Ay! tha's getten bet-ter feesh ta fry, Aw reacon. Soa thaa con dew baat uz," she said with some asperity, as she stopped opposite her own door.

Sniggy shyly hung his head in shame, but more for her than for himself. So she misunderstood the action, and went on—

"Tha's na need ta leuk loike that; Aw know wot's i' th' rooad. Tha's gettin' thick wi' them Horrocks wenches, *Aw've* yerd abaat it."

Sniggy stood with his face looking back towards the chapel. At last he turned, and looking steadily at Lottie, said, with a significance that even a much duller person than Sam's sister could not have misunderstood—

"Lottie, Aw'm no' meytherin' efther ony women, noather Horrockses nor awmbry else. Aw'll ler *them* alooan if they'll ler me alooan."

And without waiting for a reply he moved off quickly towards home.

The sufferings of poor Sam for the next few days are better imagined than described.

II.

THE OLD LOVE.

IT was Duxbury Wakes week, and of late years this great festival had come to be regarded as, more or less, a holiday for the whole surrounding district; and in spite of many and portentous harangues from the Sunday-school desk against it, every year found an increasing number of Becksiders making it an excuse for recreation and jaunting.

The old 'bus ran from Beckside twice every day during that week, to say nothing of the Clough End waggonette, which came through the village and picked up passengers.

Of course the magnates of the Clog Shop couldn't have been induced to go to Duxbury that week on any account whatever. Not for worlds would they expose themselves to the suspicion of hankering after the flesh-pots of Egypt.

About the middle of the particular Wakes week we are speaking of, Sam Speck suddenly missed his now almost inseparable friend Sniggy, and grew, in consequence, somewhat uneasy.

He knew the kind of time Sniggy used to have in former days at these wicked Wakes. And he had heard him say that, since his conversion, he was always glad when the fair was over. But this year Sniggy had lost his mother, and was "daan i' th' maath" in consequence. People in his condition often took to drink for the sake of relief and company, and Sam was afraid lest, in his sorrow and loneliness, Sniggy had yielded to temptation.

He determined, therefore, to look him tip. He called at Sniggy's house, and tried the door. It was fast, and Sam's heart sank a little.

"Hast seen owt o' Sniggy lattly?" he asked one of his friend's former companions, who stood in a dirty-looking doorway watching him.

"Ay! Aw seed him on th' Wakes graand at Duxb'ry yesterd'y, bud Aw fancy he didna coom back last neet;" and there was a gleam of unholy satisfaction in the man's bleary eye.

Sam walked back into the road, and up the "broo" to the Clog Shop, in a very miserable state of mind; and Jabe, when he heard the tidings, was scarcely less affected.

After a lengthy conversation, Sam offered to go to Duxbury in search of Sniggy, but Jabe was by no means sure that this might not be a sly dodge on Sam's part to get an excuse for a peep at Vanity Fair, and so peremptorily dismissed the idea.

Just then Sam caught sight of Long Ben going past, and hurrying to the door, he called him in.

Ben proved "awkert." He had more faith in Sniggy than that, and didn't think it necessary to "meyther." That was always the way with Ben—he always went "collywest" to everybody else, and would "sit an' grin woll his haase wur brunnin'."

Next morning Sam arrived at the Clog Shop with the tidings that Sniggy had been home, but had gone off again, presumably to Duxbury, before daylight.

Jabe felt very ill at ease, and the holiday feeling which seemed to be in the air affected him with a strange restlessness. So, later in the day, he was standing at his shop door when the 'bus from Duxbury pulled up in the triangle. He watched the passengers alight, in the hope that Sniggy would be amongst them.

But only three persons got out, and they were all women; and Jabe had turned his eyes in another direction, and was watching a slater at work on the Fold Farm roof, when a voice he knew said, close at his side—

"Jabe, Aw want ta speik ta thi."

It was Lottie Speck, one of the passengers who had just alighted. Jabe eyed her over slowly and sourly, but did not offer to move or speak.

"Jabe, Aw've summat ta say ta thi."

"Well, wot is it?"

"Aw conna talk ta thi here; goa i' th' shop an' Aw'll tell thi."

Slowly, and with evident reluctance, Jabe led the way to the inglenook, but neither sat down himself nor invited his visitor to do so.

Lottie Speck never brought good tidings, and he had enough to think about that was troublesome without anything more.

"Jabe, Aw've bin ta Duxb'ry."

"Ay! Owder an' madder."

Lottie closed her eyes in expression of her willingness to endure even worse abuse than this if the Clogger was cruel enough to inflict it upon her. After a pause, she went on—

"Aw seed summat as thaa owt ta yer abaat at wunce."

Jabe looked impatiently out of the window, as if he neither wanted Lottie nor her communication.

"It made me fair whacker when Aw seed it."

Still the Clogger would not speak.

"Hay, dear! this is a wicked wold," and Lottie heaved a pious sigh.

"Well, wot is it, woman? Aat wi' it," snapped the Clogger petulantly.

"Jabe, Aw seed Sniggy Parkin talkie' tew a bad woman."

Jabe's heart sank within him, and he felt like crying, but he would not show it to this creature, and so, glancing at her with annihilating fierceness, he demanded—

"Well, wot's that ta dew wi' thi."

Lottie was staggered.

"Me? Nowt. Bud he's a member, isn't he?" she cried, at a loss for the moment what to say.

Jabe's anger was fast getting the better of him. If Lottie did not go, he would be saying something he should be sorry for.

"Lottie," he cried, "if tha'll give o'er melling [meddling] wi' other foak, an' leuk a bit bet-ter efther thisel', it 'ull leuk a foine seet bet-ter on thi." And after another pause he turned his back on his visitor, and, stepping over towards the other side of the shop, added gruffly—

"Tha'd bet-ter be piking."

Lottie, staggered and nonplussed by the Clogger's unusually surly manner, and yet resolved to brave it out, drew herself up to her full height, and began—

"Foaks as winks at other foaks' nowtiness"—But she got no further, for Jabe made a rush at her, and what he really intended to have done it would be impossible to say, for Lottie nimbly slipped to the door, and, giving it a spiteful bang after her, disappeared, and the Clogger stood breathless and angry in the middle of his shop floor.

Later on, in the same day, Jabe and Sam had another consultation. Lottie, defeated in her purpose with Jabe, had had her revenge on her hapless brother, and Sam, though in no way abating his concern about Sniggy, had a chastened and pensive look.

Eventually it was decided that Sam should go in the evening to Lige the road-mender's, who lived on the edge of the Brickcroft, and from this vantage point watch for the fallen Sniggy's return.

About ten o'clock he came hurrying into the Clog Shop with a pale and woebegone look. He was evidently full of some sorrowful tidings, but seeing that one or two of the cronies were still there, he suddenly checked himself, and tried to look easy.

But the Clogger was not deceived. Neither was he content to wait. The strain he had borne that day made him excessively irritable, and so, recklessly ignoring all considerations of caution, he demanded—

"Well! wot is it?"

Sam was terrified; he dodged behind Long Ben and began to motion to Jabe not to speak. But the Clogger was beyond all possibility of care now.

"Wor art pace-eggin' theer at? Aat wi' it, if tha's owt to say."

Long Ben and Jethro, who were the two present, turned round and looked at Sam, and though he did his best to appear unconcerned it was an utter failure, and a minute later they had brought him into the little circle and were demanding to know what was the matter.

Sam was bursting to tell the news, but he was also very much afraid of complicating matters. However, as everybody seemed to be waiting for him, and Jabe showed ominous signs of impatience, he blurted out—

"Sniggy's cum whoam."

"Well, wot bi that?" asked Jethro, who, of course, knew nothing of what had previously occurred, but could see that something more than common was involved.

"An' he's browt a woman wi' him—an' a chilt."

A sharp cry escaped the Clogger, and even Ben looked startled.

"Art thaa sewer?"

"Aw seed em' cum, an' goa i' th' haase; aw three on 'em."

The friends gazed at each other with shocked and sorrowful looks, but for a time nobody spoke.

At last Long Ben rose to his feet, and as it was evident where he was going, Jabe cried—

"Howd on. Aw'll goa wi' thi."

Ben hesitated, and evidently thought that he had better go alone, but the Clogger looked so very anxious that he hadn't the heart to object, although Jabe himself admitted afterwards that it was an unwise thing to do.

A few minutes later the two approached Sniggy's cottage.

They could see the flicker of the firelight on the window-blind, but there was no other sign of illumination.

Ben knocked, and immediately opened the door.

As he did so a woman, sitting before the fire, and evidently rocking a little child to sleep, turned her head towards them hastily, and then as hastily turned it away again.

"Wheer's Sniggy?" asked Ben, holding the door in his hand.

"He's nor in," replied the woman, still concealing her face.

"Haa lung will he be afoor he's back?"

"He's noa comin' back here ta-neet," was the reply.

The two visitors breathed sighs of relief, and began to feel a little like intruders, and so, with an awkward "Gooid-neet," they retired.

As they ascended the "broo," Sam Speck met them, all hurried and out of breath.

"He's yond'," he cried, suddenly discovering them in the darkness.

"Wheer?"

"At th' shop."

The three walked quickly up the little hill, and checking themselves as they drew near the Cloggery, they entered as unconcernedly as was possible under the circumstances.

"Hello, Snig!" said Sam, who was first, evidently with a desire to make the ex-pigeon-flyer feel at his ease.

But Jabe was too anxious for any subterfuge. Walking up to the fire, and fixing Sniggy with his eye, he demanded —

"Wheer's thaw bin aw wik?"

Sniggy looked up quietly, glanced round to see who the others were, and then, pointing with the stem of his pipe to the empty stools, he said—

"If yo'll sit yo' daan Aw'll tell yo' aw abaat it."

The three men sank into seats, and after waiting until they were seated and smoking, he commenced—

"Yo' known, chaps, as Aw uset be thick wi' Sally Shaw?"

"Well?" (from Jabe).

"Well, when Aw geet convarted Aw wanted her to jine tew, an' hoo wodna."

"Well?"

"Well, Aw gan o'er gooin' wi' her."

"Well?"

"An' Aw started o' pruyin' fur her—fur, hay, chaps, Aw did loike her."

"Christians conna merry wi'"—Jabe was commencing, but Ben stopped him, and Sniggy proceeded.

"Well, mooar Aw prayed th' wur hoo went, an' at th' lung last hoo geet i' trubbel, an' went away."

And then Sniggy's voice quavered, and he paused, and shaking his head earnestly, he cried—

"Hay, bud Aw did loike her."

"Well, an' wot then?"

"Well, Aw wur that ill off abaat her Aw could hardly 'bide. Aw kept on pruyin' yo' known, bud Aw ne'er yerd nowt on her. An' then my owd muther deed, an' Aw felt mooar looansomer nor iver. Well, o' Tuesday, as we wur hevin' aar breakfast i' th' shop, Aw yerd Alice Varlet' tellin' Peggy Bobby as hoo seed Sally upo' Duxb'ry Wakes graand, an' hoo wur wi' a minadgerie chap, an' leuked badly an' ill off. Hay, chaps! it went through me loike a shot. Aw couldna rest, Aw couldna sleep when neet coom. An' soa th' fost thing i' th' mornin' Aw went off fur t' seek her. Aw wur seekin' her tew days, an' this efthernoon, just when Aw wur thinkin' o' givin' it up, Aw yerd a woman shaat aat 'Snig! Snig!' an' Aw turnt me raand an' it wur her."

Then Sniggy paused, and looked round on the company, as if expecting them to look as delighted as he had evidently been himself.

Nobody spoke, however, and so presently he resumed his story.

"Hoo coom up lowfing, shy-loike, yo' known, bud when hoo geet cluse tew me, hay, chaps, hoo did leuk miserable!"

The listeners looked as if that was about the only becoming thing they had heard of her, and disappointed again in his bid for sympathy, Sniggy proceeded—

"Hoo axed me if Aw wur na gooin' fur t' pay fur a drink fur her. An' Aw leuks at her, an' Aw says, 'Neaw, wench, neaw!'

"An' then hoo leuked at me, solemn-loike, an' hoo says, 'Arta religious yet, Snig?'

"'Ay,' Aw says. An' wot dust think hoo did, Sam?"

"Aw dunno."

"Hoo tewk howd o' booath my honds, o' thisunce, an' hoo says, reglar wild-loike, 'Thank God! thank God!'" and Sniggy looked about on his friends with shining, tearful face.

Presently he resumed —

"An' then Aw tewk her tew a cook-shop, and as we wur goin' hoo stops an' hoo leuks at me solemn-loike, for a great while, an' then hoo brasts aat o' skriking, an' hoo says, 'Snig,' hoo says, 'Aw wuish *Aw* wur religious!'

"Aw wur i' th' street, men, bud Aw couldna help it, soa Aw just bells aat, 'Hallelujah!' an' th' foak aw turnt raand an' starred at me as if Aw'd gooan off it."

Sniggy was so absorbed in recalling to his mind the scene he was describing, that he forgot to proceed, until presently Sam said—

"Well, an' wot then?"

"Wot then?" cried Sniggy, astonished at the question; and then recollecting himself, he proceeded —

"Whey, Aw browt her whoam wi' me, an' hoo's i' th' haase naa. An' Aw'm goin' t' lodge wi' Bob Turner till we getter marrit."

There was no more to be said. Jabe and his friends were more proud of their recruit than they had ever been, and were profoundly touched by his simple story.

"Bud, dust think hoo's gradely repented, lad?" said the Clogger with gentle dubiousness.

"Repented? Ay, wot else? Isn't that wot Aw prayed fur?"

"An' thaa thinks as hoo's come back i' answer ta prayer, does ta?"

"Aw dew that! Doan't yo'?"

And Jabe, with a great tear on each cheek, put his hand gently on Sniggy's shoulder, and said—

"Aw dew, lad! Aw dew!"

. . . .

And a month later Sniggy and Sally were married at the chapel, and a little while after they applied for the post of chapel-keepers on the understanding that there was to be no pay —"Just ta' mak' up fur th' past," said Sally.

LIGE'S LEGACY.

I.

A LAWYER'S LETTER.

LIGE, the road-mender, was in the "doldrums." His open-air occupation exposed him to the exigencies of climate, and so, driven indoors by stress of weather, he had as usual spent most of a certain very wet afternoon at the Clog Shop.

For a man of his volatile temperament he had had very little to say all afternoon, and even when Isaac brought "baggin'" for Jabe and him, and arranged it on one of the old clog benches which served as inglenook stools, Lige only seemed faintly interested.

As nobody else was about, Jabe had departed so far from his usual custom as to make remarks once or twice about Lige's unusual flatness, but they evoked no response. These old cronies had long ago got past the stage when persons feel it necessary to maintain conversation whilst together, and so there were several long silences whilst tea was being consumed.

Presently, as Jabe was crowding into his mouth an enormous piece of toast, Lige suddenly leaned forward, and scowling with a look of relentless resolution, tapped the Clogger's knee with his teacup by way of punctuating every word he was uttering, and said—

"If hoo awses [offers] ageean, Aw'll—Aw'll leeave th' village."

Jabe, with butter-smeared lips, slowly consumed his toast without deigning even to look at Lige, who still remained in the attitude he had assumed when speaking, and continued to glare fiercely at his friend.

Then the Clogger tucked into his mouth-corner the last bit of toast, took a gulp at his tea, reached out for another slice of toast, and leaning back and thoughtfully examining it, as if doubtful about the way it had been buttered, remarked, with a jerk of his short leg—

"Th' clug's upo' th' t'other fooat if Aw know owt abaat it."

"Ay, theer thaa gooas," cried Lige impatiently; "a chap met as weel try to get warm ale aat of a alicker [vinegar] barril as get a bit o' comfort aat o' thee."

Jabe took a long pull at his teacup, and then holding it from him, and looking intently into the cup-bottom, said—

"It's no' comfort as *thaa* wants; it's a cleawt o' th' soide o' th' yed. If tha'd let th' woman alooan hoo'd let thi alooan."

"Well of aw th' aggravatin' haands"— cried Lige; but his feelings were too much for him, and he sat up and stared at the tantalising Jabe with amazement, indignant protest, reproachful expostulation, and a shade of guilty self-consciousness chasing each other on his face.

Jabe went on munching at his toast in calculated unconcern, and carefully avoided the road-mender's eye, whilst Lige, continuing his amazed and indignant look, at length gasped out—

"Tha'll threeap me daan as Aw *want* th' woman next."

And Jabe, with a look of most provoking placidity, went on slowly eating and drinking, and saying by his whole manner more plainly than words would have expressed it that that was exactly what he *did* think—which, of course, only made Lige the more uneasy and angry.

The fact was that the poor road-mender was not as consistent and steadfast a supporter of his great chief on the vexed question of women as that worthy could have desired, and this was therefore one of his modes of inflicting punishment. As a general thing Lige out-Heroded Herod in his scorn of the sex, but there were certain more or less frequent and regular backslidings, during which he was absent for days together from the Clog Shop, and was heard of in the direction of "th' Hawpenny Gate," where a certain lady leech-keeper resided, and after some four or five days he would suddenly turn up again, having a ruffled and irritable air about him, but with a new and quite suggestive readiness to abuse and scoff at the slavery of married life.

On these occasions, too, he would drop darkly mysterious hints about the "fawseniss" of women and their "invayglin'" ways, with oblique references to the fable of the spider and the fly, and it was easy to see that he wished it to be inferred that he "could a tale unfold," if he chose, from the standpoint of the fly, and that he was himself an unwilling victim of female beguilement, and only preserved his liberty by constant heroic efforts and by marvels of diplomatic checkmating.

But, like many other innocent martyrs, Lige found that his friends were unsympathetic and unbelieving, and even—such is the perverseness of human nature—undertook to defend the female he professed to be afraid of from his insinuations.

Now, these occasional lapses into amatory weakness had been going on intermittently for some eighteen months, Lige's sentiments running the whole gamut of feeling from uncompromising misogamy to ardent love-sickness every two or three months. And the Clog Shop cronies took a sort of unhallowed delight in watching the mental and conversational contortions of their friend in his laborious efforts to convince them that he was a victim to be pitied rather than a backslider to be blamed.

Now, it was perfectly well known to all the chief spirits of the Clog Shop that Lige's only reason for remaining unmarried was that the lady of his second choice objected on the very unromantic ground that the road-mender couldn't afford to keep her. In fact, she had stated as much in the plainest possible Beckside English to her ardent suitor, and the verdict of the Clog Shop was: "Hoo's a sensible body—for a woman."

But Lige scorned to attribute so sordid a motive to the lady of his heart, and, moreover, was known to be exceedingly sensitive on the question of his poverty. No one would ever have guessed from his manner that he was not as well off as any of his chums. He talked sometimes of projects involving what would be to him impossible sums of money, and always included himself in any scheme which might be under discussion as at least equal to the rest in worldly resources; and they, although grimly, almost savagely, intolerant of everything savouring of hypocrisy, actually became his accomplices in this work of self-deception, and would have lost confidence in themselves for ever if by even the slightest and most indirect reference they had shown that they were aware of any difference between him and them.

At the same time it is not to be supposed that they let him alone on this question of his weak leaning towards possible matrimony; but they confined themselves to charging him with desertion of his friends, and hypocrisy in his attitude towards the other sex, and persistently refused to believe that the lady had made any overtures to him on her own initiative, or in fact any overtures at all. And though scrupulously avoiding the least hint as to the real reason, they did not spare him on others, such, for instance, as his personal appearance and idiosyncrasies, Sam Speck being specially severe on him for his lack of manners.

The conversation with which this chapter opens is but a sample of many such between Lige and his friends. On this occasion, however, a diversion occurred which for a time put Lige's matrimonial leanings out of everybody's mind. Whilst Jabe and the road-mender were sitting thus over tea, Lige restive and indignant, and the Clogger doggèd and aggressively sarcastic, the shop door opened, and Peter the postman sauntered slowly up to the fire and began to fill his short black pipe. He had finished his long morning round some time before, and was now on his way to commence the night collection.

"Does oather o' yo' chaps know awmbry caw'd E. Howarth?" he asked, as he stooped to get a light at the fire.

"Thaa meeans Harry Howarth o' th' Brickcroft," said Jabe, looking up.

"Nay, Aw dunno; that's 'Haitch' than knows, an' this is 'Hee.' Besides, it's a lawyer's letter, an' Harry ne'er gets inta ony lumber. He's as quiet as an owd sheep."

"A lawyer's letter?" cried Jabe; "less lewk at it."

Peter produced the letter—a long, blue packet, with a terribly legal look about it, and embossed on the back, Briggs, Barber, and Briggs, Solicitors, Whipham."

On the other side it was directed to Mr. E. Howarth, Beckside, Brogden, near Duxbury.

Jabe read the name on the back of the envelope several times over, and then turned the packet over and scrutinised the directions. Then he limped across the shop for his spectacles, carefully rubbed them on his red cotton handkerchief, put them on, and once more examined the missive back and front. Then he held it at arm's-length, and looking thoughtfully at it, murmured ponderingly—

"Hee Howarth! Hee Howarth! Whoaiver is it fur?"

"It meeans trubbel fur sumbry, that's sartin," said Lige. "Less leuk at it."

He knew it was useless to hope to obtain possession of the packet, and so he contented himself with stepping upon a stool and looking over the Clogger's shoulder.

"Th' felley con wroite at ony rate," he commented, scanning the directions with knitted brows.

But at that moment in walked Sam Speck. Peter the postman, when in difficulties about the ownership of a letter, often resorted to that fountain of local knowledge, the Clog Shop, for help, and so Sam was not greatly surprised to find his comrades thus engaged. Lige's elevated position, however, struck him as irregular, and as indicative of something interesting, and so, as the road-mender held the point of vantage over the Clogger's shoulder, Sam, when the situation had been explained to him, bent down upon his haunches, and whilst Jabe and Lige were scrutinising the directions he was examining the embossed stamp on the under side. A look of alarm came into his eyes, and he gave vent to a prolonged whistle, as he discovered that the letter emanated from a lawyer.

"By gum, lads, there's sumbry in for it! Hee Howarth. Hee Howarth," he went on, scratching his head and knitting his brows, "Hee How— Whey, Lige, thaa bermyed, it's *thee.*"

Lige started with a short cry. The letter slipped from Jabe's suddenly nerveless fingers and fluttered to the ground, and both the Clogger and the postman turned quickly round and stared at Lige in fear and sorrow.

Lige dropped from the stool and sat down with a sudden flop, and, shrinking back as if he were afraid of the letter making for him, cried out—

"It *isna* me! It *isna* me! *Aw've* done nowt. Aw hav'na! Aw hav'na!!"

There was a moment of awful stillness, and then Sam Speck stooped and picked up the now terrifying letter, and carefully read the directions once more.

"Ay! " he said, with a great sigh; "it's reet!"

"Hee, that's 'Elijah,' an' 'Howarth'—it's thee, lad," and the tone of the remark conveyed the idea that Sam felt that some awful mysterious trouble had overtaken his old friend.

With another heavy sigh, Sam held out the letter to Lige, but the road-mender shrank back on his stool as if afraid of being burned, and wildly waving his hands, he cried—

"It *isna* me! It isna"—And then with a pathetic break in his voice—
"Haa con to say soa, Sam?"

Just then Long Ben entered, and having been made acquainted with
the trouble in hand, he stood and looked at Lige with the same
pitiful commiseration in his eyes that showed in the faces of the
others.

Then he took the letter and examined it carefully.

"Briggs, Barber, and Briggs," he cogitated, and then he stopped and
his jaw dropped. The look of pity in his eyes deepened into alarm,
and he suddenly checked himself of an intention to speak, for he had
just remembered that Mr. Barber, the senior living partner of the firm
from which the letter had come, was the clerk to the magistrates at
Whipham. A deep sigh escaped him, and he held out the letter to
the frightened Lige.

But the poor road-mender shrank away from it, and burying his
head in his hands, groaned out a sort of smothered sob. The rest
stood looking at Lige with disturbed and anxious faces, and at last
Jabe burst out—

"Liger, hast bin foomart huntin'?"

"Neaw! neaw! " cried Lige intensely; "Aw've bin noawheer, an'
Aw've done nowt to noabry."

Jabe paused a minute, eyeing the road-mender meditatively the
while, and then remembering one of Lige's youthful besetments, he
asked—

"Hast bin pooachin' then?"

"Neaw; Aw've bin noawheer, Aw tell thi," and Lige gave vent to
another dismal groan.

"Give o'er wi' thi, Lige," cried Jabe, now nearly as agitated as his friend. "Sithi, lad. Wheer thaa goas, Aw goa; an' aw th' lyin' lawyers i' Lancashire shanna hurt thi."

"Haa yo' meyther," broke in Peter the postman; "it's happen nubbut a jury summons or a subpeeny."

"Nay," said Jabe, with a perplexed sigh, "th' bobbies [police] brings them, thaa knows."

But the suggestion of other causes for lawyers' letters than transgression of the law opened a new field of speculation, and so Sam Speck brightened up suddenly and cried—

"It's happen a fortin as sumbry's left thi, Lige."

But Lige only shook his head wearily, and groaned again.

Then Long Ben drew Jabe aside and whispered—

"Dust think he's paid his rates?"

But Ben was a poor whisperer, and before Jabe could reply Lige groaned out from between his fingers—

"Aw pay 'em i' th' rent."

This state of things was fast becoming unbearable. Jabe especially seemed scarcely able to control himself, and so he cried, though not without secret misgivings—

"Lige, ger up wi' thi an' oppen this letter. If thaa doesn't Aw'st oppen it mysel'."

"Tak' it aat o' my seet!" cried Lige, with a fresh gesture of fear.

Jabe took hold of the letter.

"It's nowt," he cried, with an affectation of contempt which he did not quite feel; but he lingered a long time with the packet, handling it with great care and turning it over and over again, and it would have been difficult to say whether fear or curiosity was stronger in him.

Then he examined the flap of the envelope, and remarked that if it had had "owt woth owt" in it, it would have been sealed. After toying with it a moment or two longer, he stepped across the shop floor and lighted a candle, and then selecting very deliberately one of his knives, and carefully cleaning it, he picked up the candle, brought it near the fire, gave it to the postman to hold, and making a sudden dash, cut open the letter.

Now it is quite certain that the Clogger did not really comprehend one word of the document the first time he read it. His business seems to have been to discover not what it was, but what it was not, and this he managed so successfully that he turned round to his woebegone friend, and cried with a sudden accession of confidence—

"Ger up, thaa ninny hommer, ther's nowt to be feart on here."

Lige did not move, but only emitted a slightly lighter groan, but Long Ben and Sam drew nearer, and looking over the Clogger's shoulder, prompted and corrected as he read out as follows, much as if he were a town crier:—

"To MR. ELIJAH HOWARTH, BECKSIDE.

(Another groan from the poor road-mender.)

"SIR,—Our late client, Mr. Abram Howarth, who died recently in this town, left a will in which you are named sole executor and legatee. If you will call at our office on Saturday morning between ten and one, we shall be pleased to explain the will and take your esteemed commands thereupon.

"We are, dear Sir, your obedient servants,

"BRIGGS, BARBER, AND BRIGGS."

It is beyond the power of the present reporter to describe the faces of the little company when Jabe finished reading. He took off his glasses and blinked his grey eyes at Ben in speechless wonder, and Ben returned the look with a dull, uncomprehending stare. The postman burst into a loud laugh, and Sam Speck, after looking from one to the other of his friends to make sure that they had heard, suddenly pushed Ben aside, and standing over the still bent form of Lige, smote him heavily between the shoulders, and shouted —

"Speik, mon! Didn't Aw tell thi it wur a fortin?"

It was some time before the road-mender could realise the meaning of the letter, and when he did, he stood up and gazed abstractedly into the fire, apparently oblivious both of the congratulations that were offered to him, and the wild guesses in which his comrades indulged as to the amount of the legacy.

After the excitement had abated somewhat, they found their accustomed places round the fire, and the pipes having been lighted, the situation was discussed in all its bearings. Lige said very little for the first hour or so, but he amply atoned for his silence afterwards by monopolising nearly all the conversation.

Then the talk turned upon the old man who had died, and whom most of the company remembered with recollections the reverse of pleasant. Lige confessed that he had only seen his deceased relative some half a dozen times, and had not exchanged twenty words with him in his life. Nobody knew anything good of him, saving always this last most commendable act of his. Then guesses were made as to the probable amount of the bequest, and memories were raked to recall the various small properties which it was known the old man had purchased during his lifetime.

Sam Speck, who seemed to be touched with a little envious jealousy of Lige's newly-acquired importance, opined that most of the property had "summat on it," and might not realise much after all; but Jabe, after a cold, withering look at the evil-minded detractor, turned to Lige, and said—

"It's a lung loan [lane] as niver hes a turn, lad; if tha'rt woth a penny tha'rt woth a paand a wik," and had the sum been a million a week Jabe could not have made a more impressive mouthful of it. Then the conversation took a practical turn, and as Lige did not seem to have quite recovered his fear of the lawyers, it was arranged that two of his friends should accompany him next morning to Whipham; and retribution now overtook the envious Sam, for he was omitted from this important deputation, though he was admittedly Lige's very closest friend.

Lige lived on the edge of the Brickcroft, and, of course, went home the same way as Ben.

When they had parted at the carpenter's gate, and Ben had reached his own front door, he heard Lige, who had suddenly turned back, calling him. When they met at the garden gate Lige seemed to have forgotten what he wanted to say. He stood back a moment, looked round on the dim outlines of the buildings about him, and then said, though not as indifferently as he intended—

"Ben, when my owd woman deed and hoo worn't i' th' club, an' Aw'd nowt ta bury her wi', an' when Aw went raand after th' buryin' ta ax them foak ta gi' me toime an' Aw'd pay 'em, they aw said as a chap 'ud bin afoor me, an' paid 'em aw. Dust know whoa that chap wur?"

Ben seemed suddenly to have become intensely interested in a little dim far-away star, the only one visible that cloudy night, and so he answered, with a fair pretence of preoccupation—

"Nay! Haa dew Aw know?"

Then Lige took another look round at the shadowy building, and went on—

"An' when Aw wur aat o' wark for eighteen wik, an' wur feart o' my loife o' being turnt aat o' th' haase fur rent, an' when Aw started o' rooad-mendin' fur th' parish, an' began a shapin' fur t' pay my back rent up, Owd Croppy towd me as it 'ud bin paid ivery wik. Thaa doesn't know whoa did that, Aw reacon?"

"Nay, Liger; dunno! Thi brass is makkin' thee suspeecious. Howd thi bother, mon!"

"Bother! Ay, ther'll be some bother, Aw con tell thi, if this comes aat reet. Ben Barber 'ull ha' to build a new haase fur Mestur *Hee*. An' ov a Setterday mornin', when Ben Barber has na getten paid fur his wark an' conna foind wages fur his men, th' fat 'ull be i' th' feire if he doesna ger it off Mestur *Hee*. Naa, moind thi, fro' this day henceforth an' for iver—a-a—partly wot, Ben Barber's banker's Mestur Hee—Mestur Hee."

And with a glow of triumph at his own brilliant effort, Lige plunged into the darkness and disappeared.

Next morning three solemn-looking figures, dressed in funereal black, and with long grave faces to match, stood by the Clog Shop door waiting for the Duxbury coach. Their three hats all belonged to the same bygone period of fashion, and Lige's had a most suggestive and transient shininess about it. His best coat also was distinguished from the others by a more pronounced greenness of colour, and this was made the more noticeable by the fact that Jonas Tatlock's trousers, which had been lent to the new man of property for this great occasion, were nearly new and of a glossy black.

As the coach came into sight, Sam Speck joined the company. He seemed to have got over his pique, and was inclined to chaff.

He called Lige "Mestur Howarth," and then on sudden recollection tried "Mestur Hee," but neither this, nor his warning that it was

Duxbury Wakes, and they were not to "chuck th' fortin away at ghooast shows and hot pey staws" before they came home, raised a smile, and the coach moved off presently carrying three men with faces of owlish solemnity.

Arrived at Whipham, an argument arose as to who should lead the way into the office. Lige seemed astonished that the question should be raised at all, and looking at the Clogger with an injured, reproachful look, he demanded—

"Wot hast come fur if tha winna leead up?"

"It's no' my fortin," protested Jabe indignantly. "It's thee they wanton, nor uz." And he might have been disavowing a great crime to judge by the earnestness of his protestation.

Lige took a long, hesitant look: from one to the other of his friends, then turned and gazed earnestly at the green baize inner door of the office; then glanced apprehensively up and down the street, and finally cried, with desperate resolution—

"Aw'st no' goa in fost for noather on yo'. Aw'll lose th' fortin fost."

After a few minutes more of wrangling, during which Lige became more and more terrified at the thought of facing the lawyer, and more and more reckless as to what became of the fortune, Jabe suddenly broke away from the other two, and began limping up the steps so earnestly that they only caught him as he was pushing open the dingy green door.

"Is th' mestur in?" he demanded, glaring fiercely at the clerks.

"Yes, sir," said a fussy penman, whom Lige immediately began to regard with strong suspicion. "Have you an appointment?"

"Neaw; we wanten t' see th' mestur." And then, turning half round to Lige, he demanded, "Where's th' letter, Liger?"

The clerk glanced at the packet. "Oh, come this way, gentlemen."

"Mr. Howarth, of Beckside, sir," he called out, raising his voice a little, and addressing some invisible personage.

It took a little time to get the three villagers piloted round desk ends, through counter flaps, and behind dirty red curtains, and when it was successfully accomplished, and they stood before the great Mr. Barber, Lige, at any rate, looked as if he were come to make confession of some awful crime, whilst Jabe took off his hat and rubbed his perspiring face and head with his red handkerchief.

The lawyer began by addressing Jabe as Mr. Howarth, and when that error had been corrected, and Lige had been dragged to the front like a reluctant culprit, the business began. It was soon made clear that there was no doubt about the reality of Lige's good fortune. He actually was sole heir of the late Abram Howarth, his uncle. The estate consisted chiefly of small properties, mostly in or about Brogden Clough, and would bring in about twenty-five shillings per week. There would be certain formalities to be gone through, probate, etc., would have to be paid, and then Mr. Barber told Lige he would be able to enter into formal possession of a nice little inheritance. Mr. Barber was also happy to tell Mr. Howarth that there was a good round sum of hard cash in the Duxbury Bank, which would pay all expenses and leave a comfortable margin.

By this time Lige began to feel his new importance, and talked with most surprising freedom to the solicitor. The lawyer congratulated Lige again, and cracked a little joke, at which Jabe and Long Ben smiled with dignified condescension, and Lige laughed uproariously.

As they were leaving, Mr. Barber called them back.

"If you want a little cash for immediate use, you know, Mr. Howarth," he began; but Lige received a sharp kick on the right foot from Jabe, and a gentle nudge on the left elbow from Ben, and so, without giving the least sign that he understood, he answered, as if cash were the very last thing in the world he either needed or cared for—

"Neaw, neaw! toime enuff ta bother wi' that when Aw've getten it gradely."

And then Lige had a sudden sense of having outwitted a man of law, and was so elated thereat, that, as he was going through the outer office, he turned, and, surveying the clerks with a glance of magnificent condescension, he asked—

"Which o' yo' chaps wor it as wrate that letter ta me?"

"I, sir," said the fussy clerk who had introduced them to the lawyer, and who evidently saw signs of a tip.

"Thee, wor it! Well, th' next toime as tha sends me a letter, send it ta 'Liger Howarth,' an' nooan o' thi 'Mestur Hee's';" and with a glance of mingled scorn and warning, Lige followed his friends into the street.

II.

A QUESTION OF CONSCIENCE.

THERE was no help for it. Sam Speck was being driven into cynicism in spite of himself. It was his duty, he knew, to fight against the tendency, and he did so, but sometimes circumstances seemed altogether too strong for him. Here was a case in point. He thought he knew his old friend Lige. He boasted, in fact, that he could read him like a book. Nothing, he thought, would ever change Lige much; and here, as soon as ever there was a prospect of an improvement in his financial position, he was becoming sly and mysterious, and was changing from the most open-hearted and least worldly of spirits, to a calculating, reticent, and money-loving soul.

Lige's sudden enrichment was, of course, the chief topic of conversation round the Clog Shop fire, but Sam marked with concern that whilst the road-mender was ready enough to hear others discuss his prospects, he said very little about them himself, and it was not until about nine o'clock in the evening, when the company was largest and discussion most stimulating, that Lige opened his mind about his future intentions at all. When thus temporarily elated by congratulations and encouragements, Lige would assert vociferously what he intended to do, but Sam observed with misgivings that he not only made no allusions to his intentions next morning, but could not be drawn to speak about them at all.

For instance, Lige had been apprehensive for some time that his "rheumatiz " would before long prevent him working, and compel him to relinquish his situation; and now, when he had ample means to keep him without work, he seemed to have become suddenly very much in love with it. Two or three times Sam had turned the conversation so as to bring this question to the front, and under the influence of popular opinion Lige had resolved to give up his employment. On one or two occasions he had got excited about the matter, and had openly declared, "Aw'll niver breik another stooan woll Aw'm wik." But next morning Sam had discovered him hammering away as usual on a heap of stones, or digging clumps of weeds out of the gutters.

And now Lige had actually come into possession of his fortune, and Sam had been with him to make the final call upon the lawyer at Whipham, and to bring his cash and deposit it in the Duxbury Bank.

It was long past noon by the time they had finished their business, and Sam was hungry. Two or three times he had dropped palpable hints about his condition, but Lige only seemed to understand when the hints became plain unvarnished avowals of hunger; and, even then, instead of taking him to a decent inn, Lige led him off to an old-fashioned cookshop, and ordered, as if he had been calling for turtle soup, "Tew plates o' tatey pie—big uns." And Sam noticed, as a painful confirmation of his fears, that though the road-mender had twenty pounds to his certain knowledge in a little bag in his left-hand pocket, yet he paid for the repast out of the few spare pence he carried in the other pocket.

After dinner, as they had to wait a couple of hours for the coach, they walked about the town and inspected the shops. Sam pulled up before every clothier's shop he came to, but neither broad hints nor excessive commendation of certain patterns of cloth and suits of clothes had the least effect on Lige; and when Sam, exercised in his mind about the rapid deterioration and threatened spiritual destruction of a man who had grown miserly on the very first day of his affluence, pointedly admired a certain stylish overcoat and recommended its prompt purchase, Lige seemed to become suddenly suspicious and sly, and wriggled out of making the purchase on some most trivial pretext. And, of course, Sam could not tell his friend plain out that his best clothes had been green and shabby for years.

All these things were very depressing to our mercurial friend; but when he discovered that Lige was going back to Beckside on the day when he had come into formal possession of his inheritance, and with twenty pounds sterling in his pocket, without taking even so much as half a pound of tobacco back to his friends at the Clog Shop wherewith to celebrate the occasion, he came dangerously near to wishing that his old friend had remained poor, and was almost thankful that the fortune had not come to himself to tempt him. Two or three times, as they travelled home on the coach, he glanced thoughtfully at the road-mender's face, and was almost certain that he perceived signs there that the hardening process had already begun.

Sitting at the Clog Shop fire that night, Sam kept a careful watch on Lige, making as he did so many pessimistic notes on the weakness of human nature.

Lige received the congratulations of his friends with a becoming show of meekness, took all chaff in good part, and even joked himself about his good luck; but, for all that, Sam could see that he was a changed man, and was fast becoming grasping and worldly.

As the evening went on, Sam resolved that he would remain behind and inform Jabe of his suspicions. But the rest would not go. Lige—

an early riser, and therefore one of the first to depart of an evening—would not go, and Long Ben, who was supposed to live in wholesome fear of his wife, seemed also reluctant to leave; and when Sam remarked, as a kind of suggestive hint, that it was "toime to be piking," he was provoked and perplexed to see both Lige and the carpenter deliberately commence recharging their pipes.

To make it worse, as he had himself started the movement for home, he found himself obliged in common consistency to follow it up, and so, after standing about for a little time, and going to the door and then coming back again some two or three times, he was reluctantly compelled to depart, leaving Lige sitting in most aggravating contentment by the fire.

When he reached his own door, which was on the other side of the road going to the mill, he still felt uneasy, and most unaccountably, curious, and when he saw Long Ben leave the Clog Shop a minute or two later, and realised that now Lige and Jabe would be alone, it was all he could do to restrain himself from going back and bursting in upon them, excuse or no excuse,

Meanwhile Jabe and Lige sat quietly smoking in the inglenook, Lige having a very abstracted look on his face. The Clogger eyed him over with quiet interest, two or three times, as if speculating as to what was going on in his mind; but neither spoke. Presently, however, Lige leaned back in the nook, and putting his feet on the bench on which he sat, he asked, taking his pipe out of his mouth, and putting his head slightly on one side in an argumentative attitude—

"Naa, has mitch a wik dust think a chap loike me owt ta give away, Jabe?"

"Wot!" cried the Clogger, with a curl of his lip, "is thi brass brunnin' thi pockets aat awready?"

"Aw'd rayther it ud brun my pocket nor freeze my soul," was the reply.

After a moment's silence, Jabe said—

"Th' Jews uset give a tenth."

"Haa mitch is a tenth o' twenty-five shillin'?" was the next question.

"Hawf a craan." [Half a crown]

And now it was time for Lige's lip to curl, and it did so until he looked positively fierce with scorn.

"Aw allis thowt them Jews wur skinny uns —but that cops aw—the greedy wastrils."

"Whey, wot does thaa think foak owt ta give?" asked Jabe, in lazy curiosity.

"T'oan hawf bi' th' t'other, fur sure" (a fair half), was the reply.

Jabe burst into a great laugh—a laugh which somehow *had* to be very loud in order to prevent it becoming something quite different. In the midst of it, however, a thought seemed to strike him, and, bending forward, he asked very seriously—

"Thaa's browt sum brass whoam wi' thi taday, hast na?"

"Ay," said Lige; "twenty paand," and he hit the outside of his trousers-pocket to indicate that he had it with him.

"Thaa'd better leeave it wi' me ta tak' cur on fur thi."

Now, though he made this proposal very seriously, the Clogger did not really expect that Lige would comply; and so he was a little taken aback when the road-mender drew a greasy bag out of his pocket and handed it to him.

"Jabe, owd lad," he said softly, "Aw hevna spent a penny o' my fortin yet, an' Aw'm no' goin' ta dew till th' Lord's hed the fost pick.

Ther's twenty paand i' that bag, an' Aw want th' trustees ta bey a new coffee-pot fur th' Communion table—solid goold if it 'ull reich tew it!"

Jabe stared at his friend in amazement; but Lige was proceeding—

"When Aw wur th' poor steward twenty ye'r sin', an' th' plate box wur kept at aar haase, aar Jane uset say, when hoo wur cleanin' th' vessils, as if hoo had th' brass hoo'd tak' cur as they shouldna put 'th' best wine o' th' kingdom' into a pewter pot as if it were sixpenny ale. An' iver sin' hoo deed Aw've bin livin' i' hoapes o' seeing her ageean; an' up yond' wheer hoo is they known abaat this fortin o' moine, an' aar Jane's tellin' 'em aw 'He'll be gettin' summat gradely ta put th' wine in, yo'll see.' An' if Aw donna, Jabe, Aw darna face her up, an' that's God's trewth, lad."

The Clogger had no answer to an argument like this. He stared before him, and sniffed and cleared his throat, and in the end had to get up and turn his back on his companion.

When he recovered himself, he said—

"Aw ne'er yerd o' noa goold Communion sarvices. They allis user silver. Bud thaa con bey a woll set, thaa knows."

And so it was settled; and as Lige left the Cloggery he was astonished at the Clogger, who actually took him by the hand and gave it a limp, timid sort of shake, as if he were unable to resist doing so, and yet felt ashamed of it, murmuring huskily, as he did so—

"God bless thi, lad! Aw dunno think thi brass 'ull spile thi."

When Sam Speck heard of Lige's proposal his feelings were very much divided. He was inclined to feel injured that Lige had not taken him into his confidence about the matter, and yet he felt so ashamed of himself for having harboured suspicions of his friend that he refused himself the pleasure of rating Lige about it as a sort of penance. Still, there was one thing that greatly exercised his mind. Why did not Lige give up his employment? He talked of doing so, vowed again and again he would do it, fixed the time for so doing more than once, and yet every morning found him going forth, as usual, with pick and shovel and long-shafted hammer, to his work.

A week or two passed, and still no signs of Lige's retirement, and at last, unable longer to endure, Sam opened out upon his friend as they sat by the Clog Shop fire—

"Tha'rt a bonny mon to be takkin' th' meit aat o' foak's maaths."

Lige looked up in wonder. He had a feeling that somehow the relations between him and his friend were not so cordial as they used to be, but he could think of no cause for it, and so he answered rather curtly—

"Naa wot's up wi' thi?"

Sam cocked his elbow on his knee and steadied his pipe in his mouth, and then, removing it for a moment, went on—

"A chap as hez twenty-five shillin' a wik comin' in, an' a hunderd paand i' th' bank, leuks well breiking stooans an' fillip' cart-ruts, and takkin' wage as other foaks are starvin' fur."

Lige winced, but he wasn't going to be taught his duty by so comparatively juvenile a person as Sam, and so he replied—

"Aw reacon thaa wants th' job thisel'! Thaa leuks loike a felley as is starvin', sure*li*."

"Aw tell thi," persisted Sam, "as there's three on 'em as Aw know on as is waitin' fur th' shop [situation], an' it's nowt bud robbery."

Sam spoke with warmth, and the situation was getting somewhat strained, and so Long Ben, from the inside corner of the nook, chimed in, to create a diversion —

"Hast bin to th' Hawpenny Gate lately, Liger?"

But this subject seemed to be quite as troublesome to Lige as the one Sam had started, and so, to escape further banterings, he remembered "a bit of a arrand," and disappeared, leaving Sam receiving a mild reproof from the carpenter.

But Lige could not quite get rid of the question Sam had thus pointedly raised, and as he stood next day on the top of a heap of stones, a little higher up the road than the chapel, he mused thoughtfully on the previous night's conversation.

The fact was, now that he had the chance of giving up work altogether, he discovered an interest in it which he had never realised before, and found himself strangely reluctant to change. And then he was more jealous of any tendency to get vain because of his riches than ever Sam could be for him, and suspected himself of all sorts of grasping propensities, and was rather glad therefore to continue his work as a means of keeping the natural man in subjection.

The point raised by Sam had never occurred to him, and he at once began to feel very guilty about it. Then the remembrance of Ben's interjected question came back to him. Away from the curious eyes of his associates he could afford to think as long and as freely as he liked on the matter, and a smirk of satisfaction came upon his face as he realised that his change of fortune had immensely improved his matrimonial prospects.

But all at once the smile vanished from his lips. A look of perplexity came into his plain old face, as if he were trying to recall something that eluded his pursuit. Then his face became portentously long, a deep sigh escaped him, and, limply dropping his hammer, he got down from the stone heap and propped himself against the wall to think. But the more he thought the worse he became. He passed his hands over his brow, rubbed uneasily at his stubbly chin, scratched both sides of his head at once, and wriggled and twisted as if in the grip of someone who was torturing him. Then he stepped into the middle of the road, looked dazedly round at the horizon with a helpless, appealing sort of look, and a moment later he plunged off down the "broo" in a walk which only just escaped being a trot.

He was making, of course, for the Clog Shop, and as he reached it, he burst open the door, and, ignoring the fact that Jabe was serving a customer, cried excitedly—

"Whey, Jabe, the fortin isna moine."

Now the customer was a new-comer in the village, and was rashly attempting to banter the Clogger about the price charged for clogging—a thing which every Becksider knew better than do—and she had consequently stirred up the old Adam in him. And so he replied in his crustiest tones—

"Whoas else is it, thaa lumpyed?"

But seeing that Lige was very much excited, lie added more mildly-

"Goa an' sit daan wi' thi."

But Lige was too distressed to sit, and so, staring wildly at Jabe, he cried out, almost in tears—

"Hey, mon, it's hers."

Jabe now realised that the matter was serious; and so, entirely ignoring the astounded customer, he put on his spectacles, and, carefully surveying the road-mender, demanded—

"Whoas?"

"Hers, Aw tell thi," shouted Lige, almost beside himself. "Jane Ann's, thaa knows. Hast forgotten as hoo wur his chance-chilt. It's hers, mon. It's no' moine at aw."

Jabe carefully counted out the change for the customer, and then actually came round the corner of the counter to open the door for her. Then he carefully closed it, walked back to his place again, and turning round, looked Lige steadily in the face.

The fact was that, for once, speech had entirely forsaken the old Clogger. The Jane Ann alluded to was the very leech-keeping woman whom Lige had been so unsuccessfully wooing, and whose origin had been almost forgotten at the end of her forty odd years of life; and when Jabe really grasped the whole situation as it spread itself before his mind, it simply took away both breath and speech.

Presently, more to relieve the tension than with any idea that he was helping matters, he said—

"Haa can it be hers when it wur left ta thee?"

And Lige replied as Jabe knew he would, when he said—

"Hers! It *is* hers. Hoo's his dowter, mon!"

Jabe's perplexity was so sore that it galled and vexed him, and so he replied hotly—

"Wot's left ta thee's thine, isn't it, thaa numskull?"

But Lige was indignant with an indignation curiously blended with reluctance, and so he replied, as if there was some sort of melancholy gratification to be got out of making the facts look as inexorable as possible—

"Her fayther robbed her, an' naa Aw mun rob her—is that what thaa meeans?"

With a gesture of despairing anger, Jabe turned his back on his friend, and limping heavily to the fire, dropped down upon a stool, looking the very picture of helpless distress, and in a moment or so Lige joined him, looking if possible more miserable still.

After sitting staring into the fire for a long time, Jabe in surly tones ordered Isaac to fetch Long Ben. This was no time for half-measures. Jabe was on the rack, and if he felt like that, what must Lige be enduring.

It seemed as though Ben would never come, although he had started the moment he was summoned. But when he did arrive, and had been put in possession of the facts of the case, the look on his face banished from Jabe's heart any hope that his more resourceful friend would be able to find a way out.

There the three sat. Each man knew how easy and natural it would be to take the way of the world and its legal sanctions, and be satisfied, or at most make some little allowance to the neglected and overlooked daughter. But each man saw also the inexorable requirements of righteousness, and to say that they quailed before it is but to say that they were men.

"He happen hed some reeason fur no' leeavin' it to her," said Jabe at length, more to start discussion than from any faith in his own argument.

"Hoo ne'er did nowt to hurt him in her loife," said Lige sternly, "nobbut keepin' on livin'."

"Well, thaa con give her summat—soa mitch a wik, or summat."

"Ay, or else mak' a will an' leeave it aw tew her," added Ben.

Lige lifted up a haggard face and asked quietly—

"Wod *yo'*?"

The countenances of the two friends dropped again, and there was a long silence. At last Lige lifted his head and asked, with an effort—

"Which on yo's goin' to the lawyer's wi' me i' th' morn?"

A startled look came into Jabe's eyes. He jumped to his feet—

"Liger," he cried, with intense earnestness, "promise me tew things. Fost, as tha'll wait a wik afoor thaa does owt; an' second, as tha'll no' mention it to a soul till th' wik's up. Naa, promise."

A week's respite seemed a little heaven to Long Ben, and so he earnestly supported Jabe's request; and truth to tell, poor Lige was not unwilling to postpone so momentous a decision. Then Ben said he must go back to work, and Lige decided to do the same, and as he passed the shop window with strained and heavy look, Jabe, gazing sorrowfully after him, murmured—

"God help thi, Liger! Tha'rt poor an' owd an' simple, bud if thaa comes aat o' this o' th' reet soide, tha'll be th' best mon amung uz."

III.

HOW THE NEW PLATE WAS BOUGHT.

THERE was no more work for poor Lige that day. He tried; but he found himself pausing every few moments, and in his still bent position staring at the stones under his feet, in set, absorbed preoccupation.

Before he had been at work half an hour, he stopped and started for the Clog Shop once more, and was soon laying before Jabe some new aspect of the case. After a while he returned to his employment, but in a few minutes he was again in consultation with his friend. This sort of thing was repeated three or four times as the day went on.

On one of these interviews, just as Lige was returning to his work again, he suddenly turned back, and leaning his body over the counter until his mouth nearly touched the Clogger's ear, he charged him in a thick dramatic whisper to keep the whole thing from "th' chaps," and especially from Sam Speck.

As evening drew near, Lige's excitement became almost uncontrollable. He was afraid to stay at the Clog Shop lest he should be compelled to confess his trouble to someone, and yet he was afraid to be alone and have to fight his mental conflicts by himself. And somehow, though he felt sure his friends would all advise him to let things alone, he was more confident of his power to resist temptation when in company than when alone.

Then he was afraid, too, that "th' chaps" would by some means get the secret out of Jabe, or even out of Long Ben, though he had much more confidence in the latter than in the former. And so he wanted to be near at hand, that his presence might be a restraint on the Clogger.

Altogether Lige was in a most restless state of mind, and throughout the early part of the evening was passing in and out of the Clog Shop every few minutes, one moment raising some new point with the Clogger, and the next charging him by most solemn warnings not to let anybody even suspect what was the matter. Then he would be seen posting off in haste for home, which he never reached, and a few minutes later he would come hurrying up the hill with the inspiration of some totally new phase of the case within him.

Strange to say, the peppery Clogger bore it all with a patience that was quite remarkable. But the fact was, the problem so entirely absorbed his own thoughts, that he answered Lige's questions and instructions in a dazed mechanical sort of way.

As the road-mender was stretching over the counter, and warning Jabe, for at least the fifth time, of the danger of letting Sam know anything about it, a sharp voice suddenly broke on his ear, and Lige, hastily straightening himself, turned round to face the very person he was speaking of.

Lige made his face as straight as he could, and tried to look easy and unconcerned; but it was a complete failure. Sam saw instantly that something of very unusual interest was affecting his friend, and also that Lige was very anxious to conceal it from him.

Sam promptly suggested a "smook," and Lige was so afraid of crossing him that he agreed, and sat down to the first pipe he had tried that day. He perched himself for a few moments on a stool, where he could keep his eye on both Sam and the Clogger, and thus prevent any secret signalling between them.

Presently, however, Sam drew him into conversation, and the two got gradually farther and farther into the inglenook, until the Clogger could not hear what they were saying. Then they dropped their voices still lower, and Jabe was tantalised by the feeling that the lowering of their voices meant the deepening of their interest in the subject under discussion, of which he could not hear a word.

All at once, however, there was an amazed cry from out of the nook, and Sam could be seen standing up, and looking excitedly from Lige to Jabe, and from Jabe back to Lige, as though he could not decide which of them was the more demented. Then he began to laugh—an ironical unbelieving sort of snigger.

"Give it up, hay!" he cried. "Aw'm loike as if Aw seed thi."

And then, taking his breath for a moment, and eyeing the road-mender slyly over, he shook his head in a waggish sort of way, saying, as he did so—

"Hay, Liger, tha'rt an owd brid tew!"

"Aw see nowt else fur it," sighed Lige, ignoring Sam's chaffing tone, and evidently very miserable.

Sam whisked round in a manner expressive at once of impatience and intolerance of contradiction.

"Dunna meyther, mon. Wot's thine's thine, isna it?"

"Aw tell thi it *isna* moine: it's hers; an' Aw'm robbin' th' woman, an' nowt else."

There was an exclamation from Jabe at his bench, and petulantly flinging down his tools, he came and joined the others at the fire, and for the next hour the whole question was threshed out again.

Sam was incredulous, then angry and abusive, and finally he settled down into doggèd, unconvincible opposition, declaring again and again that Lige's proposed surrender of his "fortin" was "fair flyin' i' th' face o' Providence."

Jabe said comparatively little. The crisis was beyond him. He longed with all his heart to find some way of dealing with the matter less drastic than the extreme step of surrendering the whole property. But all his efforts so far had been vain, and so he listened to Sam much more carefully than usual, in the hope that he might be able to suggest something that would relieve the situation.

And Sam, when once he had become convinced that Lige was serious, certainly was ingenious in his suggestions, though Jabe was shocked to find how little scruple he seemed to have about the spirit of the moral law.

To every one of Sam's ideas, however, Lige opposed the same relentless answer, and Jabe never acknowledged truth more reluctantly than he did on this occasion, when his conscience pulled one way and his interest in his friend the other.

Presently the company began to assemble for the evening, and it turned out to be, perhaps, the longest night ever spent round the Clog Shop fire. Everything was dull and flat; so much so, in fact, that the more casual of the attendees moved homewards very early, and by nine o'clock Jabe and Lige, Long Ben and Sam, had the inglenook to themselves.

To Jabe the situation was fast becoming unbearable. He marvelled at and secretly gloried in Lige's uncompromising attitude; but he felt somehow that the actual performance of this act of sacrifice was intolerable to him. He was distressed, also, at the effect the struggle was having upon his old friend. He looked aged and haggard. The old wrinkles on his face seemed suddenly to have been reinforced by a number of new ones, whilst the veins on his forehead stood out in alarming prominence.

Under these circumstances he felt that Lige ought to be taken care of by somebody. He had not been really home all the day, although he had started half a dozen times. He had eaten nothing, and if he went home to a cold house, and then supperless to bed, the consequences might be serious.

Jabe waited, therefore, until Ben had drawn the old road-mender into conversation, and then, taking Sam aside, he instructed him to go and spend the night with "th' owd lad," and any other nights possible whilst Lige remained in this disturbed condition.

When Sam, who fell into the scheme somewhat reluctantly, had coaxed Lige to go, Jabe and Ben leaned forward on their seats, with elbows on knees and arm-propped chins, discussing with an earnestness that was almost grim the crisis that had just arisen. When Jabe described the doggedness of Lige's adherence to his own view of the case, and the immovability of his purpose to carry out what he felt to be right, the two looked at each other with shining eyes which expressed a sort of holy delight in their old friend that no possible circumstance would have compelled them to acknowledge in words.

"Aw wuish we'd ne'er yerd of his plaguey fortin," said Jabe at length, with a perplexed sigh.

"Ay," was Ben's response. "If he'd ne'er a hed it he'd ne'er a missed it. But it's hard wark givin' up aw his little plans an' schames."

"Ay; an' he'll ha' to keep on workin' tew," sighed Jabe.

There was a long silence. The fire fell together, and they both turned abstractedly to look at it. Some internal commotion seemed to be going on in Ben, and at last, standing up and shaking his fist at Jabe as if he were Lige's cruel oppressor, he cried, with a sudden fierce gush of tears—

"He'll no' wark noa mooar, fortin or noa fortin."

Jabe sat glowering into the red fire with a look which was an emphatic endorsement of Ben's declaration. Ben stooped for a clog-chip and relighted his pipe, and then he said—

"It'll be hard wark givin' up his new haase an' aw th' things he wur goin' ta dew."

"Hay, mon," answered the Clogger, "it's no' that he's botherin' abaat. It's th' Communion plate. He thinks mooar o' that nor aw th' t'other put together."

"Aw believe thi, lad," murmured Ben, after musing on the information for a minute.

Another long silence ensued, and after a while Jabe, who was unusually subdued for him, knitted his brows, and looking up at his friend, asked—

"Well, is ther' *nowt* we con dew?"

"We met get th' lawyer's opinion abaat it," said Ben tentatively.

"Neaw! neaw! yo' known wheer yo' begin wi' them chaps, but yo' niver known wheer yo' stop."

"Well," sighed Ben presently, "Aw con think o' nowt else."

"Neaw," said Jabe disappointedly, "that's loike thee. Thaa con think fast enough if it's ony lumber tha'rt up tew. Bud thaa con think o' nowt when tha'rt wanted."

Ben as a rule took no heed to his friend's railings, but to-night, chafing under a sense of powerlessness, he answered somewhat sharply—

"Well, thee think o' summat then?"

"Ay," snarled the Clogger, "*me* ageean. A bonny lot o' numyeds yo'd be baat me."

Ben sighed again, slowly knocked the ash out of his pipe, and said, as he rose to go—

"Theer's nobbut wun thing left as Aw con see."

"Wot's that?" asked Jabe, subdued again by Ben's grave tone.

"Th' owd Beuk says as 'Unto the righteous there ariseth light in the darkness,' an' we'en getten ta wait till it does," and with another sigh Ben sauntered off home.

The clogging business suffered during the next three days. Jabe found it simply impossible to give his mind to his work. To make matters worse, Lige, after two or three attempts, had given up the idea of working until some settlement was arrived at, and wandered in and out of the Clog Shop all day long, alternately anathematising a fate that compelled him to make so momentous a decision, and praying under his breath for Divine guidance.

Sam Speck, in his character as Lige's keeper, scarcely ever left him, and kept up also a persistent assault on the position Lige had taken up on the question of his inheritance. To Sam that position was simply ridiculous. If the money was properly and legally left to him, what right had he to bother any further about it? And as for Lige's notion that Jane Ann, the leech-woman, was the rightful owner, Sam simply laughed at it.

"Whey, mon! t'oan hawf th' brass i' th' country 'ud ha' to swop hons if thot wor th' way o' doin' it. Ha' some sense, mon! Tha'rt goin' dateliss."

As for Lige, it was simply pitiable to see him. He forgot his half-weekly shave. His face wore a worried, almost haunted look, and his eyes were faded and watery in the morning, and bright and restless in the evening. Every few hours the arguments pro and con were rehearsed again by himself and some one or other of those in the secret, but always with the same result, and the Clogger grew peevish under the continued strain.

Every night since the discovery of Lige's dilemma, the four who knew of it remained behind after the others had gone, and went over the whole question again from beginning to end, but with a disheartening lack of definite result.

"Aw'll tell thi wot it is," cried Sam Speck, at the close of one of his many attacks upon Lige's position, "it's nowt else but a judgment on her. Hoo turned up her nooase at thi, an' wo'dn't ha' thi at ony price. Well, hoo's cut her oan throttle—an' sarve her reet."

This certainly was a new idea, and Jabe and Ben were inclined to see something in it; but Lige only shook his head and groaned—

"Hoo's his dowter, an' wotiver hoo does conna mak' her onybody else's dowter." And with a face of deepening gloom he bent over the fire as if he were cold.

But the idea had set Long Ben thinking, and after a more or less sleepless night he was at the Clog Shop before Jabe had finished his breakfast, with at any rate a gleam of light in his mind.

Now Jabe had felt from the beginning that if ever a solution of the difficulty was reached it would have to come from Ben, and so he sat up in his arm-chair in the parlour and set his loose leg a-going in eager anticipation the moment he set his eyes on the carpenter.

"Aw think wee'st ha' rain," began Ben, trying to look easy, and glancing carelessly through the parlour window.

"Ler it rain!" exclaimed Jabe impatiently. "Wot dust want?"

"Naa, Aw wur nobbut wondering whether we met square this thing"—and Ben put his hands behind him and turned his back to the fire.

"Goa on!" rasped out Jabe, scarcely able to contain himself. "Lige 'ull be here in a jiffy."

Ben glanced out of the window again, looked demurely round the room, and then said—

"Thaa knows Jane Ann, dust na?"

"Ay! wot bi that?" and the Clogger looked as though he would have liked to drag the slowly flowing words out of Ben's hesitating mouth.

"Is hoo a dacent woman, dust think?" was Ben's next venture.

"Ay! hoo's reet enuff. Goa on, mon. Wot art dreivin' at?" and Jabe's short leg was riding up and down with frantic excitement.

Ben looked round the house again, rolled his carpenter's apron round his waist, and proceeded—

"He's promised no' ta speik abaat it fur a wik, hasna he?"

"Well, well!" and Jabe had to seize hold of the chair-arms to keep down his irritation at Ben's deliberateness.

"If hoo could be getten ta hev him afoor th' wik's aat"—

Jabe jumped to his feet with a shout, and giving Ben a push which nearly caused him to sit down on the parlour fire, he cried—

"By gum, tha's getten it, lad!"

Then he stood back, and was evidently thinking rapidly.

"Howd on!" he cried suddenly, raising his hand as if he were signalling. "Hoo'd happen throw him o'er when hoo geet howd o' th' brass."

"Wot! When hoo knowed wot he'd done fur her? Beside, we met happen guard ageean that."

"Haa?"

"By axin' her if hoo'd owt ageean him but his pawverty."

"An' wot then?"

"Well, if hoo hadna, we met tell her as he's better off nor he uset be."

The Clogger eyed Ben over with an eager, gloating sort of look, and then, slapping him on the shoulder, he broke through the principles of a lifetime by giving expression to feelings of unfeigned and proud admiration of his friend—

"Ben thaa licks Owd Scratch fur schamin'—thaa does, for sure."

But, though this was Ben's plan in outline, there were details wherein he saw possible difficulties, and so, sitting down, he and Jabe went over them one by one, enlarging and perfecting the scheme.

"When mun we start?" asked Ben at last.

"The sewner the better," was the emphatic reply.

"Then tha'd better pike off ta-day."

"Me! me goa! Wot th' ferrups art talkin' abaat, Ben?"

"Well, thaa knows her, an' Aw dunno."

"Bud Aw'm an owd bachelor. Aw know nowt abaat women, an' Aw dunno want t' dew nother. Tha'rt maddlet, mon."

But Ben stuck to his point, and it soon began to be clear that there was no other way out of the difficulty. Jabe at first refused peremptorily. He stormed. He called Ben all the usual names of opprobrium, and invented several new ones for the occasion. Lige's fortune might go to Hanover for him. And he got angrier and angrier as the inevitableness of Ben's suggestion became clearer to him.

Ben, relying on his old friend's strong attachment to Lige, and his general willingness to help anyone in need, held quietly to his point, and at last, after the longest and toughest struggle these two old gladiators ever had together, Ben departed, leaving Jabe vowing more vociferously than ever that he would not go a yard, but feeling certain all the same that he would go.

And sure enough early in the afternoon of that same day the trees and hedges along the lanes to the Halfpenny Gate beheld the fierce woman-hating old Clogger limping doggedly along on an errand of love, and he who never courted fair woman for himself was actually going a-wooing for another.

The details of that memorable interview have never been fully divulged by either of the parties who shared it, but sufficient is known for the purposes of this story.

Jane Ann received Jabe quite effusively, and, though they were but slightly acquainted, insisted on his having tea with her. Jabe persistently declared his inability to stay, as was the proper thing to do in the Clough, and several times tried to bring round the conversation to the subject of his visit. But Lige seemed so unimportant a person to the leech-woman in comparison with her present guest that she could not be induced to talk about him, and was demonstrative enough in her attentions to make the Clogger feel uneasy and suspicious. When tea-time came Jabe had not even mentioned his real business, and so was compelled, in spite of himself, to accept Jane Ann's most pressing invitation, and he sat at the table in a state of nervous apprehension lest someone should suddenly open the door and find him in this most compromising position.

Towards the end of the meal he managed to introduce Abram Howarth's name, and discovered that his hostess knew all about the matter. She seemed strangely unconcerned about it, Jabe thought, and even then he could obtain no clue as to her feelings about poor Lige.

What the Clogger suffered in the interest of his friend that day will never be known, but presently, excited and afraid for himself, and anxious to get the interview over, but dodged and eluded by Jane Ann at every turn, he eventually grew desperate and blurted out the whole truth, and threw himself and his friend on the lady's mercy.

The leech-keeper suddenly became very quiet and hurried into the back-yard—to feed the hens, she said; but really to conceal very genuine emotion and to collect her thoughts.

When she came back her manner towards the Clogger had undergone a decided change, and she raised no objection to his proposed departure.

Jabe was not quite satisfied, for though the lady now seemed willing, and almost eager, to see Lige, she would give no promise as to how she would treat him, and absolutely refused to bind herself in any way. At the same time, as Jabe seemed so anxious, she allowed him to conclude that the road-mender would not suffer by being left in her hands.

The expedition was not wholly satisfactory, Jabe mused as he went home. And Long Ben's mode of receiving his account of it tended to confirm this impression. But there was nothing for it now but to go on with the scheme, and the next question was how they were to deal with Lige.

This proved by no means an easy problem, but at last they decided that, whilst concealing Jabe's visit from him, they would persuade him to go and see Jane Ann first instead of the lawyer, and they would for his own sake encourage him to act as soon as the week's grace was up.

Lige was surprised and suspicious when that very evening they put on an air of reluctant resignation as if already accepting the inevitable, and he began to feel very lonely as he found them disposed to push him on in his resolution instead of trying to dissuade him as heretofore. For some time he held out resolutely against going to see Jane Ann at all, and declared he would hand everything over to the lawyer, and "ha' dun wi' it." But eventually the dexterously managed pressure of his friends prevailed, and the course they recommended was decided upon.

Two days yet remained of the terrible week, and the way Lige seemed to be suffering as the time drew nearer made Jabe and Ben feel very guilty, whilst at the same time it gave encouragement to Sam to think that his arguments were prevailing. Of course, Sam knew nothing of Jabe's visit to the Halfpenny Gate, and Jabe and the carpenter found his ignorance very useful to their scheme.

All morning on the day after the expiration of the week, Lige sat groaning and sighing over the Clog Shop fire, wishing he had never been born, and denouncing the departed Abram as if he had done him some deadly injury.

He seemed to grow more settled towards noon, and having dined at the Clog Shop, he hurriedly started off home, and half an hour afterwards, carefully dressed, and wearing once more Jonas's "blacks," he made his way on his fateful errand.

He went very slowly, and stopped and talked to himself and prayed in the quiet lanes, but at length he dragged his reluctant legs to the cottage of his lady-love, and knocked and entered without waiting for permission—

"Well, haa arta, wench?" he asked in a low sad voice that failed to conceal his agitation.

Jane Ann was ironing, and glancing carelessly up, she answered—

"Aw'm reet enuff."

Lige was trembling now, but Jane Ann didn't appear to notice. Neither did she ask him to sit down, and so from sheer weakness he moved towards a chair, and dropping into it, faltered faintly—

"Aw want ta speik ta thi, Jane Ann."

"Then donna! Aw've towd thi afoor, an' Aw meean it."

Lige's pale face became ashy as he answered—

"It's no' that, wench, this toime. Aw've cum ta speik abaat thi fayther."

"Tha's no need; tha con tell me nowt good abaat him."

"Thaa knows as he's deead, Aw reacon?"

"Ay!" and the tone of the admission sounded as if she were reluctant to admit even so much.

"Dust know whoa he left his brass tew?"

"Ay," and Jane Ann went to change her flatiron at the fire, showing by her whole manner that she wished him to understand that the subject was distasteful to her.

But Lige was in it now, and intended to make an end.

"Well, it's no' moine, thaa knows; it's thoine," he said, leaning forward on his stick.

"It *isna* moine, an' Aw shanna hev it."

"Bud thaa *mun* hev it; thaa'll *ha'* ta hev it," and Lige became momentarily quite aggressive.

"Shall Aw?" And Jane Ann tossed her head defiantly, and began to rub her flat-iron on the smoothing blanket.

There was silence for a moment, for Lige was quite nonplussed. At last he said coaxingly—

"Jane Ann, it isna my fawt as he left it ta me. Aw knew nowt abaat it till efther he wor deead."

"Whoa said it wur?"

"Well, tak' it then, will ta?

Then Jane Ann wheeled round, and, looking Lige steadily in the face, said, holding the iron away from her—

"Liger Howarth, Aw'st never tak' a hawpenny on it if thaa talks till t' Judgment Day. Soa theer!"

Lige was amazed and distressed, and all the more so as he felt the old Adam in him rejoicing over Jane Ann's obstinacy. He sat looking at the flat-irons in the bars of the fire for some time, and then he asked, hesitantly, as if ashamed of the suggestion

"Well, wilt tak' th' hawf on it!"

"Aw tell thi, Aw winna tak' a fardin."

There was another uncomfortable pause, and then Lige ventured—

"Wilt tak' them tew haases at th' bottom o' th' gate yond'?"

Then Jane Ann seemed really angry, and replied—

"Aw've towd thi wunce fer aw, Aw'st ha' *nowt*, an' if thaa conna be said tha'd better be shuntin'."

Lige was abashed. He sat for a long time trying to think of something else to propose, but as nothing came, he rose reluctantly to leave, saying, as he did so—

"Well, Aw'll be goin'. But Aw'll gi' thi a fortnit to think abaat it, and then Aw'll come ageean."

"If thaa gi'es me twenty ye'r, it 'ull mak' noa difference," and Jane Ann rubbed resolutely at her ironing-cloth.

Lige moved slowly to the door, unwilling to go, but afraid to stay. He was just raising the latch and clearing his throat for a last word, when Jane Ann, with a face hot with ironing, and perhaps also with something else, bent low over her work, and said more softly than she had yet spoken—

"Liger."

"Wot?"

"Ther's wun thing Aw'll hev, if tha'll ax me."

Lige brightened up and turned back into the house again, and asked eagerly—

"Wot's that?"

"*Thee.*"

. . . . .

There is really no more to be told. Lige the road-mender had never had any attractions for Jane Ann, and Lige, her father's heir and her supplanter, had become an object of aversion. But the Lige whose simple honesty and rare conscientiousness had prompted him to make so great a sacrifice for justice and righteousness' sake became suddenly very noble in her eyes, and the road-mender went back to Beckside an accepted suitor and a very happy man. And the first business of Jane Ann after she came to Beckside to live was to order the new Communion plate for the chapel.

THE MEMORY OF THE JUST.

I.

A FATHER'S HONOUR.

"PUZZLES! they arr that! They're Chinese puzzles, women arr! It teuk th' 'owd lad' ta foind th' fost on 'em aat, an' it tak's him ta dew it yet. Some on 'em's simple an' some on 'em's sawft, bud then aw tremenjous deep."

The speaker, of course, was Jabe. Raising himself up to straighten his back as he stood with braces hung down at his side, over the clog-shaping bench, and using the last half-finished sole to emphasise his observations, he was addressing himself apparently to vacancy, for the rest of the company were sitting deep into the Ingle, and were invisible behind clouds of smoke.

"Wot does thaa know abaat women?" came from somewhere behind the smoke-cloud, in tones very like those of the erstwhile road-mender and recent bridegroom, Lige.

"Aw know wun on 'em as hez made a sawft yed sawfter lattly."

There was a sort of sputter of laughter in the nook, and the voice of Sam Speck cried delightedly —

"Goo' lad, Jabe! By gum — that's a nobbler fur thee, Liger!"

But Lige was very easy-going in these days of his prosperity, and was, moreover, interested in the topic which had provoked the Clogger's tirade, and so he brought the conversation back by observing —

"Thaa happen feart her, Jabe. Women wants handlin' gently, than knows."

"Feart her? Aw will fear her if hoo comes ony of her stuck-up ways wi' me. Aw tell thi they'r clemmin' i' th' haase, and hoo comes an' slaps her brass daan i' th' frunt o' me as if hoo hed a milliond."

"Ay, an' they sticken ta they'r oan pew, an' pay fur it. An' they spend as mitch brass i' donning up th' owd chap's grave as 'ud keep wun on 'em—partly wot," added Sam Speck sternly.

After a short pause, Lige observed reflectively—

"Well, if ther' is a grave i' that yard as owt ta be kept noice it's owd Abil's; it 'ull be a lung toime afoor ther's another loike him i' Beckside.

But Jabe was out of all patience, and all the more so as he was somewhat uneasy in his own mind.

"Ha' some sense, will yo'!" he cried. Tummy Nibble towd me hissel' as aw th' butcher's meit they iver han is tewpennorth o' liver at th' wik end, an' a pennorth o' cratchins o' Wednesdays. An' wun Setterday when he awsed ta give Jinny a bit o' briskit as he couldna sell, hoo threw it back i' th' cart an' welly slapped him i' th' face."

"It's pride! sinful pride, an' nowt else," cried Sam with stern indignant emphasis, and Jabe thus encouraged, proceeded—

"Dun yo' know haa it is as they cum'n ta th' chapel wun at wunce naa? It's 'cause they'n nobbut wun bonnet between 'em. An' aar Judy says as that's bin awtered an' awtered till it winna awter. Isn't that pride?"

And Lige sighed and shook his head, as a sign that he would be very reluctant indeed to believe the charge. And the Clogger, though he sat down in the circle of smoke and lighted his pipe, still showed where his thoughts were by the uneasy motions of his short leg.

The subjects of this conversation were two middle-aged females named Horrocks, who were generally known as "Rhoda an' Jinny Abil" — Abel being the name of their father, now long deceased.

They lived in what had once been the prettiest cottage in Beckside. It stood in the midst of a rather large garden just beyond the schoolhouse, going up the "broo" to Knob Top. Unlike most of the other cottages in the hamlet it was built of stone, and the windows, where climbing plants did not prevent, were rimmed round with a framework of whitewash. The ground rose at the back and screened the cottage from the east wind, and for many years the neatly-kept little house, with its gay and fruitful garden, had been a grateful sight to any one entering Beckside from that end of the village.

Old Abel, who built and owned it, was a mason by trade, and one of the mainstays of the chapel in the days when Jabe and his friends were young. He was a man of high character and gentle, kindly ways. His goodness seemed to shine out of his ruddy face, and he was known as one of the most upright and honourable men in the community. He was the associate and coadjutor of Jabe's father, John Longworth, and when he died he was so sincerely respected and beloved that the chapel people had by special contributions erected what was even in Jabe's later days by far the most pretentious tombstone in the graveyard. And when old John Longworth, declaring that he couldn't think of a text of Scripture, or a verse of a hymn, good enough to express the virtues of their departed friend, finally wrote out in his painful roundhand for the stone-carver's instruction, "Mark the perfect man and behold the upright," everybody felt that John had been specially guided and had made the only adequate selection.

Old Abel left three children, a son and two daughters, and these, though quiet retiring people, followed in their father's footsteps, at any rate so far as a deep attachment to the chapel and an interest in its welfare were concerned.

The son, Abel the younger, was the mill joiner, and Rhoda and Jinny were weavers, and so they were regarded as pretty well off, though now and again the extra sharp ones of the village pretended to have noticed odd and unexpected signs of pinching and even poverty about them.

Then young Abel died, and the girls were left behind. They owned the house they lived in, and had three looms each at the mill, and so must still have a good income; but notwithstanding all this they did not seem really comfortable, and every now and again little incidents occurred which made people wonder whether "Abil wenches" were really as well off as they were supposed to be, and as they always took pains to appear to be.

The one weakness of these two plain women was their quiet pride in their father's memory, together with the manifestation of that pride in fastidious and unremitting care for his grave. The stone was always kept scrupulously clean, and the little flower-bed before it always showed that careful and loving hands constantly tended it.

Now, it was a moot point in Beckside theology whether it was quite right to show excessive interest, especially of the mournful kind, in graves, there being a sort of feeling that people ought to rejoice at the translation of their friends, especially if they were uncommonly good. And so the conduct of "Abil wenches" attracted more notice than it ordinarily would have done, and it was feared that they were giving way to the "sorrow of the world."

It was noticed also that the two women had aged very rapidly since their brother's death, and the most diligent care on their part did not conceal the fact that they were getting poorer. Rhoda, the eldest, had begun to look quite old, and there were already indications of a premature breaking up of her constitution. At the same time she became shyer, and gradually changed from a calm, self-possessed Lancashire lass into a fretful, jaded, worn-looking and suspicious woman.

Then she became unable to work at the mill, and the burden of maintenance fell entirely on the younger and less energetic Jinny.

And now, as their poverty had an explainable cause, and could no longer be matter of doubt, tentative offers of help were made, but in every case they were hotly and almost fiercely rejected, as if, in fact, poverty were a terrible crime which they would rather die than confess to.

The night before the one on which our story opens, Jabe had been holding his class.

It was ticket night, and the leader, when receiving the class moneys after the minister's departure, left Jinny's lying on the table, and detained Jinny herself in conversation until the rest were gone, when he picked up the shilling and was quietly slipping it into her hands again. But she would not understand, and when the Clogger was compelled—not too gently, it is to be feared—to explain that he couldn't allow her to pay, as he felt sure she couldn't afford, Jinny flushed, and then turning white with fear and resentment, cried, eyeing Jabe over with keen suspicion as she did so—

"Haa does thaa know we're poor? Whoas towd thi?"

"Know? Aw con see, woman, sure*li*!" cried Jabe, with rising choler.

"See! Ay, tha'rt allis pooakin' thi nooase inta sumbry's business. But let me tell thi, Abil Horrocks allis held his yed up i' th' wold, an' his dowters art na goin fur t' disgrace his name. Moind that, naa!"

Jabe's feelings were divided between anger at the woman's obstinacy and pride, and a strong secret sympathy with her feelings about her father, and the respect that should be shown to his memory, and so he said, half apologetically

"Well, wench, Aw meant noa harm."

"Well, then, ler uz alooan, an' tell t'othcrs ta ler uz alooan. We'en getten ta tak' cur o' my fayther's name, and we'll dew it—ay, dew it if we dee dewing it"—and then Jinny burst into tears and hurried out of the vestry.

But she did not go home. She walked up the road a little way, and turned into a by-lane, where she slowly dried her tears. Then when she thought Jabe would be gone she came back to the chapel. It was a cloudy night, with an intermittent moon, and putting her clog toe into a hole in the wall, Jinny, as if she were accustomed to enter the graveyard that way, climbed quickly over, and was soon kneeling by her father's tombstone.

She looked up for the moon, but it was hidden for a moment behind a cloud, and she knelt there in an attitude of prayer, but though her lips moved rapidly, not a sound came from them. Presently she became more excited, and at length, turning her face up passionately to the clouds, she cried, clenching her hands with intense resolution—

"They shanna know, fayther; they shall niver know."

At that moment the moon came into sight for a moment, and, as its pale, cold beams fell on the stone, Jinny lifted her head and looked at it. Then she got up and dusted the already spotless surface just where it was lettered, much as another woman would have cleaned an expensive piece of pottery or a large mirror. And then she put one arm over the top of it, and stooping down, she read the precious lines once more, and then, still hanging over it, she fondly kissed the letters, and, turning her white face up till the moonlight fell across it and made it almost ghastly in its paleness, she cried, with a sudden burst of tears—

"It's theer yet, fayther! An' they shanna tak' it off. They can murther uz if they'n a moind, but they shanna tak' it off. Thaa *wur* parfect; than wur hupright; let clubs an' accaant beuks say wod they'n a moind."

When Jinny reached home that night, she found her sister huddling over a very small slack fire, and trying to get some little heat into her thin shrunken limbs.

Rhoda did not move when her sister entered, but when Jinny had drawn her chair beside her, and told the story of her interview with Jabe, she broke out—

"We'est ne'er dew it, wench! Summat's bin tellin' me as we shanna for mony a wik. We'en scratted an' we'en clemm't ta clew it, an' we shanna dew it efther aw."

Jinny muttered something.

"Nobbut ten paand! It met as weel be a hunderd, wench. We'est ne'er raise it. Aw'm deein'; Aw know Aw'm deein'; an' then my fayther's stooan 'ull be a lyin' stooan fur iver an' iver." And poor Rhoda beat on the sanded floor with her feet, and rocked herself in an agony of tearless grief.

After a while she stopped suddenly, a look of resolution that was almost fierce came into her eyes, and, after wrestling with deep feeling for a moment or two more, she jumped to her feet, and, clenching her fist and stamping emphatically on the floor, she cried—

"Bud we mun, Jinny, we mun! Aw conna dee till it's done. We'll sell ivery stick we han bud we'll dew it." And then clasping her hands together, and holding them over her head, whilst a look of tender melting love came into her eyes, she cried—

"An' then, fayther, we'est see yo'—'wheer the wicked cease fro' troublin', an' the weary are at rest.' An' then yo'll know as we tewk cur o' yo'r name. An' that 'ull be heaven fur uz. Ay! that 'ull be heaven for uz."

But next day, and many days after, poor Rhoda kept her bed. At first Jinny was able to leave her and go to the mill, but presently she grew feebler, and at the same time so excitable, that it was not safe to leave her, and Jinny had to stay at home and nurse her. Neighbours came to offer help, but they were suspiciously and almost rudely repulsed by Jinny, in a perfect fever of fear and apprehension; and day after day she watched over her dying sister, and lived no one knew how.

II.

OWD CROPPY'S ERRAND.

SEVERAL, anxious consultations were held at the Clog Shop about the Horrockses, but the only result of them was that Dr. Walmsley went to the cottage, and insisted, almost by on seeing the invalid. And the doctor reported that though there was no particular evidence of disease in the patient, and no very clear sign of poverty in the house, yet the woman was evidently dying, and dying of weakness and trouble.

Jabe was nearly beside himself, and made all sorts of wild suggestions for compelling the Horrockses to open their minds. At last one night, as Long Ben was going home from the usual rendezvous, he saw a woman, with a shawl over her head, standing hesitantly at the garden gate of his house.

"Is that thee, Ben?" she asked timidly, as he came up.

"Ay; is that thee, Jinny?"

"Ay! Ben, aar Rhoda wants thi."

"Naa?"

"Ay, naa. An' fur marcy's sake come."

Ben closed the gate and went along with poor Jinny. They walked rapidly but silently towards Abel's cottage.

"Is hoo wur?" asked the carpenter, as they neared the Beck bridge.

"Wur? Ay, hoo's deein', Ben," and Jinny burst into a cry that was somehow too terrible for tears.

When they reached the cottage, they found Rhoda sitting up in bed, and evidently waiting for them. Her face was haggard and pale, but her eyes were bright with excitement.

Ben sometimes did a little furniture brokering, and so, as he began to inquire after Rhoda's health, she impatiently waved the subject aside, as if it were too trivial, and began —

"Ben, Aw want thi to tell me haa mitch theas bits o' things o' aars are woth."

Ben looked round, seemed to hesitate for a moment, and then answered —

"Aw durn't know; wot art botherin' abaat? Wot dust want to sell 'em fur?"

But Jinny, stepping behind, pulled his coat tail, and so Ben, guessing that he was required to humour the patient, went on with a sudden assumption of business shrewdness —

"Haa mitch dust want fur 'em?"

Ben expected that Rhoda would begin to "haggle" with him, but instead of that she leaned forward with eager eyes and lips dry from excitement, and cried, "Ten paand. They're woth ten paand, arna they?"

Now, seeing that the dying woman really wanted to sell, Ben would probably have agreed if the sum demanded had been double what it was, and so he answered promptly —

"Ay, Aw'll gi' thi ten paand an' chonce it."

Rhoda put out a thin blue-lined hand, and cried, "Tak' 'em then, an' gi' me th' brass."

"Brass? Aw hevna getten it wi' me. Dust want it naa?"

"Naa! Ay, naa! Aw'm deein', mon. Naa! Naa!!" And the excited woman wrung her hands in intense impatience.

"Aw con fotch it thi, if tha's a moind," said Ben hesitatingly, and knowing full well that he hadn't half the sum, and couldn't think where to procure it at that late hour.

"Fotch it, then. Fotch it, an' be slippy, mon! Or else Aw'st be deead afoor it comes." And with a gleam of eager joy that did not appear to Ben to be quite sane, she went on "Just let me get a seet on it an' howd it in my hond fur wun little minute, an' then, an' then— Aw'll—

'Clap my glad wings and sooar away,
An' mingle with the blaze of day.'"

And flinging up her arms and falling back on her pillow, she lay there panting and exhausted.

Jinny made attempts to soothe her sister. Tucking the bedclothes around her and shaking up the pillow, and wetting her lips with cold tea, she crooned over her in an anxious endeavour to calm the sufferer's agitation.

After a few minutes of apparent unconsciousness, the sick one suddenly opened her eyes, and sat bolt upright again. Seeing Ben still standing there, she put out her open hand as if to receive something, and cried—

"Hast getten it, lad? Give it me; give it me!"

"Tak' thi toime, woman; he's gooin' fur it naa!" said Jinny coaxingly.

"Toime! Aw've toime fur nowt. Fotch it, Ben; fur marcy's sake fotch it. Aw'st dee ba'at knowing it's paid if thaa doesna."

And then, checking herself suddenly, she gazed at Ben with the searching, suspicious look he had so often seen in these women's faces of late years.

On Rhoda promising to be still and quiet, Ben and Jinny went downstairs.

"Does hoo oft wandther loike that?" asked Ben softly as they reached the lower room.

"Wandther? Hoo's no' wandthering, Ben;" and then, in an agony of fear and anxiety too stern and imperious to conceal, she cried—

"We mun hev' it, mon; chuse wheer it comes fro'. Hoo conna dee till hoo knows it's reet, or if hoo dees ba'at knowing ther'll be a ghooast i' Beckside, fur hoo'll niver rest in her grave."

The look of tortured fear on poor Jinny's face went to Ben's heart, and in an impulse of wonder and pity he cried, though he would have given his ears to recall the word when it had gone—

"Wot dun yo' want it fur?"

Jinny stopped her wailing, and shot into Ben's face another of those terrified, suspicious looks he had grown familiar with, and after studying his face for a moment or two, and appearing to be relieved by what she saw, she at length said—

"Aw conna tell thi, Ben; Aw wouldna tell thi to save my soul. An' if iver thaa knaws, tha'll wuish thaa hadna known. But thaa shanna know! Noabry shall iver know." And for a moment Jinny looked as fierce as her sister.

Ben was puzzled and distressed, but realising both the uselessness and the unkindness of pressing the matter, he hastened away to find the money.

After crossing the bridge in profound agitation, he remembered Lige's many offers of help if he ever needed it, and turned in by the Brickcroft corner, and stopped at the road-mender's door. He raised the latch, but the door would not open; and he then remembered that Lige and his wife had gone to Duxbury about the sale of a piece of property, and had announced their intention of staying the week-end.

Where must he go next? He had not more than three pounds in his pocket. He shrank from exciting the dangerous curiosity of Sam Speck about the matter, and so, after many a misgiving, he turned up the "broo" toward the Clog Shop, preparing to make a clean breast of everything, and induce the Clogger to join him in his strange speculation.

Jabe's face as Ben told his story was a study. First it was mockingly scornful. Then, when the money question was raised, it became a picture of unconvincible obstinacy. Then, as Ben detailed the painful agitation of the women, Jabe's eyes began to blink rapidly, and he blew his nose with most unnecessary violence, and finally every other expression was swallowed up in one of open-eyed and wondering curiosity, as Ben described with significant nods and winks the strange enigmatical hints which had dropped from the women, and the air of mystery with which the whole question seemed enveloped.

And this provided Ben with a way of escape, for Jabe's chronic anger with Ben for his "sawftniss," and his indignation with the women for their pride, were both forgotten in the presence of an object which excited at once genuine anxiety and keen, wondering curiosity.

But, unfortunately, Jabe had very little ready money in the house—less than two pounds, in fact—having that day paid a heavy bill for "owler" wood.

Ben seemed inclined to rest awhile and discuss the situation, but Jabe positively could not sit still, and in a few moments they were on their way to Nathan's.

Nathan had gone to the Clog Shop, Tatty said, but as they had not met him, it was certain he must have made a call somewhere. When they reached the smithy yard gate, and were standing and discussing where Nathan would most likely be, they heard a panting gasp behind them, and the agitated voice of "Jinny Abil" cried —

"Hast getten it, Ben?" And then, as if unable to control her feelings, she stood back, and, wringing her hands, cried—

"Oh, dunna say thaa hasna! for God's sake, dunna say that! "

"Dunna, wench; dunna," said Ben soothingly. "Aw'm gooin' efther it naa."

"Then thaa hasna getten it! Oh, efther aw theeas ye'rs, efther aw theeas ye'rs," and Jinny wrung her hands again in helpless, piteous despair.

She continued clasping her hands and twisting her body as if in intense pain, until Jabe could bear it no longer, and so, hastily drawing Ben aside, he whispered —

"Tak' her whoam. Aw'll goa and get it somewheer."

Ben turned round to persuade Jinny to go home with him, but he was saved the trouble, for all at once the distressed woman burst out—

"Hoo's gooin'! Hoo's gooin'? Hoo'll be deein' bi hersel'," and with another piteous wail she darted off down the hill towards home.

Ben, after another hasty word with his friend, followed closely behind.

"Mun Aw tell her Aw've getten th' brass?" he asked as they went along.

"Bud thaa hasna."

"Neaw, bud Aw shall hev' i' th' morn."

"Morn!" was the almost fierce reply; "hoo wants ta see it. See it afore hoo dees. Hoo could dee an' be dun wi' it, then. Ay! an' soa could Aw, an' be thankful."

They had just reached the bridge. The waters of the Beck were brawling over the stones underneath, the stone parapet was bathed in moonlight, and not a soul was in sight.

"Jinny," said Ben, stopping suddenly, and speaking with great impressiveness, "wot's aw this meean? Ther's summat wrung; naa wot is it? Owd Abil's childer doesna need ta want nowt i' Beckside sure*li*."

But at the mention of her father's name Jinny gave another bitter cry, and started once more for home.

When she reached the cottage, Jinny passed right upstairs, but Ben remained standing before the expiring fire, and waiting a summons to the bed-chamber, listening one moment to the sounds above, and the next to everything outside that suggested the coming of the Clogger.

Presently he was relieved to hear someone approaching the house, but the next moment his pleasure was dashed by the discovery that it was not the irregular click-clack of a clog, but the duller thud of a boot that he heard, which made him aware that the new-comer could not be the Clogger.

A peculiar, sharp, single tap on the door announced the presence of "Owd Croppy," the Brogden and Duxbury rent and debt collector. Whatever could he be doing in Beckside at this time of night?

He stared when Ben opened the door, and looked impatient and disappointed, as if he had something to communicate which was very good and which he longed to utter.

"Hello!" he cried; "wheer arr they? Wheer's Rhoda? Wheer's Jinny?"

A sudden seriousness came over the old collector as he learned the facts of the case and the condition of poor Rhoda.

"Well," he said, after ruminating with pursed lips for a moment or two, and following Ben's example by speaking under his breath, "Aw mun see 'em! Aw've getten some news as winna keep! "

"Howd on," replied Ben, holding up his hands deprecatingly and still speaking in a whisper, "it met kill 'em, or" —and then he paused, and as all the stray words and unintentional hints the women had dropped came back to him all at once, he continued—"or else cure 'em. By th' mon, Croppy, th' Lord's sent thee here ta-neet."

Croppy wasn't at all sure of this. His face seemed to say that he was much more accustomed to commissions from an opposite source, but before he could answer Jinny came hurrying downstairs.

She uttered a despairing cry as she saw the debt collector.

"Wot! Awready! Thaa met a letten her dee fost. Wun on us 'ud a getten aat on it at ony rate. But thaa shall be paid. Aw'll pay thi if Aw hev ta sell th' last rag o' my back. An' then Aw'll goa to th' bastile an' dee. Ay, an' be rare an' fain ta dee tew!"

"Jinny," cried Croppy, ashamed for once of his profession, "Aw hev'na come abaat brass. Aw've come wi' some queer news. Good news tew, Aw darr say!"

Just then the high ringing voice of the feverish sufferer upstairs was heard. "Jin ler him come up; ler him come up, Jin."

Jinny stepped to the bottom of the stairs and told her sister who the visitor was.

"Dust think Aw conna yer whoa it is? He met a waited till Aw wur cowd, bud ler him come up."

Jinny beckoned Croppy to follow her, and they both ascended to the bedroom.

At this moment Jabe gently raised the latch. Ben could see at a glance that he had not been successful. He motioned the Clogger to be silent, and then drew him out of the house again and expressed his conviction that they wouldn't be needed any more that night. But Jabe was hard to convince. His curiosity was so thoroughly aroused that it took all Ben's arguments and persuasions to induce him to leave the sisters until the morning; and but for the fact that he had no money to offer them, he would undoubtedly have held out. It was late, however; Croppy's business was evidently very important, and might take a long time, and so, with a painful and snappish reluctance, Jabe at last consented, and the two, after shouting "Gooidneet!" up the stairs, and getting a reassuring "Gooid-neet" in Jinny's own voice in reply, made their way across the bridge and up the "broo."

III.

JOY COMETH IN THE MORNING.

NEXT morning Jabe had Ben up earlier than usual, and the two made their way to the Horrockses. To their surprise, the curtains were drawn up and the door was open.

Jabe's nervousness made him bashful, and so he stopped on the threshold and knocked.

Hurried feet came noisily downstairs, and as soon as she saw them, Jinny, who had a dishevelled and up-all-night appearance, cried out, whilst tears of evident joy welled up into her eyes—

"Hay, chaps, come in; bless yo', come in. Aw feel as if it wur th' resurrection mornin', an' Aw'd just come aat of a grave. Bless th' Lord Bless th' Lord!"

And, as Jabe and Ben looked at each other in astonishment, Jinny's cry was feebly repeated upstairs—"Bless th' Lord! Bless th' Lord!"

"Wotiver's ta dew, wench?" cried Jabe, in amazement.

"Ta dew? Ther's iverything ta dew. Summer i' th' middle of winter; midsummer in November. It's heaven upo' 'arth; heaven upo' 'arth!"

"Whey, wotiver's happened?" and Ben lifted his eyebrows and looked at Jabe, and muttered under his breath, "Th' poor crayter's gooan off it."

"Ler me tell 'em, Jin—ler me tell 'em. Bless th' Lord!" came feebly downstairs.

"Yo'll ha' ta goa upst'irs, chaps," said Jinny, actually smiling. "Hoo allis hed her own rooad, yo' known."

In obedience, therefore, to these directions, the Clogger and his friend made their way to the bedroom, where they found Rhoda still in bed, but looking like a transfigured being.

"Sit yo' daan," she said, as they entered, and then she looked from one to the other with eager, beaming eyes, and burst out, "Bless th' Lord! Bless th' Lord!"

When they were seated, and were looking hard at the sick woman in whom so strange a transformation had taken place, she suddenly turned in her bed, and looking at Jabe, demanded—

"Jabe, wot wur it as yo' put upo' my fayther's stooan?"

"'Mark the perfect man and behold the upright,'" said Jabe.

"An' wor it trew? Wor he parfect an' upright? Wor he?"

"He wur that," answered Ben fervently.

"A foine seet better nor ony 'at's abaat naa," added Jabe as a clincher.

"Bless th' Lord! He wur! He wur!" And the two women looked at each other, apparently gloating over the words they had heard.

Then Rhoda's face suddenly darkened again. She seemed to be collecting her powers for a difficult task, and at last she said impressively—

"Jabe, iver sin th' wik efther it wur put up we'en bin feart it wur a lyin' stooan."

"Naay, *Aw* ne'er wur," cried Jinny, through glistening tears.

"Whey, it *wur* thee," cried Rhoda in astonishment. "Aw knew betther aw th' toime."

"Naay, it wur thee; no' me."

But just then Ben chimed in: "If iver a grave-stooan i' this wold towd trew, it wur that."

"Trew? It wur na hawf trew eneuff," added Jabe emphatically.

Rhoda paused in a listening attitude, as if she were hearing enthralling music, and presently she went on—

"Th' wik efther th' stooan were put up, a felley cum fro' Duxbury an' said as th' club beuks as my fayther used t' have wur wrung, an' hed bin fur mony a munth."

"Wrung?" cried both men at once, in amazed indignation.

"Ay, wrung! An' if Aw hedna bin i' th' haase aar Abil 'ud a felled him. But Aw sattled Abil a bit, an' then th' chap axed him fur t' goa ta Duxbury an' see th' beuks fur hissel'.'"

There was a sound of long, laborious breath being drawn, and Jabe and his friend looked at each other in fierce indignation.

"Well," Rhoda proceeded, "he went, an' when he coom back he wur loike a deead un. He sat daan afoor th' feire an' started a whackering and skriking an' couldna tell us a thing. Well, at th' lung last, he said as it were trew, an' mi fayther 'ud bin takkin' th' club brass for ye'rs."

Rhoda paused for a moment to give her hearers time to realise the awful communication she had made. Then she wiped her perspiring face with a spotted cotton handkerchief, and, leaning towards the Clogger, whose short leg had already kicked the bed-stock several times, she went on—

"Sithi, Jabe; Aw could ha' torn aar Abil to pieces when he said that." And then, after a moment's silence, "Poor lad, it kilt him."

"Well, yo' known," she proceeded, after a moment's mournful thought, "we couldna believe it of aar fayther, but Abil stuck aat as it wur trew, an' we wur that feart on it gettin' aat we darrna speik abaat it ta awmbry. So we morgiged th' haase an' paid it,—welly sixty paand,—an' th' felley said as he'd keep it quiet."

"Thaa lumpyed! whey didn't thaa cum an' tell me?" interrupted Jabe in stern indignation.

"Aw know'd it wur wrung aw th' toime, an' Aw wouldna hev' agreed ta pay it, chuse wot they'd said, ony fur that text upo' th' gravestooan," answered Rhoda. And then, after another pause, she proceeded—

"Well, six munths efther, th' felley coom an' said as they'd fun' some mooar aat. Hay, Ben, Aw thowt as mi hest 'ud a bust. We prayed till we couldna pray, an' we skriked till we wur blind. An' aw th' toime foak were talkin' abaat th' grave-stooan, an' sayin' has trew it wur. An' we knowed as it wur aarsel's, but we couldna prove it, an' we wur feart aat of aar wits on it bein' fun' aat.

"Well, we borrad th' second lot o' brass off Owd Croppy at a big interest, an' wot wi' th' debt an' wot wi' th' interest we'en bin payin' it off iver sin'. It kilt aar Abil, an' it wur killin' me. Th' last ten paand we couldna raise; we'en bin tryin' for welly tew ye'r. An' Croppy saused uz ivery toime he coom. An' we wur that feart of owt cumin' aat, as we darrna leuk poor. An' then Aw geet badly, an' Aw wur feart o' deein' afoor it wur paid. It ud aw a come aat if Aw hed, happen. But Aw, couldna keep up. Aw felt Aw wur dun fur. An' Aw wur welly crazy maddlet ta get th' brass, an' save my fayther's name."

Then she paused for a moment, out of breath. Both Ben and Jinny began to exhort her to rest a little, but she stopped them with an impatient gesture and proceeded—

"At last aar Jin an' me made it up as hoo should goa i' lodgings, or else to th' bastile, when Aw wur deead, an' sell aw th' furniture ta pay wi'. Aw couldna dee, yo' known, till mi fayther's name wur saved—an' it is saved naa. Bless th' Lord!"

"Thi fayther's name ne'er wanted savin'," jerked out Jabe; "bud goa on an' finish this nominny."

"Well," resumed Rhoda, "when Aw know'd Aw wur struck wi' death, Aw felt Aw couldna goa till Aw know'd as it wur aw reet an' safe. An' soa Aw sent fur thee, Ben, last neet. Thaa allis hed a koind hert, lad. An' thaa cum, an' went away ta fetch th' brass, and when Aw wur waitin' upst'irs fur thi ta cum back, Aw yerd Owd Croppy daanst'irs, and then he cum up. An' hay, Aw wur feart! But he said as he'd some news fur me. Aw didn't want ony news, but Aw darrna say so. Soa he cum an' he stood jist where tha'rt sittin' naa, Ben, an' he leuked at me, an' he said, 'Amos Bobby wur kilt this mornin'.'

"Amos wur my fayther's pardner i' th' club stewardship, thaa knows. Well, Aw thowt as they'd fun' summat else aat, an' Aw skriked aat, but Croppy said as when he wur deein' Amos sent fur him an' towd him he'd summat ta get off his soul afore he faced his Maker. An' wot dun yo' think it wur?"

Both men were watching Rhoda with a stern eagerness that was painful, but neither spoke.

"He towd Croppy as he'd awtered th' beuks ta pay his dog-runnin' debts, an' then when my fayther deead suddin he couldna foind th' brass, an' soa he leet it goa upo' th' deead mon. An' soa, yo' see, his name's saved at last. Hay, Aw know'd it couldna be mi fayther; bud we'en saved his name! We'en saved his name! And naa Aw con goa ta me grave contented."

But she didn't. At first it seemed very doubtful whether she would rally, but the vindication of her father's honour, and the removal of her own intolerable burden, seemed to give her new life, and in a short time she was going to the mill again, looking younger and stronger than she had done for years.

ISAAC'S ANGEL.

I.

LOVE AND MUSIC.

ISAAC, the Clogger's apprentice, sat at his work before the back window of the shop one balmy day in the early summer. He had opened the window, thereby letting in the scent of wallflowers and the hum of bees.

Jabe was out, for it was the first working day after the Whitsuntide holidays, and the Clogger, though he would certainly not have admitted the fact, was feeling the effects of the holiday and the school treat, and so, being in no humour for work, had gone down to Long Ben's to "sattle up" about the previous day's proceedings.

And Isaac seemed to have caught some of the restlessness of his master, and was getting on very slowly with his work.

He held a clog-top between his knees, and was making a show of stitching it, but when he had drawn the tatching ends through their holes, and stretched out his arms to pull them tight, he kept them thus extended, and sat gazing out of the window with a far-away, melancholy, and dispirited look on his face.

Then as he sat gazing out of the window at the tree-tops on the ridge of the Clough, he would every now and again heave a heavy sigh, then start suddenly as he discovered that he was idling, and hurriedly resume his stitching, casting as he did so furtive glances towards the inglenook, where Sam Speck sat enjoying a meditative pipe.

Presently Isaac's sighs became quite demonstrative, and were evidently somewhat artificially produced for the purpose of attracting attention. If so, they entirely failed, for Sam, half-asleep, was not in the least affected by them. A few minutes later Sam began to nod, which seemed to quite disturb poor Isaac. Then his pipe dropped out of his mouth, and that awoke him, and as he was picking it up, Isaac, to prevent him dozing off again, broke out—

"Sam!"

"Wot?"

"Aw've yerd bet-ter hanthums tin that we hed o' Sunday neet."

"Wot's thaa know abaat hanthums?"

Isaac seemed not to hear this rough answer, and proceeded—

"Aw loiked it weel enuff i' perts, bud Aw thowt as th' solo spilet it, thaa knows."

"Spilet it, thaa bermyed, whey it wur the best pert on it."

Isaac seemed very uncomfortable, and the face that gazed out through the window looked quite wretched.

"Ay! Aw darr say it's reet enuff if it 'ud bin sung owt like"—and Isaac stole a long sly look at Sam.

"Sung! whey, it wur sung grand! He's a throit like a throstle, Joe hes."

A spasm of pain shot across Isaac's homely countenance, as if Sam's words were so many twists of a thumbscrew or other dreadful instrument of torture. For a moment or two he seemed unable to speak. His lips tightened, and then suddenly relaxed and quivered, and as he gazed abstractedly at the distant treetops once more, something very like tears swam into his eyes.

Presently, with a manifest effort, he asked—

"Did—did—t'other singers loike th' solo?"

"Aw reacon thaa meeans did Lizer Tatlock loike it? Well, hoo did. Hoo gan him some peppermint humbugs when it wur o'er."

Isaac went very red about the neck and ears. His eyes filled again, and looking with a sort of desperation through his tears at the distant trees once more, he said slowly and falteringly, and in a tone which even the most credulous would have found it difficult to believe in—

"Aw cur nowt abaat Lizer Tatlock."

Sam laughed—a great, ironical, unbelieving laugh. "Neaw," he cried, "an' tha'rt no' jealous o' Joe, arta? Oh neaw! sartinly not!" and Sam grinned again in relish of his own rough irony.

There was another pause, during which Isaac was evidently trying to get himself well in hand again, but in spite of all he could do a great tear splashed down upon his hand as he was boring a hole in the clog-top with his awl.

Now Sam saw this tear, and it was the first indication he had had of the depth of Isaac's feelings on the matter of their conversation, and so, after watching the apprentice meditatively for some time, he changed his tone and said, with an assumption of stern impatience—

"Whey doesn't thaa shape, mon, an' get th' wench if thaa wants her? Hoo conna be so bad to pleeas when hoo tak's up wi' Joe."

Isaac took another long stare through the window, and then, speaking like a man who was absorbingly preoccupied, he murmured dejectedly—

"Joe's bet-ter leukin' nor me, an' mooar of a scholard—beside his singin'" and then, after a pondering, dreamy pause, "Hay! Lizer does loike music."

"Hoo wouldna be Jonas's wench if hoo didna," cried Sam; "but whey doesn't *thaa* start o' singin'?"

150

And Isaac, with a despondent shake of the head and a voice of profound melancholy, replied—

"Aw conna sing a nooat, Sam."

Sam sat up, as if to think more rapidly, seemed about to speak once or twice, and then checked himself; but at length he suggested, though not very confidently—

"Start o' playin' then, mon. Thaa met ger i' th' band, thaa knows, an' that 'ud fotch her off her pierch."

An eager light came into Isaac's eyes. This was evidently what he would like most of all, but a moment later he shook his head sadly and said—

"Aw'm sitchen a numyed, thaa knows, Sam; besides, whoa'd larn me?"

Sam evidently agreed with Isaac as to his lack of power to acquire knowledge, but he also sympathised with him in his trouble, and so he said at last—

"Well, if thaa loikes fur t' try th' voiolin, Aw'll larn thi."

Isaac accepted this with great eagerness and many clumsy expressions of gratitude. And in response to it Sam offered to get him a fiddle and allow him to pay for it as he was able, which, as Isaac was poor and had a sick mother, was a great relief to him.

Then there came the question as to where the practising should take place. Sam was so dubious about his pupil that he insisted on the lessons being given secretly. They couldn't be given at his house, for his tyrant housekeeper and sister would not, he knew, tolerate them for an hour.

After much discussion, a disused hencote at the bottom of the yard wherein Isaac's mother's cottage stood, and which belonged to the cottage, was decided upon, and it was arranged that lessons should commence at once.

Many and many a time did poor Sam repent of his bargain during the next few months, for Isaac fully justified his own account of himself, and proved a most trying pupil.

In course of time, however, some little progress was made, and almost every night during the following winter any person going down Shaving Lane would have heard certain peculiar sounds coming from the outbuildings abutting upon the lane, and if they had peeped, as more than one curious Becksider did, through one of the many holes in the wall, they would have seen a tall, long-necked youth, with very short hair, mending a broken string, or resining a fiddle-bow, or producing, with fearful facial contortions and grotesque protrusions of tongue, certain weird, indescribable sounds, which every now and again very distantly suggested a tune.

As the springtime came round again the practices became more frequent, and Sam was sometimes on the point of giving his pupil up altogether, and sometimes prophesied that he would "mak' a fiddler efther aw."

One day, however, Sam effected his grand *coup*. It was the second practice night at the Clog Shop preparatory to the "Sarmons," and things could not be said to be going at all well. The instrumentalists struggled bravely with the new piece of anthem music, but when at last they had got through it, every man finished with that irritated and discouraged feeling so usual in the earlier stages of musical preparation. This was Sam's opportunity.

"Aw'll tell yo' wot it is, chaps," he cried, straightening himself and brandishing his fiddle-bow to emphasise his argument, "th' fost fiddles isna strung enuff, an' wot's mooar, they ne'er han bin strung enuff sin owd Job gan up."

"They makken neyse [noise] enuff, at ony rate," snarled Jabe from behind his 'cello; "it's no neyse we wanten, it's music."

"Yo' conna foind fiddlers upo' ivery hedge backin," said Jethro impressively.

"We met ax fat Joss," suggested Jonas the leader.

"Wot! Theer's noa ale-hawse fiddler goin' fur t' play i' aar chapil," cried Jabe, with fierce resolution.

There was a pause, broken by the strumming of strings in process of tuning, and then Sam said as carelessly as he could —

"We met tak' a young un an' larn him."

"Ay," retorted Jabe sarcastically, "we did that when we teuk thee, an' a bonny bargin thaa wur tew."

But the others, who evidently thought there was something to be said for Sam's suggestion, looked at him as if expecting him to proceed, and when he did not, Jonas, as leader, demanded —

"Aat wi' it, Sam; wot art dreivin' at?"

Sam became all at once deeply engrossed in tightening his fiddle-bow, and as he bent his head over it he said, in a low, hesitant tone —

"Isaac con fiddle a bit."

"That wastril!" cried Jabe, rising to his feet in supreme indignation; and in a moment everybody was speaking at once, and all agreed in denouncing the idea as absurd in the extreme. But Sam stuck to his point, and after a long strenuous argument, which sadly interfered with the practice, reluctant and tentative consent was given for Isaac to come to the next practice and try.

When Sam late that night communicated the intelligence to his pupil in the hencote, Isaac was overjoyed.

"Hay, lad," he cried, "when hoo sees me stonnin' i' th' band at th' Sarmons, an' fiddlin' away loike—loike—winkin'—wot'll hoo think on me then?"

And Sam, though with certain misgivings, catching for the moment some of Isaac's enthusiasm, replied—

"Joe Gullett's dun fur ony minit."

It was a trying ordeal through which poor Isaac passed next day. All day long Jabe was lecturing him on the difficulties of the task he was undertaking, and the utter impossibility of his being able to play creditably alongside such accomplished exponents of the art as the members of the band. And when the evening came, and eight sternly-critical judges listened to Isaac's initiatory performance with heads held sideways and nodding marks of time, the verdict, though not definite and final, was anything but hopeful. At any rate, when the practice was over, and Isaac, after waiting for the verdict for a long time, at last rose to go, he asked, with his hand on the latch— "Mun Aw cum ageean?"

Nobody seemed inclined to answer, until Jonas, who as leader was expected to reply, answered somewhat surlily—

"Thaa con pleeas thisel'."

Of course Isaac continued to attend, but his case was never regarded as a hopeful one. Just when he ought to have been showing most improvement he became somehow most stupid, and his inclusion in the band for the great "Sarmons" day was an unsettled question to the very last. In fact, had it not been that Long Ben and Jethro discovered that Isaac did not dream of being left out, but was looking forward to his first public appearance with an eagerness they could not bear to disappoint, it is absolutely certain that Jabe would have had his way and the young clogger would have been summarily dismissed.

A week before the great event Jonas undertook to give Isaac a little private instruction, to prevent a *fiasco* at the last, and the only point in this arrangement that struck Isaac was that he had become a pupil of "Lizer's" father, and might even meet her in the house when he went for his lessons.

But the young lady was somehow always absent, and eventually he began to regard this as a fortunate circumstance, as his appearance in the band on the great Sunday would be all the greater surprise to her.

There was one drawback, however, to the completeness of Isaac's joy on the occasion. It was an unwritten law in Beckside that everybody with any pretence to respectability—at any rate every young person—must appear on Whit Sunday in new clothes, and had Isaac been able to add this additional glory to the triumphs of the day, his cup would have been about full. But his mother's illness had made that impossible. He would have to wear his old suit on this greatest occasion of his life, and just on the top of one knee his trousers had had to be darned, and the darn would be shockingly conspicuous, and he would sit where everybody could see him. But even this great difficulty did not daunt him. He got a new "dicky," a new bright blue necktie, with white spots in it, and a new billy-cock, and sat up until long after midnight in the hencote going over again and again the pieces to be played on the glorious morrow, finally going to bed to think and dream and do everything except sleep.

The Sunday proved wonderfully fine, though hot, and a great crowd assembled.

Very shyly poor Isaac insinuated himself into the vestry appropriated for the use of the band, and turned red and pale and pale and red again as he followed the procession of instrumentalists into the chapel.

Isaac was placed at the corner of the Communion rail, with Sam Speck at one side of him and Jimmy Juddy at the other. The players had their backs to the congregation, and their faces towards the stage on which sat rows of girls in white. In the bottom row, but on the other side of the pulpit from Isaac, sat Eliza Tatlock, whose dancing black eyes and arch roguish face had entirely bewitched the poor apprentice.

Having found out exactly where she was, Isaac began to make every possible use of his great opportunity. When he commenced to tune his fiddle, it was done pointedly at her, as if the exercise were a tribute to her beauty, rather than a mere musical preliminary. When the hymn was given out, and the band stood up and struck off with the tune, every stroke of Isaac's fiddle-bow which could possibly be made to do so went in Eliza's direction, and in all the succeeding parts of the service Isaac played palpably, and most enthusiastically, at the queen of his heart. Sad to say, though he never took his eyes from her except to look at his notes during the whole service, the hard-hearted beauty never deigned him so much as a single glance, whilst he twice caught her smiling in the direction of Joe Gullett.

Except for this circumstance, Isaac was perfectly satisfied with the service, and felt it, therefore, a great compliment when, immediately after dinner, Jonas Tatlock came down to him, and drilled him for a whole hour in his part for the evening service.

And poor Isaac did not know that this was done to appease the wrath of the Clogger, who was denouncing his apprentice in most violent language, and insisting on his being kept out of the evening's performance.

But the morning's service was merely a skirmish, and even the afternoon was not regarded by the band as of much importance, as they took but a very secondary part in it. The grand display, of course, was always reserved for night, and as the time drew near Isaac made his way in a high state of nervous perspiration to the band vestry.

Had he been less preoccupied he might have noticed that his fellow-players all looked at him with cold averted faces, except Sam Speck, who looked so bad that Isaac asked him if he'd got the "toothwarch."

Presently the Clogger entered the vestry. "Sithi'," he cried, as soon as he caught sight of his apprentice, "it's aither neck or nowt wi' thee ta-neet. If thaa shapes ta-neet loike thaa did this mornin' Aw'll— Aw'll brast thi fiddle fur thee."

Isaac smiled sheepishly, and tried to imagine how ashamed of himself his master would be when the service was over.

In a few moments they adjourned to the chapel, and Isaac, glancing up, saw that "Lizer" was there, looking as saucy and wicked as ever, and that Joe Gullett had changed places, and was just at Lizer's feet.

The great musical event of the day was the anthem of the evening service, and Isaac, turning round for an instant, saw all the musical critics of Brogden, Clough End, Halfpenny Gate, and the neighbourhood, sitting behind him with uncompromising faces.

At last the anthem was called for, and the band and choir stood up to perform. Just as Isaac was settling his fiddle to his chin he caught sight of Lizer looking straight at him. He felt that look right down to his toes. Now for it! The music commenced, and in a moment or two Isaac was sawing away for dear life, glancing every bar or two towards his lady-love to see how she was taking it. He saw her frown once. Then she blushed, and smiled very strangely. Then she went red again, and then, after biting her lip for a time, she presently laughed outright, and Isaac, excited almost beyond himself, put all he knew into the last grand fortissimo, and sat down, feeling that his work was done and his victory complete.

But somehow the band was very badly behaved that evening. Even Jabe was muttering and setting his teeth about something all through the sermon, and the rest hung down their heads and scowled; and when the last hymn came they played as if all life had gone out of them.

Isaac was surprised and grieved, and made up his mind to admonish his seniors gently when he got into the vestry. He had done his part. What was the matter with all the rest of them?

As the congregation dispersed, the band played a selection, and Isaac, in the confidence of a great sense of victory, extemporised a little, putting in several fine grace notes; and congratulated himself that everybody was noticing him, as indeed they were. He almost blushed as he discovered going out that all the musical critics in the congregation were looking at him in wonder, and, he doubted not, in envy too.

Poor Isaac! scarcely had he got inside the vestry when Jabe, almost purple with wrath, fell furiously upon him.

"Thee play!" he cried indignantly. "Ther's as mitch music i' thee as they' is in a cracked weshing-mug! Dun? Tha's spilt the best hanthum we'en iver hed, an' th' collection's daan three paand; that's wot tha's done! Pike off whooam, thaa scraping scarrcrow thaa!"

And glaring angrily at him, whilst the rest looked on with pained, resentful looks, Jabe pointed to the door, and stood in the middle of the vestry, waiting for him to depart.

And as if that were not enough, as he was going dejectedly down the "broo" towards home, who should pass him but the laughing, teasing "Lizer," talking with suspicious confidence to Joe Gullett.

II.

NO PLACE LIKE HOME.

ISAAC and his mother lived in the last of three irregular little one-storey cottages at the corner of Shaving Lane. He had got within a few steps of home when the teasing "Lizer" and her companion, Joe Gullett, passed him.

When he saw them thus in company, and heard the young lady's titter, he nearly stopped. A great lump came into his throat, and he struggled vainly to keep back hot, angry tears. Absorbed in watching his rival, he forgot to look where he was going, and a moment later he had stumbled over the remains of an ancient kerbstone, and his fiddle went flying from under his arm and clattering along the road, whilst Isaac himself went sprawling into the ditch.

He was up again in an instant with a great slit in his trousers, just across the top of the knee where they had been darned. He was covered all over with dust, and felt that he had scraped the skin off his shin. But that was nothing to the anger and bitter shame that raged within him as "Lizer" and Joe, just as they were turning the corner of Shaving Lane, looked at him. Concern and sympathy shot into "Lizer's" dark eyes, but at that instant Joe made some remark, which Isaac did not hear, but which set "Lizer" off giggling, and even after they had disappeared round the corner Isaac could hear her rippling laugh.

Sore, ashamed, and bitterly angry with all the world, Isaac picked up his instrument and walked slowly towards the house, knocking the dust off his clothes as he went, and struggling hard to keep back tears of pain and anger.

He steadied himself for a moment ere he opened the cottage door, waited until he could command his countenance, and then quietly lifted the latch.

The cottage was poorly furnished but spotlessly clean, and on the far side of the fireplace stood an old four-post bedstead carefully hung with pink and white bed-hangings of ancient pattern. Isaac never looked at the bed. He took off his hat and laid it on the edge of an old chest, ready to be taken up into the attic when he retired to rest. Then he carefully put away his fiddle in a little green bag and hung it in the chimney corner nearest the bed. Then he sat down before the fire and made a show of poking it, though the evening was most uncomfortably warm. In a moment or two he got up, walked to the window, and appeared to be interested in examining a couple of potted plants.

As he did so, a dismal chirp was heard just above his head, and a young "throstle" in a little cage hanging against the window-jamb began to show signs of recognition and gladness. But even this did not interest him, and instead of giving the expectant bird a responsive whistle, he stood blankly staring at it, as if it had committed some shocking crime, and then abstractedly turned away again and sat down once more by the fire.

All this time, as Isaac was well aware, a pair of anxious, pain-faded eyes had been watching him from the bed, and as they watched they grew darker and more distressful, and when he finally sat down before the fire, evidently very unhappy, the sad eyes grew softer, a melting light came into them, and many a wistful glance was cast towards him.

No sign or sound was there beside. Isaac was still in dreamland, and a dark and dreary dreamland it must have been, to judge by his face and the gloomy stillness in which he sat.

Presently there was a movement in the bed, accompanied by a groan which the sufferer tried hard but vainly to suppress. She now lay on her back gazing earnestly at the joists above her head, and after a pause she said in a low, gentle voice—

"Hay, Aw'm a praad woman ta-day."

But Isaac neither moved nor spoke, and so after another pause, she went on—

"Sum women's sons 'as bin i' th' ale-haase an' th' skittle alley an' tossin' an' swurrin' [swearing] aw day, an' moine's bin playin' hanthums at th' annivarsary. Bless th' Lord!"

Isaac gave a gasp, and a great gush of tears rose into his eyes, but he never spoke.

The sufferer on the bed was listening intently, and waiting for him to speak, but as he did not, she began to prepare her next remark; looking steadily at the joists, and apparently absorbed in conversation with the Great Unseen, she moved her twisted hands and said—

"Ay, Lord, th' herps of goold an' th' angils' singin' 'ull be varry grand, bud—Aw'd rayther yer aar Isaac playin' i' th' annivarsary."

And then she added in a soft, apologetic undertone—

"Yo' mun excuse me, Lord; Aw'm his mother."

Isaac was crying now. Not with the hot, hard tears of disappointment and shame, but the soft, gentle overflowings of relief and sympathy. He sat for some time undisguisedly wiping his eyes and sighing. Then he resumed his steady stare into the fire, but never a word did he speak,

"Aw reacon Aw'st ne'er yer na mooar hanthums till Aw get to the bet-ter land," murmured the sufferer on the bed, still apparently speaking to the Unseen or to herself.

And now for the first time Isaac turned and glanced towards his mother, but almost immediately resumed his glowering into the fire.

"Ne'er moind," came from the bed again. "Ther's plenty as hez yerd him play, if Aw hevna. Bud Aw'st be a hangil afoor lung, wi' wings an' noa rheumatiz, an' Aw'st goa to aw th' Sarmons as aar Isaac plays at."

And the afflicted one turned over on her side with her face to the wall, and shut her eyes as if in pain.

At this Isaac turned again and looked towards his mother, and once more resumed his gazing in the fire. Then he looked again with a wistful, anxious look. A long pause followed, and at length the young clogger rose to his feet and reached out his hand for his violin. He tuned it in a slow, absent sort of manner. Then he drew the bow across the strings aimlessly, and at last, turning his back towards the bed, he began to play, carefully and nervously at first, but soon with confidence and then with abandon, and with an accuracy and skill which would have greatly astonished his tutors and fellow-bandsmen. Finally he finished up with a grand, triumphant flourish.

During the playing of this anthem Isaac's mother did not move, and even when he had finished she gave no sign at all. Isaac stood for a moment expecting her to say something, and when she did not, he grew uneasy, and crept round the foot of the bed, with the fiddle still at his chin, to steal a look at her. Still she neither moved nor spoke. Had she gone to sleep whilst he played? He stepped nearer, passed the scullery door, stole along the other side of the bed, stooped over and looked down. And there lay a woman with a face worn with long and terrible suffering, but which now shone with a light that was scarcely earthly, whilst the pillow under her cheek was wet with gracious tears. As he bent over her she moved and opened her eyes. Then she smiled. Such a smile! Isaac had never seen anything like it before.

"Haa's yo'r pain, muther?" he asked, for the sake of saying something.

"Pain, lad? Aw know nowt abaat pain! Aw'm i' heaven. Hay, Isaac! Aw've bin i' heaven."

A great glow of comfort and gladness suddenly gushed into Isaac's heart, and, partly to hide his emotion and partly to continue his mother's pleasure, he perched himself on the edge of the bed and played one of the anniversary hymns. When that was finished he played another, and then a third, and by this time his mother was sitting up and watching him in the twilight with admiring and grateful eyes.

When he had finished he walked back to his place by the now dead fire. A great peace was in his heart. He had found a vocation, and even his expulsion from the band began to look a less dreadful thing to him.

Then he got his mother a little food, and went out and fetched a jug of skimmed milk, and with that in one hand and a piece of oatcake in the other he sat down at the bedside to talk.

"Hay, Isaac; thaa hez capt me ta-neet," began his mother. "Aw ne'er thowt as thaa could play loike that."

"Aw'll gi' yo' sum mooar when Aw've hed mi supper," said the easily-encouraged fiddler.

"Nay, lad, tha'rt tired ta-neet."

"Tired? Aw cud play aw neet!" And, putting down his empty milk-basin, he picked up his fiddle, though it was now quite dusk, and said —

"Naa, muther, what wed yo' loike?"

The bedridden woman seemed to hesitate. Then she looked at her son through the gloaming, and said —

"Yo' grand players dunno bother wi' childer's tunes, dun yo'?"

The subtle flattery of these words was like healing balm to Isaac's sore heart, and he said cheerfully —

"Childer's tunes? Ay, wot yo' loike, if Aw know it?"

"Can thaa play, 'Aw want to be a hangil'? When Aw uset t' yer that Aw could fair yer th' angils singin' and see 'em comin' tew me."

Of course Isaac knew that tune, and so he began to play, whilst his mother fell back on her pillow to listen. When he had got through the simple little melody he commenced again, and then again, and at last, after a particularly loud and flourishing wind up, he dropped upon the bed, crying, —

"Well, muther, will that dew?"

By this time it was so dark that he could not see his mother's face, except by going close to her. And as he bent over her he thought she looked almost beautiful, and an impulse came over him to kiss her. But he had never done such a thing in his life that he could remember, and blushed at his own thought.

Just then his mother moved.

"Huish!" she cried in subdued, reverent tones; "they're theer! They're theer, Isaac!"

And then she closed her eyes again, and sighed, and smiled, and Isaac crept off the bed and stood in the darkness alone.

Then he slipped off his boots, and was creeping up into his little attic, when a soft voice said, "Isaac!"

"Wot?"

"Wilta bring th' angils tew me ageean some day?"

"Ay, muther; ivery day if yo'n a moind an' if fiddlin' 'ull dew it."

And with that he climbed his little ladder, and crept into his bed a comforted and even thankful young man.

Next day was the school treat, and of course a holiday, but Isaac had no heart for the festivities, and shrank timidly from the chaff he knew would be dealt out to him. So he stayed at home. All morning he was "fettlin' up" the little cottage, although it was already spotless, and in the afternoon, whilst the scholars were enjoying themselves in the Fold Farm field, Isaac was playing to his mother. Though the cottage door was kept open because of the heat, he kept carefully out of sight, and watchfully avoided both seeing and being seen.

When he retired that night, he spent a long time before he went to sleep picturing to himself the ordeal he would have to pass through on the morrow at the Clog Shop, and it took all the comfort he had got from his mother's appreciation to nerve him to face the fiery trial.

But the anticipation proved as usual worse than the reality. Jabe treated him with a dignified indifference, never even alluding to Sunday, and the other frequenters of the Clog Shop seemed more inclined to pity than to scold him.

For the next two months Isaac spent most of his spare time at his mother's bedside, and the fiddle was in constant use, although Isaac had often to confess to himself that he had never played the anthem so well as he did on that first sad night.

But now other things began to trouble him. He thought he perceived a change in his mother, and at last he mustered courage to ask the doctor about it.

"She might linger for some time," was the doctor's verdict, "but at longest she will scarcely see the next winter through."

Poor Isaac! It was hard work playing with this fear on his mind. He had got so used to his mother being in bed, that it seemed as if she always had been there, and always would be. What should he do if she were taken? There would be nobody to live for and nobody to play for then. Life would be a blank.

One night, some three weeks after Isaac's consultation with Dr. Walmsley, he had been kept rather later than usual at the Clog Shop by pressure of business. When he got home he found his mother strangely changed. She seemed greatly oppressed with the heat and very restless. By this time Isaac's faith in the power of his fiddle was almost boundless, and so in a few minutes he was sitting in his old place by the bedside and fiddling away at the simple melodies his mother liked. For a time the music seemed to excite rather than soothe. She sat up two or three times and looked at him earnestly, and then fell back with a gasp on her pillow. This alarmed Isaac more than he cared to show, and he glided off into Sunday-school tunes, carefully reserving his one unfailing little hymn until the last.

"Arr they comin', muther?" he said, in a loud whisper, as he reached the end of "The realms of the blest," and a faint voice replied—

"Bless thi, lad! Bless thi!"

Isaac tried another tune, and then a third.

"Con yo' see 'em, muther?"

"Bless thi, lad!" came back through the twilight in a faint gasp.

As he played "There is a happy land," Isaac inwardly resolved that if he did not get a more satisfactory answer from his mother next time, he would plunge right away into the irresistible "I want to be an angel," and when he got through the tune and bent forward, he noticed that his mother was sitting up, and leaning towards him, and gazing at him with a strange intentness.

"Con yo' see 'em yet?" he asked, in hushed tones.

The suffering woman bent farther forward and took his face between her hands, and, looking with burning gaze into his eyes, she said earnestly—

"See 'em! Well, Aw con see *wun* on 'em at ony rate. Aw th' angils i' heaven arna as bonny to me as my oan fiddlin' clogger lad; an' they hevna done mooar fur me, nayther."

Isaac was startled. It was a most unusual action on the part of his mother, and her words were more strange than her deeds. But for all that those words sent a warm gush into his heart, and so, to relieve his feelings, he dashed off once more into "I want to be an angel."

Before he had got through, his mother had dropped back upon her pillow, and Isaac, taking this for a good sign, began again. Then he tried a third and even a fourth tune, and when at last he stopped, he discovered that his mother was asleep. Softly putting his fiddle away, and lighting a candle, he approached the bedside. His mother was apparently in deep slumber, but such a peaceful, happy sleep it seemed. She almost seemed to be smiling, and once more the temptation to kiss the pain-worn face came to the bashful lad, but only to be resisted, as before.

Then he stole off to bed, and when, next morning, he came to the bedside to greet his parent, he found that she had had her desire, and gone to see the angels. Isaac stood for a moment stunned; then, uttering a great, dreadful cry, he flew off to the Clog Shop.

Jabe, Aunt Judy, and Sam Speck were soon on hand to render all possible help, and deep, though almost wordless, sympathy. Three days later, his mother was laid in the chapel yard, and Isaac, refusing several rudely-tender offers of at least temporary lodgings, went back to live by himself in his mother's cottage.

For a whole month he never touched his fiddle, but spent his spare time gathering together the few little knick-knacks belonging to his mother, and arranging and rearranging them in an old box covered with wall-paper.

One sultry evening he felt more pensive than usual. Somehow the box failed to interest him for once, and he wandered about the house in a restless, uneasy manner.

Presently he turned towards the mantelpiece, and, after hesitating a moment, reached down his fiddle, and drew the bow gently across the strings. The instrument gave forth a most plaintive note. That touched him. He felt his hand shake, and so, with a heavy sigh, he put the fiddle back into its bag and hung it up again.

But he was now more restless than ever. He went to the open door and stood looking moodily up and down the road. Then he came back and stood in the middle of the floor. A feeling of intolerable loneliness came over him. He looked round the room again and again as if seeking someone, and then, drawing a long breath, he moaned out, "Aw am looansome"; and then, after a pause, "Aw wuish mi muther's angels 'ud come."

And as he stood there in his misery, a thought suddenly struck him.

"They'll happen come if Aw play," he cried, and snatched down his fiddle. "Hoo'll happen come hersel'. Hay, Aw wuish hoo wod, bless her!"

Then he commenced to play. The twilight was just gathering in, and but for the open door the small-windowed house would have been almost in darkness.

As Isaac played, his spirits rose. He began to think that perhaps the angels would come, and so he played on and felt relieved and cheered. Tune after tune was gone through, the music moving the lonely, fretful heart of the young clogger, until it grew strangely light and warm. As he played, he glanced round into the darker corners of the room as if expecting to see someone. Still he played, getting lighter-hearted and more hopeful almost every moment. Just as he was turning upon what he had reserved as usual for the last, a shadow fell across the doorway. He did not see it for a moment, and had got into the second line of his tune, when, turning towards the doorway, he stopped suddenly, and cried, in undisguised astonishment

"Lizer!

Yes, there she was. The same black-eyed, bewitching beauty upon whom he had once so fondly looked with hope. But her face was grave—a strange thing indeed for her. She also seemed a little shy and embarrassed.

"Ay, it's me, lad," she said, in answer to Isaac's startled question; and even he could not help noticing that there was a tone of kindness and sympathy in her voice.

Isaac pointed to a chair, but she blushed and shook her head, glancing the while at the door as if meditating flight.

Isaac noted this, and was just about to beg her not to go so soon, when she stopped him by asking—

"Artna looansome livin' here by thisel'?"

"Hay, Aw am that," said Isaac, and the look he cast at her would have melted a heart of stone.

There was an awkward pause, during which Eliza was drawing figures on the sanded floor with the iron of a dainty clog.

"Wot wur that thaa wur playin'?" she asked, although the wicked puss knew as well as he did.

"'Aw want to be a hangil,' my muther's tune, thaa knows."

"Did thi mother loike it?"

"Ay, hoo did that; hoo uset say it browt th' angils tew her. Aw thowt it 'ud happen bring 'em to me."

There was another long pause, and more clog-iron sketching on the floor. Presently, after looking at him steadily for a moment, she resumed her drawing, saying as she did so—

"Wot dust want angils fur?"

"'Cause Aw'm sa looansome. They uset comfort my muther, and they'd happen comfort me."

The pause that followed was longer than ever, and by the way Eliza kept glancing towards the door, Isaac expected every moment to see her dart away through it and vanish. But presently she bent her pretty head, and a great blush began to rise up her white neck—

"Aw wuish Aw wur a hangil," she stammered, and then snatching up her little white apron, she hid her hot face in it and seemed about to begin to cry.

But even then the stupid Isaac could not see, and so, looking up with dull astonishment, he asked—

"Wot does *thaa* want ta be a hangil fur?"

But Eliza was already trembling with the thought of her own boldness, and so there came out of the crumpled apron the single word—

"Nowt."

And then the slow lover seemed to guess something, only it was altogether too wonderful and astonishing to be true; but presently he ventured—

"Thaa could be mooar nor a hangil ta me if thaa nobbut wod."

"Wot?"

"A woife."

And "Lizer" didn't "fly up," as he had expected; she didn't even run away. She just stood there and cried, and seemed to be waiting to be taken possession of. And at last Isaac ventured; but how it was done, and how Eliza responded is really too private a matter to be detailed in print.

An hour later, Isaac stood at Jonas Tatlock's garden gate, talking brightly to his sweetheart, even then scarcely able to believe in his luck.

"Lizer," he said, "Aw allis thowt as thaa looked daan o' me an' loufed at me."

"Aw'st louf at thi ageean mony a toime afoor Aw've dun wi' thi," was the saucy reply.

"Bud, Lizer, did thaa cum ta see me ta-neet 'cause thaa yerd Aw wur looansome?"

"Neaw."

"Wot then?"

"Well, thaa knows, when thi muther deed, foak were aw saying haa thaa'd tan cur o' thi muther an' fiddled to her aw neet o'er?"

"Well, wot bi that?"

Lizer hesitated, looked down into Isaac's homely face for a moment, and then gazing right before her, said hesitatingly—

"Well, thaa knows, Aw thowt as a lad as teuk cur of an owd woman 'ud happen tak' cur of a young un tew."

ISAAC'S FIDDLE.

I.

ROCKS AHEAD.

HO! ho! ho! hoo'll ha' me! Hoo'll ha' me! Hoo *says* hoo'll ha' me!" laughed Isaac to himself, as he walked down the "broo" homewards, on the night of Lizer's acceptance of him.

His head rolled about, his hands were thrust deep into his greasy fustian trousers, and he seemed to walk on air; whilst every limb of his body appeared to be working on springs. His delight was almost uncontrollable.

When he had got past Long Ben's he stopped and looked up. The sky was full of soft light, and though it was not yet dark, the stars seemed so close and bright that they appeared to challenge him, and so, lifting his head, he cried joyfully—

"Capt? Ay, Aw'st think yo' arr capt. Aw'm capt mysel'! Bud it's trew! Hoo'll ha' me. *Me!* Aw tell yo'. Hoo said hoo wod hersel'," and he burst out into a great triumphant laugh.

A moment later he had reached his own little dwelling, the door of which he had left open on departing to see Lizer home.

On the threshold he stopped and pointed to a flag a yard or two nearer the fireplace.

"It wur theer," he cried, "just theer. Hoo wur stonnin' o' thatunce," and the foolish fellow produced a grotesque imitation of Eliza's naturally graceful attitude. "An' hoo said it hersel'. An' hay, hoo did say it noice; hoo did fur shure."

The house seemed strangely empty and unresponsive. Isaac felt he must give expression to his feelings, and there was nobody to talk to. Just then he spied the birdcage hanging in the inside of the chimney-jamb with its dropsical-looking occupant fast asleep. Even a bird was better than nothing to tell his happiness to.

"Naa, then," he cried, giving the cage a sharp rap. "Wakken up, wilta. Did t'yer what hoo said? Tha owt to sing, mon! Sing till tha brasts thisel'. Hoo says hoo'll ha' me. Bi th' mon, if hoo does Aw'll bey thi a new cage."

The bird, startled out of its sleep, hopped clumsily into the middle of its little house, opened the eye nearest to Isaac with a startled protesting look, and then drowsily closing it again, dozed off once more to sleep.

Isaac turned away and went and stood in the doorway. By this time it was as dark as it ever would be that night, and the village sounded strangely still. Leaning against the doorpost, Isaac glanced up and down the road two or three times as if seeking someone to whom to tell his great secret; but not a soul seemed to be stirring.

Then he stepped out gently, closed the door after him, and, crossing the road, turned hurriedly into "Sally's Entry," and hastened through the mill yard and along the mill lane, and in a moment or two was standing under the lilac tree at the bottom of Jonas's garden.

For several minutes he stood looking in a sort of triumphant ecstasy at the windows, first downstairs and then up. He had never even heard of serenading, and couldn't have sung if he had, so he propped his chin on the flag fence under the lilac bush, and, looking from one window to another, he murmured thickly—

"Tak' cur on her, Lord! Tak' cur on her! Tha's tan wun guardian hangil off me, bud Tha's gan mi anuther."

Then he paused, and looking over his shoulder as if to answer some invisible objector, he went on.

173

"Simple? Aw know Aw'm a bit simple, bud *hoo* isna? Hoo's as sharp as a weasel, an' as bonny as a rooase, and hoo says hoo'll ha' me, an' Aw cur fur nowt nor noabry if hoo does." And suppressing with difficulty another great laugh, he moved away towards home, stopping every now and then as he went along, and glancing proudly back at Jonas's windows.

His heart gave a little leap as he passed the Clog Shop, for he suddenly noticed by the starlight that Jabe was standing smoking at the shop door, and great as was his joy and confidence, the sight of that terrible form quite chilled him.

He had not altogether recovered when he reached home, and on entering the cottage he carefully closed the door as if apprehensive that his master might be following him.

Standing on the hearthstone, and looking round in the dim light, he noticed a little can of milk, and, picking it hastily up, he "swigged" away at it until the last drop was gone.

As he put the can down again slowly and meditatively in the faint light he touched something that gave forth an indistinct strumming sound. It was his old fiddle.

The preoccupied look which had been on his face ever since he had seen his master vanished like magic, a gleam of eager joy came into his eyes, and, groping about on the table, first for the instrument and then for its bow, he cried delightedly

"Hay! is that thee, owd lad? Come here wi' thi," and snatching it up and holding it out eagerly, whilst his face beamed with admiration and gratitude, he cried—

"Sithi! If Aw didna want to play on thi Aw'd ha' thi framed. Bless thi owd hert, dust know wot tha's dun? Tha's getten me a sweetheart, mon! Th' bonniest wench i' th' Clough. Ay, or i' th' country oather. Hay, bud thwart a grand un. Aw nobbut gan three shillin' fur thi, bud Aw wodna tak' ten paand this varry minute."

And then he grasped it again between his fists, and shook it as a sign of excessive affection, and holding his coat sleeve in its place by doubling his hand over it, he gently polished the already shining back, and looked as though he would kiss it.

"Sithi," he cried at last, holding it out at arm's-length and gazing at it with ardent admiration, "Aw wodna part wi' thi fur aw th' instruments th' Clog Shop iver hed in it, an' wotiver comes an' wotiver goos, thee and me niver parts—niver, neaw niver!"

Poor Isaac! If he had known—but fortunately he did not. And so, after polishing it and caressing it and doing all sorts of ridiculous things with it to show his affection, he finally put it tenderly away in the chimney-corner, and went to bed.

Next morning, in spite of a restless, almost sleepless night, Isaac was in, if possible, higher spirits than ever. Rising earlier than usual, he waylaid Old Jethro on his knocking-up rounds, and dragged him into the cottage to have a cup of hot coffee, and when the old man was departing he called him back, and with an air of mingled mystery and delight, said eagerly—

"Jethro, afoor th' wik's aat yo'll yer summat. An' it's trew, moind yo', every wod on it," and then darting indoors, he banged the door upon his old friend and set up another great laugh.

Then he tried to engage the "throstle" in a whistling competition, but his own notes were so loud and shrill from sheer excess of happiness that the poor bird realised at once that he had no chance, and retiring from the contest, stood looking at Isaac in amazement and apparent perplexity.

Ten minutes to six found our young clogger dodging up and down Mill Lane, in the hope of seeing, and maybe even speaking to his sweetheart, but when she at last appeared he had to resist a sudden temptation to run away. And as Lizer caught sight of him, and actually left the two girls she was walking with and crossed the lane to speak to him, even the exhortation she gave him to "goa whoam, and donna mak' a foo' o' thisel'," failed to damp his joy, and he went down the "broo" again, struggling with a great desire to shout.

At seven o'clock he went to the Clog Shop, and after opening the shutters and lighting Jabe's parlour fire and putting on the kettle, he sat down before the back window to work.

But he was very restless. Taking a partly-finished clog between his knees, he sat looking musingly at it and smiling every now and again at his evidently delightful thoughts.

Presently he got up, threw open his window, and seeing a cluster of roses hanging over the window frame, he plucked one, and filling the bottom part of an old oil-can with water, stuck the flower in it and set it on the bench before him. Then he began to work again in a sudden hurry, and as he worked he whistled. Then the whistle grew into a hum, and in a few moments, in entire forgetfulness of everything but his own great happiness, he burst out singing— if singing it could be called.

The sun was pouring its warm rays through the window and bathing him in golden light, the waving corn on the hillside beyond his master's garden seemed to smile with him, the birds were singing blithely in the trees that fringed the garden in evident sympathy, and all nature seemed to him to felicitate him on his great gladness. The singer, though his tones were harsh and unmusical, had thrown back his head, and was almost shouting in the excess of his joy, when suddenly a whole shower of clog-tops came flying at his head.

He stopped, and, with his mouth still open, turned in the direction from whence the missiles came, and lo! quite near to him was his dread master, standing glaring at him in the parlour doorway.

Jabe was very scantily apparelled. His stockings had been pulled hastily upon his legs, the feet part of them still flapping about. His blue-striped shirt was stuffed hurriedly into his trousers, which were held in their place by a single brace, the remaining one hanging down behind and dangling about his legs. He still wore his red-tasselled nightcap, and the face below that headdress was something terrible to behold in its indignant sternness.

"Wot's to dew wi' thi, thaa yowling swelled yed?" he demanded in gruffest anger.

Isaac felt a momentary shock at the sound of his master's voice, but his joy was so great that even this fearful apparition could not daunt him, and so, dropping the clog he was working upon, he rose hastily to his feet and cried—

"Aw conna help it, mestur. Aw'st brast if Aw dunna sing. Hoo'll ha' me! Hoo says hoo'll ha' me!"

Jabe stood in the doorway glaring at his apprentice with fixed, stony gaze, but not a word did he utter.

"Lizer, mestur! Lizer Tatlock. Hoo says hoo'll ha' me."

Jabe's face became grimmer and stonier than ever, every muscle seeming to be perfectly rigid.

"Hay, mestur, Lizer'ud mak' a—a—a—wheelbarrow sing. Hoo'd mak' _yo'_ sing if hoo said hood hev yo'."

The grotesque figure in the doorway neither moved nor spoke, but still stood gazing in annihilating scorn on the poor apprentice.

Presently the short leg gave a sort of premonitory jerk, the eyelids twitched rapidly, and at last, in tones of withering rebuke, the Clogger said—

"Isaac, women's bin makkin' gradely men inta foo's iver sin' th' wold began, bud naa they've started a makkin' foo's inta bigger foo's. Tha's bin totterin' upo' th' edge o' Bedlam iver sin' Aw know'd thi, an' th' fost bit of a wench as leuks at thi picks thi straight in."

And drawing himself up to his full height, and putting on, if possible, a grimmer look, Jabe transfixed poor Isaac with a stony eye, and then solemnly stepped back into the parlour and banged the door.

When Jabe came downstairs into the parlour, after completing his morning toilet, the look of stern anger had entirely disappeared from his rugged countenance, and a pleasant, even amused, expression had taken its place.

The fact was that the indignation that made him look so terrible to poor Isaac had been almost entirely assumed, in conformity with the general principles of his workshop discipline.

As he mashed his tea and cut his bread and butter a look of mischievous enjoyment gleamed out of the corners of his eyes, and now and then a soft relishful chuckle escaped him. As he consumed his breakfast his merriment increased, and he more than once burst into a laugh, whilst he slapped his thigh in keenest enjoyment, his short leg becoming increasingly demonstrative as he mused.

"Well dun, Isaac," he chuckled, "tha's byetten [beaten] th' fawsest woman i' Beckside aw ta Hinters. Bi th' ferrups! bud hoo'll mak' a shindy abaat this."

And then he rose from his chair, put on his leathern apron, lighted his pipe, and assuming once more a grim, surly air, walked into the shop.

All that day poor Isaac was subjected to a constant fire of raillery.

At one time the ridiculous and impudent presumption of "'prentice lads" and "little two-loom wayvers reaconing to cooart" was scoffed at.

"Sich childer! wee'st ha' hawf-timers puttin' in th' axins next."

Then the folly of marriage under any circumstances was set forth, and dwelt upon with becoming length and exhaustiveness. Isaac's mentor then passed by a natural and easy transition to a diatribe on the ways and wiles of women.

Soon the tormentor became ironical, and pretended to offer his misguided apprentice sincere commiseration on his reckless act and its terrible consequences, and finally he dropped into a humorous vein, and affected curiosity as to the art and mystery of courtship.

All this Isaac bore with buoyant equanimity, having, in fact, anticipated something very much worse. Late in the afternoon the unusually garrulous Clogger started a new line of thought. He had been sitting in the inglenook chatting with Sam Speck, after baggin', and when his visitor had departed he still sat musing in the fireless corner. All at once, however, he whisked round, and eyeing his apprentice with a look of stern reprobation, said—

"Tha'rt a bonny mon ta steil anuther felley's wench, artna; an' thee a member tew."

The self-complacent, almost consequential, simper which Isaac's plain face had worn most of the day suddenly vanished, and in its place came an expression of blank surprise and sorrow. For, in all the hours of his happiness since Lizer's acceptance of him, strange though it may appear, he had never once thought seriously of Joe Gullett, and now that he was suddenly reminded of him, the sun of his gladness suffered an almost instantaneous eclipse.

A customer came in just at that moment who had left a pair of clogs to be reclogged, which Jabe had decided were not worth it, and as this meant a battle royal, exactly to the pugnacious Clogger's heart, poor Isaac was left for a while to his own painful reflections.

"Hay, dear!" he sighed forlornly, looking out through his little window, "happiness doesn't last lung! Wheniver Aw wur a bit marlocky my muther uset say as Aw shud sewn hev' a clewt at th' t'other soide o' mi yed; an' it is sa." And then after a moment or two of most melancholy musing, he groaned—

"Poor Joe!"

Presently he began to see himself as an interloper and thief. He had stolen an old friend's sweetheart. Basely stolen her! And not fairly either. Hadn't he employed the subtle and irresistible witchery of fiddling to accomplish his selfish purpose? And he began to feel much as a person would do who had obtained some coveted possession by basely resorting to sorcery.

But just then the memory of certain quite irresistible glances and certain most seductive tones which he had seen and heard the night before under the lilac tree came back to him, and sent such a sweet thrill through him that in a moment or two Isaac found himself contemplating a certain young clogger so bound in the enslavements of love that he had become utterly reckless of all moral or spiritual considerations whatsoever, and this, as it intensified his sense of guiltiness, compelled him to regard himself as a mass of meanness, selfishness, and treachery.

Just as he felt himself sinking deeper and deeper into this slough of iniquity, he suddenly heard a loud whisper—

"Isaac!"

Isaac started guiltily, made a fussy pretence to be working, and then glanced furtively round to see who was calling him.

It was Sam Speck. Jabe was still engaged in a loud unsparing denunciation of the "scrattin' ways" of the owner of the condemned clogs, and so Sam had come in and taken his seat in the fireless inglenook without being noticed. He was perched on the outermost edge of a superannuated clog bench, which now did duty as a fireside seat, and was leaning forward as far as he could so as to be able to whisper to Isaac without being heard. And as Isaac glanced round in response to the call, he put his hand to his mouth and called out quickly—

"Tha'll cop it, lad! Bet Gullett's fair raving yond'! Hoo says hoo'll leather thi," and then as the door banged to, and Jabe's customer, vanquished and humbled, left the shop, Sam turned round to conceal what he had been doing, and entered into conversation with his chief, whilst Isaac was left to his own tormenting reflections.

Betty Gullett was the village termagant, and a terror to all peaceable people. The one soft place in her heart was that filled by her son Joe, and Isaac suddenly realised that he had made a most formidable enemy, who would stick at nothing to accomplish her revenge.

Isaac was not, of course, afraid of any mere physical castigation that might be in store for him, but in his excited fancy he saw himself attacked on the road, or outside the chapel, or even in his own house, by a fearful woman whose very husband had run away to America years ago to be out of reach of her tongue and temper.

By this time he was in a cold sweat. The hand that limply held the clog-top he was stitching positively shook, and his emotions were so distracting that he could neither work nor think. He felt sick, and for the first time in his life he could not cry to relieve his distress.

He had sat in his place fighting, now with a reproaching conscience and then with his own quaking fears, for some time, when presently he became dimly conscious that he was being made the subject of a muttered conversation in the inglenook. And now Sam Speck and his gruff employer suddenly appeared to his distorted fancy as kind friends, instead of the cynical critics he had ever regarded them. He would sooner face them a hundred times than endure one five minutes of Betty Gullett.

Another moment, and in his anguish he would have got up and unbosomed himself to them, and thrown himself on their pity and protection; but just then others of the Clog Shop cronies came in, and Isaac, with a despairing gasp, shrank back into himself again.

The hour that followed was probably the longest of Isaac's life. Would "knocking off" time never come? One five minutes he was working desperately; the next he was gazing out of his window with a woeful, desolate look.

Oh, what a wretch he had been to steal another lad's wench! What would people think of him? He would never be able to hold his head up in Beckside again. But he was being most deservedly punished. Judgment had overtaken him with most exemplary swiftness; and as the squat form and red face of Mrs. Gullett rose before his mind, she appeared to him as an awful avenging sprite. Then he fell to pitying himself as an unlucky wight, and a poor friendless orphan, and here relief would have come, for he felt he could cry but for the close proximity of so many unfeeling men. Oh that he could be alone, just to relieve his heart, as he longed to do!

And "at lung last" the old long-cased clock just inside the parlour door began to growl as an introduction to barking — that is striking; and by the time the latter operation was concluded, Isaac was out of the shop and hurrying down the "broo" to the little cottage where he knew he would be alone.

And now an extraordinary thing happened. As Isaac turned homewards, with his head down and his heart thumping at his side, he began to pray, and as he prayed he reached the cottage door and commenced fumbling in his pocket for the lever of the latch, which was the only form of key he used. And if any curious reader interested in spiritualistic manifestations will make a journey to Beckside, the present occupant of the Clog Shop will tell him that just as he was putting the sneck into the door on that memorable evening, he distinctly heard a voice say to him, "Goa ta Lizer," and he will ask you, in a voice that rebukes all scepticism, "Wurn't that a hanser ta pruyer?"

Answer or no, voice or no, it came to poor buffeted Isaac as a revelation.

Of course! Why had he never thought of it before? Lizer was equal to anything—equal to anything—even to Betty Gullett.

It took only a very few minutes for him to get some hasty apology for a supper.

A great load had been taken off his mind. Leaving Lizer to deal with his terrible she-enemy, and relying on old acquaintanceship and a close knowledge of Joe's disposition, he would do his best to conciliate his rival. He would apologise. If absolutely necessary, and Lizer didn't object, he would tell Joe the whole truth as to how he came to get Lizer at all, and surely that would pacify him.

But his first duty was to see Lizer, and after Lizer, Joe.

With these thoughts in his mind, he started for his sweetheart's house. Perfectly satisfied and at ease as to Lizer's ability to deal with the greater enemy, he began to arrange in his mind his own interview with the injured Joe. He grew surer and surer that he could mollify Joe. He would seek him out immediately after seeing Lizer, and get it done with and off his mind.

He hoped he would be able to find Joe. It would be disappointing if he couldn't, or if Joe wouldn't talk to him when he did find him, but he would hope for the best.

Hello! Isaac had by this time nearly reached Tatlock's house, and was stepping forward at much more than his usual pace, when lo! right under the lilac tree, the scene of last night's great happiness, stood Joe himself.

Isaac pulled up suddenly; his heart gave a great leap; he began to shake from head to foot. Joe had seen him, and was actually coming towards him, so that the interview so eagerly desired a moment ago would be got over at once. Isaac hesitated a moment, tried to move, but felt as if he could not; put his hand to his head, grabbed frantically at his cap, and the next moment, cap in hand, he was fleeing along Mill Lane as fast as his shaking legs could carry him.

II.

REMORSE.

DOWN the lane, through the mill yard and along Sally's Entry, rushed poor Isaac, evidently making for home. As he neared that haven, however, he began to have misgivings as to its security as a place of refuge, and so, when he reached it, he rushed past and down the "broo" and over the bridge, turning to the right on the other side, and scudding along the path up the Beck side, glancing apprehensively around every few yards to see if he were being followed.

When he had got some half a mile up the Clough he slackened pace, for no pursuer was in sight. Then he sat down on the Beck side to get his breath, moaning and groaning in self-disgust and fear. Then he grew quieter, and, as it was now nearly dark, he began to pick his way across the stones in the Beck, and to steal slowly but fearfully homeward.

He hesitated for some time before approaching the cottage, but now the desire to see Lizer, and the fear of what she would say, first of his absence and then of his cowardly flight before his rival, were urging him forward as strongly as his fear of meeting Joe was holding him back.

Very cautiously he approached the backyard wall in Shaving Lane. Then he climbed clumsily over it into the disused hencote, where he would fain have rested; but by this time his concern about Lizer had grown so strong that he could not keep still, and in a few moments he had re-climbed the back wall, scudded along the lane again, and striking the footpath that led up into the Duxbury Road, he was soon stealing carefully past the chapel and the Clog Shop on his way to Tatlock's house.

"Isaac!"

The young clogger nearly jumped out of his skin. The voice came from somewhere behind him, and as he remembered the voice he suddenly realised that he must have passed Lizer somewhere and never seen her. The girl was standing with a shawl over her head, under the hedge of a garden, and he must have almost touched her as he passed.

She was evidently shaking with quiet laughter, and began to question him quite innocently as to where he had been, and why he had passed her "sa independent."

Now Isaac had vowed half a dozen times within the half-hour that no power under the sun should ever induce him to tell Lizer why he had so ignominiously fled, and so in a clumsy fashion he tried to fence. And Lizer only laughed a soft delightful sort of laugh, and pretended to be quite satisfied with his lame and contradictory explanation.

But, somehow,—Isaac never could understand how it came about,— ten minutes later, as they stood once more under the lilac, he was telling his sweetheart, without ever being asked to do so, all that he had suffered during the day, not omitting his terror of Mrs. Gullett, and his sudden flight from the presence of Joe.

Sad to relate, Lizer laughed, and not a mere good-behaviour laugh either. Under a surface of demure sobriety, even Isaac could see that she was secretly revelling in amusement and delight. She enjoyed his description of his many misgivings and heartrendings; she enjoyed even more his terror of Mrs. Gullett; but when it came to his pathetic and sympathy-seeking account of his flight from Joe, the hard-hearted little "hussy" could no longer control herself, and broke out into a long rippling laugh—a laugh which made her little body shake all over, and even brought tears of delight into her eyes.

Isaac felt chagrined, and had to struggle more than once to overcome that unfortunate tendency of his to tears. And then Lizer seemed to understand, and lightly changed her manner, so that by the time they parted that night she had somehow contrived to inspire her lover with some of her own contempt for the terrible Betty, and had also impressed upon him the necessity of doing all he could to comfort the forlorn Joe.

Now this last idea was so much in harmony with his own feelings that Isaac readily promised and resolutely determined to carry it out. But though he told himself twenty times a day how eager he was to meet young Gullett, it was odd that no opportunity seemed to present itself, and when it came to actually setting out to look for Joe, it was astonishing how many things came to prevent him, and how easily he allowed himself to be overcome by them. Saturday night came, and he had not even seen his rival. Moreover, do as he would, he could not get over his terror of the terrible Betty, and every time the Clog Shop door opened he gave a nervous start, and held his breath in torturing suspense until he heard the actual voice of the new-comer and was reassured. Not once in those days did he dare turn round to see who the visitor might be.

Saturday and Sunday nights were regarded as the great courting nights in Beckside, and Isaac spent the whole of the former evening in most delightful intercourse with his lady-love, and was in a seventh heaven of delight.

Next morning, however, there came a change. Isaac had for some few weeks now been taking the violin part in the singing-pew, but that morning as he went into school Lizer's youngest brother, Jacky, stopped him, and told him that his father wished him to keep away from the singing-pew that day. That sounded ominous, and Isaac became at once very uneasy.

When chapel commenced he saw with alarm that Joe's place amongst the singers was vacant, as was also that of Sophia Gullett, Joe's sister.

A minute later, Isaac felt a "crill" run down his spine as Mrs. Gullett, accompanied by her only son, stalked into the pew immediately in front of his. Twice, at least, during the singing of the first hymn Mrs.

Gullett turned half round, and stared coolly and contemptuously at poor Isaac, each time sending him into a cold sweat.

Then in the prayer Isaac heard Joe sigh, and this made him feel worse than ever. Once he caught Sophia looking at him as if he were some awful monster, and the sorrowful reproachfulness of her glance as she turned away nearly brought the ever-ready tears into his eyes.

Oh dear! what a miserable fellow he was! But it was only another illustration of his master's oft-repeated proverb that "the way of transgressors is hard." As the service proceeded, Joe kept sighing, and every sigh seemed to go through the unhappy Isaac, his only consolation in these painful moments being to take long reassuring looks at his sweetheart.

The service seemed a terrible length, and towards the end of it another tormenting thought took possession of him. Mrs. Gullett would be sure to attack him when the service was over, perhaps in the very chapel itself. There was nothing for it but to go out before the service closed. But no; that would be to openly manifest his cowardice, and Lizer wouldn't like that.

What must he do? They were singing the last hymn. Another moment and it would be too late. The music stopped, and the people began to kneel.

Now for it! Isaac slid his hand softly down over the side of the pew door. He partly opened the door. Mrs. Gullett was moving. He grabbed at his Sunday "crow" (hat), rose softly to his feet, and made a rush.

Alas! alas! the matting outside the door had puckered, and as poor Isaac started down the narrow aisle, his Sunday boot caught in a fold, and he went sprawling full length on the floor.

How he got up, and out, and home that day he never knew. And in the afternoon the chaff to which he was subjected nearly drove him, as he said, "maddlet." To make matters worse, Lizer seemed actually to have enjoyed his ignominious downfall, and did nothing but titter and laugh as he poured out to her the tale of his woes. Nay, to crown all, as he was leaving her that night she gave him a sharp little lecture, and bade him "be a gradely mon, an' nor a dateliss gawmlin."

Another miserable night for poor Isaac, and next day the attack was renewed.

As soon as he got to his work in the morning old Jabe began to "bullyrag" him as a disturber of divine worship, and an enemy of the church's peace; and later in the day, Sam Speck, in a loud voice, informed the Clogger that Joe Gullett was "takkin' lessons i' boxin' off little Eli."

By evening, Isaac, made desperate from sheer misery, was driven to the resolution to end the matter one way or the other. All the night, therefore, after ceasing work, he was hunting for Joe. He dared not go to the house, but he visited every other place where it was at all likely that his rival might be found, but all to no purpose. Then he went and hid himself in a dark corner, opposite Joe's residence, to watch for him coming home. But though he watched long and anxiously until one by one every light in the Gullett house had been extinguished, no Joe turned up, and the suffering lad had perforce to go home and brood over his sorrows.

During that long night, as he lay tossing about in bed, alternately lamenting his fate and praying for help and deliverance, a great thought came to him. It made him sick as he faced it, but slowly it took an inexorable grip of him, and after fighting with it for an hour or more, he realised that the path of duty had been laid before him and that there was no escape.

As soon as it grew light enough he got up and fetched his fiddle upstairs, and then lay back in bed looking lovingly at it and groaning, and every now and again drawing the bow gently across the strings in an absent, pensive sort of way.

Then he got out of bed again and went downstairs, returning almost immediately with some rubbing cloths and a bottle of little Eli's wonderful furniture polish.

Then sitting on the bedside in his shirt,—he had never possessed a night-shirt,—he began to take the fiddle to pieces and clean and polish it, part by part. Carefully and lovingly putting it together again, and replacing an imperfect string, he then began to play, slowly and pensively at first, but as his interest in the music deepened he grew earnest and then excited, until, as he finished an encore on his mother's favourite tune, he suddenly discovered that it was almost time to be at work. So, hastily dressing, he took the instrument downstairs again, hung it carefully in its place, and then standing away from it and looking sorrow-looking fully at it, he cried hoarsely—

"Aw conna help it, lad! Aw'm shawmed to leuk at thi, bud Aw conna, conna help it."

And then he turned hastily away, and wiping his eyes with the back of his hand, hurried out to his work.

III.

THE SACRIFICE.

TWICE that day Isaac saw Joe Gullett, and Joe saw him, but now, strange to say, the youth who was supposed to be almost thirsting for poor Isaac's blood hurried away before Isaac could get near him.

But Isaac was not to be baulked. Having once realised that the step he contemplated was inevitable, he watched eagerly for his opportunity.

He happened to be getting in the Clog Shop coals that afternoon, and so as the mill was "loosing" he spied Sophia Gullett going home from her work.

Isaac dared not wait to think, and without a moment's hesitation he darted across the road.

The girl pulled up as he drew near, and hastily drew her shawl more tightly round her arms,

"S'phia," began Isaac, with an attempt at a coaxing smile, "wilt dew summat for me?"

Sophia, who had had in her secret heart a sort of fancy for Isaac for herself, and therefore felt the more aggrieved at the choice he had made, drew a step back, and then asked, with a tentative inflexion in her voice—

"Wot is it?"

Isaac felt the unspoken rebuff, but dared not draw back now, and so, with quivering lips, he stammered—

"Aw want ta speik ta your Joe ta-neet. Wilt ax him ta cum daan ta aar haase? Do, wench, wilta?"

Sophia was tender-hearted, and felt herself giving way, but remembering the necessity of being loyal to her brother, she tossed her head again, dodged past Isaac, and started homewards, simply saying as she did so, with a look that gave, Isaac no clue whatever as to her intention—

"Happen Aw will, an' happen Aw winna."

The young clogger went back to his coal-carrying very despondently. There was no knowing what Sophia would do, and it seemed very probable that he would not get rest to his troubled mind that night, in spite of all his resolutions and efforts.

However, when work was over he made for home. There he busied himself "fettlin' up" the house. Then he fetched in a couple of bottles of little Eli's famous "Yarb beer," and then taking down his fiddle, he laid it tenderly on the table and sat down to wait.

He had set the door open that he might see anyone who passed, and moving his chair so as to command as much of the road as possible without being too conspicuous, he began his watch.

But the time passed and no Joe appeared. Isaac began to fidget. Several times he was on the point of picking up his violin, but restrained himself. Then he began to walk about the house. Then, as impatience and excitement grew upon him, he tried to whistle and even to sing, but there was no heart in his effort, and his music soon ceased.

Presently he sauntered to the door, and, putting on a laboured look of indifference, stood propping the doorway with his elbows. Still no Joe, and it began to grow dark. He had not explained his last night's absence to Lizer, and this was evidently going to be a second wasted evening.

To a girl of Lizer's spirit this was a serious thing. Oh, what an unlucky wretch he—

Ah! Sure enough, right up the "broo" was coming the long-expected Joe, but he was sauntering along as if he were going nowhere. Isaac's heart went thump! thump! His legs began to tremble. An almost irresistible desire to flee, or to go inside and bolt the door, came over him, but struggling earnestly against it, he held his post.

Joe drew nearer, and Isaac had a good view of him. He appeared to be just taking an easy evening stroll. His mouth was puckered as if he were softly whistling, and he was turning his head and glancing at the housetops, first on one side of the street, and then on the other, as though he were looking for a stray pigeon, or were interested in smoky chimneys.

And the nearer he came to Isaac the more engrossed he seemed to be in his elevated studies. He was now only a few yards away, but was apparently entirely oblivious of Isaac's presence.

The supreme moment had come. It was now or never, Isaac felt. And so, assuming an air of most careless unconcern, strangely unlike his actual feelings, he finally managed to squeeze out—

"Heaw dew, Joe?"

Joe did not stop, though he slackened speed somewhat. He brought his eyes slowly back from their distant occupation; an awkward smile flickered at one corner of his mouth. He shot a shy glance at his rival, and then quickly transferring his gaze to the housetops once more, he answered—

"Heaw dew?"

Then there was a pause, and Joe, to Isaac's horror, seemed to be moving on again; and so, with another great effort, he forced out the profound remark—

"Ther's a deeal o' midges abaat ta-neet."

But even this bold advance did not entirely arrest the progress of the tantalising Joe. He paused uncertainly, swung uneasily round on one leg, and at length answered very slowly—

"Ay."

And then he stopped, and the two stood with half the road between them, but for a minute or more neither of them spoke.

Presently Isaac tried again. With a sigh, and a painful effort, he ventured—

"Eli's tarrier's kilt a rotten [rat] ta-day."

"Aw've yerd sa."

And still the two were no nearer, and watching them standing awkwardly talking at each other from that distance, it would have been difficult to decide which was more uneasy.

After a while, Isaac stepped timidly down from the doorstep, and taking one stride nearer to his rival, made another remark about as interesting as those above recorded. Then, as he made a monosyllabic reply, Joe took a little step towards Isaac, and stood hesitating in the road. And so they went on, moving almost inch by inch nearer to each other, making casual and inane remarks about anything that occurred to them, until they were actually close together.

And then a spirit of dumbness seemed to have seized upon both of them, and whilst Joe looked up the road very dreely and hummed a tune, Isaac looked down the hill and seemed to be making a special study of the schoolhouse beyond the bridge.

Then Joe made his first voluntary remark, and though it was as little connected with the subject in both their minds as any of his own remarks had been, Isaac plucked up wonderfully, and at last, making a desperate plunge, he cried with quite unnecessary excitement—

"Joe, halt seen my throstle?"

Joe never had, and so a minute later he was standing in the house, waiting whilst Isaac found a candle with which more effectually to exhibit his feathered friend. The candle having been lighted, and the poor bird wakened up to be inspected, Joe passed encomiums upon it, which were a clumsy compromise between polite approval of the throstle and protest against too great familiarity with its unpardoned proprietor.

When at length ornithology had been exhausted as a topic of conversation, Isaac turned round and thrust a chair forward, so that

Joe, if he wished, could sit down. But he, somehow, could not ask him to do so.

Then he placed the candle on the table, carefully setting it so that it would show off the fiddle that was lying there. Then he espied the two bottles of "yarb beer," and with a sudden but very hollow show of cheerfulness, he gaily opened them, and handed a foaming pint pot to Joe.

But a sudden fit of taciturnity, and even melancholy, seemed to have seized Joe. For though he dropped into the chair near him, he heaved a most lugubrious sigh, and tragically waved the beer away, as though it were trifling with his lacerated feelings to offer it.

Isaac had a sudden return of his sense of guiltiness, and stood looking at his visitor with mournful eyes.

"Joe," he said presently in a low, husky voice.

"Wot?" came heavily and reluctantly from the afflicted youth.

"Aw allis loiked thee, Joe."

But Joe heaved another deep sigh, and sadly shook his head.

After another long silence, during which Isaac stood at the far side of the table, now shutting his eyes tightly as if in prayer, and now looking earnestly from the fiddle to Joe, and then from Joe to the fiddle again, he screwed his body about as if thereby to force the words out, and said in a voice the tremor of which was more eloquent than any words—

"Aw've wuished mony a toime as thee an' me wur bruthers, Joe."

Joe suddenly bent forward, and dropping his elbows on his knees, buried his head in his hands and uttered an awful groan.

Isaac stood looking wistfully at him for a moment or two, and then in a most pathetically coaxing tone he said—

"Less be friends, Joe."

Joe shook his head in a wearily decided manner, and heaved another sigh.

Isaac waited a little while, and then went on, still more anxiously—

"Joe, if tha'll be friends, dust know wot Aw'll dew?"

Isaac evidently expected that curiosity, at any rate, would make Joe speak, but he was disappointed, for he only shook his head more sadly and decidedly than ever.

"Aw'll gi' thi th' preciousest thing Aw hev' i' th' wold, Joe."

Joe raised himself slowly up, and leaned back in his chair, and partly because he felt he must say something, and partly because curiosity was, after all, beginning to assert itself within him, he said, with exaggerated indifference and melancholy—

"Dunna meyther me."

But Isaac was by this time desperate. He had worked himself up to this point of excitement, and felt that he must end it now or never, and so, seizing his cherished instrument and thrusting it feverishly into Joe's hands, he cried—

"Aw'll gi' thi me fid—fiddle, Joe," and the poor fellow burst into a passion of tears—for it was like parting with life itself.

Joe sat leaning back in his chair, and looking at the joists above his head for quite a long time. Then he suddenly rose to his feet, and awkwardly thrusting out his hand, he stammered in choking tones—

"Shak' hons, Isaac!"

Anyone could see by the way it was done that these two village lads had had little practice in this form of salutation, but as they stood together on that old sanded floor, in the dim candle-light, gripping each other's hands and looking into each other's eyes, they entered silently into a bond which neither time nor trial has been able to break.

"Aw winna tak' thi fiddle, lad," faltered Joe with his hand still in Isaac's, "bud Aw'll tak' thee. Ay, an' Aw'm suman' praad to tak' thi tew. After wot tha's dun ta-neet, Aw dunna Wunder as Lizer loikes thi. Aw'm glad tha's getten her—a—partly wot."

And in this strange interview this was the only mention made of the subject of their differences. And when, as Isaac saw his friend home, they came unexpectedly upon Lizer, and in the fulness of their hearts told her all that had taken place, the bewitching little besom called Joe a "lumpyed" in such a delightful sort of way, and gave him such a tap on the cheek where any but a Lancashire lass might have given him a kiss, that Joe, when he left the courters, went home as nearly reconciled to his fate as could well be expected.

THE HARMONIUM.

I.

AN APPLE OF DISCORD.

JABE and Long Ben had been spending a week at the seaside for the first time in their lives. Excursions of this nature were in those days very rare amongst Beckside folk, and this was brought about by Lige, the road-mender. That worthy and his wife, now retired and living comfortably in a little cottage near the "Beck," had evidently determined to enjoy themselves for the rest of their lives, and so gave way to habits which occasioned their friends much concern.

Amongst other questionable tendencies, they grew fond of making little excursions abroad on visits to friends and the like.

This was all very delightful to Lige himself, although he took his pleasure somewhat fearfully. He was troubled on every new adventure of the kind with painful misgivings as to the righteousness of such conduct, and vainly attempted to square matters with his plain-spoken conscience by extraordinary contributions to the chapel collections.

When, therefore, Jane Ann had proposed to him to go to "th' sayside," he had had a somewhat painful struggle; and, in fact, even when he had got to the watering-place, and was enjoying himself to the full, he had moments of such painful self-reproach, that he hit upon the ingenious expedient of trying to persuade the grave heads of the church at Beckside to join them in their dubious pleasure; and thus, by obtaining official sanction for his frivolities, to relieve himself of at least some of the responsibility for them.

And so Jane Ann, of whose penmanship Lige was most inordinately proud, had written a long letter, enlarging, not upon the worldly attractions of the place, but upon the marvellous eloquence of the preacher at the Methodist Chapel, and the beauty of certain new tunes which were being sung there, and closing with a most urgent request that Lige's friends would join them for a few days.

But Lige, uneasy and impatient though he was, had to wait several days for a reply, for so grave and altogether unusual a matter was not to be settled all at once.

Seaside visitation was, according to Beckside standards, a somewhat questionable practice. It savoured of pampering self-indulgence. It was extravagant and worldly, and was generally regarded as a sign of ostentation and frivolity. It was some time, therefore, before the two friends could find an excuse for the journey which satisfied themselves and those about them. What made it worse, Sam Speck had not been invited, and he was very stern and uncompromising in his maintenance of the orthodox Beckside view of the case, and came down upon any weak argument advanced by Jabe or Ben in favour of the excursion, or any such-like worldly vanities, with unexampled fierceness, and contrived to obtain the at any rate partial support of Nathan, Jonas, Jethro, and the rest.

Sam's position was made the stronger by the fact that both the Clogger and his friend found themselves surprisingly inclined to accept Lige's invitation, but were very much ashamed at being so weak and frivolous.

At last, however, Sam went too far one night, and so goaded the wavering Clogger, that he suddenly arose from his seat and announced his intention of going, whatever either Sam or anybody else might say.

Of course, if Jabe went, Ben must go too; and as Mrs. Ben rather encouraged the idea, and Jabe's mode of settling the discussion transferred the moral responsibility of the whole expedition to the Clogger's shoulders, Ben plucked up courage, and away they went.

When they arrived at their destination, they were shocked to find Lige so evidently carried away by his frivolous surroundings that he met them at the station wearing a straw hat and a thin alpaca jacket, and flourishing a rakish-looking cane. And the light-hearted manner in which their old friend walked them into lodgings of awe-inspiring grandeur, as if it were an everyday matter to him, quite took their breath away.

Well, they had spent a busy and very happy week, and, having got their faces most satisfactorily tanned, were returning on the 'bus from Duxbury to Beckside.

There was only room for one on the driver's box, and the 'bus was kept standing several minutes at the bottom of Station Road whilst Jabe and his friend settled which of them should occupy the coveted seat. Ordinarily, neither of them would have cared to travel outside, but on this occasion they were both of one mind, and neither would give way for the other—and neither would confess that the real reason of this obstinacy was an intense desire to catch the very first possible glimpse of dear old Beckside.

As the reader will guess, Jabe was the successful candidate for the outside berth; and Ben, when he got inside, went up to the far end of the vehicle and took his seat by the window, in order to have the next best possible view to Jabe's.

It was, perhaps, as well they were parted, for as they drew near home, certain painful misgivings began to exercise their minds. What had hppened to the dear old place in their careless and unnecessary absence? They were both sure they would find something wrong. And only justly so, either. They had been gadding about and seeing wonderful things, and wickedly enjoying themselves without stint, whilst the chapel had been left to take care of itself—or what might turn out even worse than that, to be managed by rash and inexperienced hands.

It would not have greatly surprised Ben to find his children all ill of fever, or his shop burned down. And Jabe was by no means sure that he should find the chapel where he left it, and all right. Ah! how wicked they had been! Why, the very evening of their arrival at the watering-place, as they were walking on the sands, Lige, the trifler, had gaily challenged Long Ben to a game at "Aunt Sally"; and Jabe was convinced that, but for his own indignant protest, Ben would have accepted, and the world would have had the scandalous spectacle of two pillars of the church throwing sticks at a big, hideous-looking wooden image with a pipe in its mouth.

On the other hand, Jabe was very uneasy lest Ben should, after all, know what he did whilst Ben and Lige were having their photos taken; and the uneasy Clogger realised that he would never be able to hold his head up in Beckside again if it got out that he had had his "bumps" felt by an itinerant phrenologist.

Neither of these men had ever been a week out of Beckside in his life before, and as the coach drew near the village they grew quite nervous and apprehensive as to what might have happened during their absence, their fears being all intensified by the painful recollections of the thoughtless and wicked gaiety in which they had been indulging.

When the 'bus reached the top of the hill, and was going down into the village, Jabe heaved a great sigh, and Long Ben, with his nose flattened against the coach window, had difficulty in keeping back his tears.

And after all nothing had happened. The chapel stood just where they had left it, and looked bonnier than ever. The buzz of the mill could be distinctly heard, and over that the c-h-e-e-t, c-h-e-e-t of the saws from Ben's sawpit; and when the conveyance stopped, and Isaac, Sam Speck, Nathan, and Jethro came rushing out to meet them, overwhelming them with questions and chaff about their sunburnt faces, Jabe, standing off from the group, and looking round with unwonted seriousness on his face, cried out—

"Th' sayside's reet enuff fur them as loikes it, but *Beckside's* good enuff fur me."

And Long Ben, turning his back to the group of friends, and looking very earnestly at the mill chimney, whilst he vainly tried to straighten a quivering face, responded—

"Ay, lad; ther's noa place loike whoam, is ther'?"

Safe home again, both our friends felt inclined to laugh at the fear that had spoilt the pleasure of the return journey, but almost immediately other thoughts began to trouble them. Jabe wondered whether Ben really did know about that phrenologist, and Ben felt himself going red about the ears as he thought of the dreadful possibility of Jabe blurting out the truth about the "Aunt Sally."

These things were too shameful even to be discussed by them, and so, though they had abundant opportunity as they came home of entering into a compact, neither of them had ventured to suggest it to the other. Fortunately Lige had stayed behind a little longer, and so could not expose them; but what if he came home and in his garrulous way blurted out the whole story?

At the Clog Shop that night there was, of course, a full assemblage, and as Jabe and Ben described what they had seen, and marked the effect of it on the company present, they forgot their pricks of conscience, and were very soon on the best of terms both with themselves and each other.

Jabe, of course, was the chief spokesman, and he sat in his shirt-sleeves with a new long pipe before him, smoking a wonderful brand of tobacco to which Lige had introduced him, and enlarging on all they had seen and heard. He dismissed the ordinary attractions of the place in a very summary manner, although Ben confessed afterwards that he "fair crilled" as Jabe mentioned "Aunt Sally" a second time. And when Jabe paused for a moment to relight his pipe, Ben seemed inclined to take up and continue the story, for he drawled—

"An' ther' wur wun o' them—them bumpfeelin' chaps—an'"—

But here Jabe broke in with most unwonted haste—

"Th' Ranters wur howdin' camp-meetin's upo' th' sonds; an' hay, wot singin'!"

Having thus got the conversation into smooth waters again, Jabe passed on to what he knew would be more interesting to the company, and described the big chapel they had attended, and the preachers, and the music; and the company noted with interest that, instead of describing the leaders of the music as the singers, he called them the "kire," and even the singing-pew itself was denominated the "horkester" —which were regarded as signs that even the sturdy ecclesiastical conservatism of Jabe had been relaxed by his short sojourn abroad.

"Haa mony wur ther' i' th' band?" asked Jethro at this point.

"Band? thaa lumpyed; it wur a horgin."

Sam Speck, who, with the memory of his late ill-treatment on his mind, had hitherto manifested an ostentatiously supercilious indifference, now suddenly woke up, and glancing significantly at young Luke Yates, who sat near him, leaned his head against the chimney, and winking mysteriously at Jonas Tatlock, said quietly—

"Ay! bands is gooin' aat o' fashion fur chapils."

"Soa mitch wur fur th' chapils, then," retorted Jabe with emphasis.

Sam and his friends glanced at each other again, and the conversation seemed somehow to have got stranded.

"We went to th' Independent Chapil i' th' afternoon; it wur th' Sarmons," —said Long Ben at length, —"an' talk abaat singin'"— But Ben could find no words in which to express his admiration, and so he nodded with most eloquent suggestiveness at Jonas.

"Wur ther'a band theer?" asked Sam, whose mind seemed somehow to run very oddly on this subject.

"Neaw; ther' wur a harmonion."

Sam's eyes sparkled, and after turning and looking significantly over his shoulder at those who sat nearest to him, he drew a long breath, and asked quietly—

"An' th' music wur tiptop, thaa says?"

"It wur that," replied the carpenter, putting as much weight into his words as he could make them carry.

Sam was conscious that Jabe was studying him curiously, and so he moved restlessly in his seat. Then, after a pause, be dropped his voice somewhat, and remarked with a very awkward attempt at indifference—

"That's wot we wanton here."

Ben opened his eyes a little, and then, looking at Sam interrogatively, he asked—

"Uz! wot dun we want?"

Sam cast another look at those nearest to him, and then, wincing as if in anticipation of a blow, he said softly—

"A harmonion."

Everyone in the company shot a quick glance at Jabe, and as quickly turned away again, whilst the possessors of those eyes held their breath as if anticipating an explosion. But the Clogger neither moved nor spoke. His rugged face became a shade sterner, but for any other sign he gave he might never have heard Sam's remark.

The silence that followed was most unpleasant, and so, to relieve it, Long Ben looked across at Sam, and asked—

"Wot dun *we* want wi' a harmonion?"

Sam stole another quick glance at Jabe, whose silence was more ominous than any speech, and answered sulkily—

"Well, we dew. Th' Clough Enders hez wun, an' th' Brogdeners hez wun, and they'n tew at Duxbury Schoo'."

Sam sat like a naughty boy expecting a box on the ear. And the rest of the company stole shy, quick glances at the Clogger, whose silence under these conditions was a sort of slow torture. Presently Ben went on—

"Dust know what harmonions cosses?" (costs).

"Cosses? Ay!" replied the now desperate Sam. "We can hev a gradely good un wi' six stops in fur ten paand, an' Jimmy Juddy says he'll gi' tew towart it."

Then two or three others added details, and for the next few minutes they talked eagerly, but somewhat nervously, on the subject, evidently unconscious of the fact that in every word uttered they were betraying themselves to the silent and inscrutable Clogger.

In the discussion thus initiated, it gradually became clear that, immediately after the departure of Jabe and Ben for "th' sayside," Sam and Luke Yates had begun to carry out a long-cherished plan of agitating for a modern musical instrument for the chapel. The suggestion had met with more encouragement than they had expected—Jethro, the knocker-up, being their only serious opponent; and, as he was not of much account, and was clearly prejudiced, they had, by the time the two excursionists returned, nearly perfected their scheme.

Amongst other things, they had got a lot of tentative promises that nearly covered the proposed outlay, and an illustrated price-list of very attractive looking instruments.

At this point, Sam produced from his pocket a gorgeous catalogue, with one of the leaves carefully turned down, and, opening the book at this particular page, he looked anxiously round for someone to whom to present it.

But, though they had all examined it several times a day for the last few days, they seemed to have suddenly lost all interest in the matter, and shrank from accepting Sam's offer under the stern eye of the terrible Clogger. Sam bent forward and nervously thrust the catalogue towards Long Ben, but that worthy looked straight before him and absolutely ignored the document. Sam was visibly agitated, and would gladly have put the list back in his pocket, but he either could not or dared not, and so he held it out hesitantly and looked at it a long time, conscious that everyone was watching him, and finally, making a desperate effort, he got up, strode across to where Jabe was sitting, and, pointing with his finger at a picture of a very imposing looking instrument, he cried

"That's it, sithi. Wee'st ha' sum music when we getten that."

Jabe was sitting with his short leg flung carelessly over the other against the opposite side of the chimney-jamb, and to everybody's surprise he put out his hand, and in a listless, indolent fashion took hold of the catalogue and glanced at the indicated picture.

Then, still holding the list between his thumb and finger, he lolled back lazily, and fixing his eye on a thick cobweb in the corner of a walled-up side window, he said, with a slow impressive shake of the head—

"Aw'll tell yo' wot, chaps; we liven i' wunderful toimes."

Everybody was surprised and mystified, and whilst one or two of the conspirators began to show an inclination to hopefulness, the more experienced hung their heads apprehensively.

Nobody replied to Jabe's enigmatical remark, and so in a moment or two he shook his head more seriously than ever, and still contemplating the cobweb, added—

"Wunderful toimes."

But, even then, nobody responded, and the older ones present glanced pityingly at Sam.

"Iverything's dun by machinery naa-a-days," continued Jabe, putting on a look of carefully simulated wonder. "We'en spinnin' machines, an' weyvin' machines, an' sewin' machines, an' weshin' machines, an' naa, bi th' ferrups, we'en getten *warshippin'* machines," — and absorbed with the contemplation of all these modern marvels, Jabe stared at the cobweb in rapt astonishment.

"Machines?" began Sam indignantly, but two or three put out their hands and checked him, whilst the Clogger, still gazing at the spider's habitation, went on with slow and painful deliberateness—

"Wee'st ha' prayin' machines an' preichin' machines next. Naa, if nobbut some handy chap 'ud mak' a machine fur turnin' sawft gawmliss bluffinyeds inta gradely felleys, Aw'd bey wun mysel'. Ther'd be plenty o' wark fur it i' Beckside."

There was a sudden sputter of half-amused, half-angry laughter, which relieved the tension somewhat. Two or three slily drew the backs of their hands across their mouths as if they had just tasted something enjoyable but forbidden, and Sam was lifting his head to reply, when Jabe went on once more in a humorously sarcastic tone—

"A harmonion, eh? We'd better send for lame Joe, an' start a concerteena band, or else a singin'-pew full o' lads wi' tin whistles an' Jews' harps."

Sam Speck, goaded to desperation, set his teeth, and, clenching his fist, brought it down heavily on the bench before him, crying in indignant anger—

"Well, we'en getten th' brass, an' wee'st ha' wun, chuse wot thaa says."

Jabe's face became suddenly very stern. The amused, contemptuous look upon it vanished, and, pursing his lips, and drawing together his brows, he said, with slow weighty emphasis—

"As lung as ther's a fiddle-string i' Beckside, or a felley as can start a chune [tune], ther'll be noa harmonion i' aar chapil."

The countenances of Sam's supporters dropped visibly, and a glint of unholy fire shot into several eyes, and as Long Ben noted this he chimed in soothingly—

"We met use it fur th' schoo', thaa knows. We'en bin rayther hard up sometimes lattly."

But the possibility of Ben's defection from his side roused Jabe, and so, jumping to his feet, he shouted in his excitement—

"Ther'll be noa barril-orgins—baat handle—i' that schoo' woll Aw'm alive," and then, after a pause—"Neaw, an' if yo' getten wun efther Aw'm gooan, bi th' mop' Aw'll cum back to yo'."

As Jabe sank back into his seat, glaring relentless resolution all around, a spirit of sulky depression seemed to fall on the company; and what should have been a highly enjoyable evening proved so disappointing, that the friends began to depart quite early, whilst those who remained looked more and more dismal.

Scarcely had the last man except Ben departed when Jabe rose to his feet, and, glaring at the companion of his recent jaunt, he cried in bitter distress—

"This is wot comes o' thi sayside maantibankin'. Didn't Aw tell thi haa it 'ud be?" And then, sinking into his seat again with a face all a-work, he cried with added bitterness—

"Aw wuish th' sayside 'ud bin at Jericho, Aw dew, fur shure."

Now, as Ben had gone to the watering-place quite as much because he thought Jabe wanted to go, but would not go alone, as because he fancied the excursion himself, and as all the warnings and misgivings had been uttered by himself, as far as he could remember, and had been received by his friend with fine scorn, he was somewhat surprised to have this charge hurled at him, but he knew his man too well to reply just then. And so, after sitting and smoking in silence for a long time, he said soothingly—

"Ne'er moind, lad; ther'll be noa harmonions i' heaven."

"Neaw, nor saysides noather," grunted Jabe.

II.

THE TRUSTEES' MEETING.

IT is perhaps necessary to explain that the musical service at the Beckside Chapel was conducted on rather free-and-easy principles. The choir was a fairly stable quantity, but the instrumental part of the service was somewhat carelessly managed. To begin with, there was only room for about four instruments in the singing-pew, and as Nathan's "'cello" was regarded as indispensable, it only left three places for all the rest. These places were filled by any members of the band who took it into their heads to attend and bring their instruments—as far, at any rate, as the limited accommodation would allow. Jonas Tatlock always kept his violin at chapel to be ready for those odd occasions when no other fiddler turned up, but the music of this instrument was usually provided by Jimmy Juddy, or Isaac the apprentice, or both. The "'cello" and the two violins were regarded as all that were absolutely necessary for an ordinary service, but on Sunday evenings, and on all special occasions, the instruments would be reinforced by, an additional "'cello," Peter Twist's clarinet, and occasionally by a double bass, or even Jethro's trombone.

When, therefore, on the very Saturday night that Jabe and his friend departed for the seaside, Sam Speck sprang upon the company assembled at the Clog Shop his revolutionary proposal to introduce a harmonium into the chapel, all the instrumentalists regarded it as a direct attack upon their order, and resented it accordingly.

"If we getten a harmonion ther'll be noa raam fur fiddles," objected Jimmy Juddy, toying with one of Jabe's hammers.

"Fiddles, thaa lumpyed! wee'st want noa fiddles when we getten a harmonion," said Sam, looking pityingly on Jimmy for his lack of comprehension.

"Dust meean to say as if th' harmonion gooas in aw th' t'other instruments 'ull ha' to cum aat?" demanded Jethro in painful surprise.

"Ay, fur shure! Wot else?"

Now, up to this point there had been a disposition to at any rate give the question a fair hearing, but now, seeing that, like Othello's, their occupation would be gone, those in the company who were accustomed to play in the chapel at once went over to the opposition. One or two, however, found their positions somewhat difficult. Jonas, for instance, who, as leader of both band and choir, was an important person, whilst conscious of a desire to experiment with a new instrument, felt that his own beloved fiddle would be displaced, and that his *protégé* and future son-in-law, Isaac, would be reduced to the rank of an unimportant private member, and so he wavered, and with him were Jimmy Juddy and one or two others.

On the other hand, Jethro, the knocker-up, in the absence of his great leader, maintained a fierce and uncompromising opposition, and so it happened that far into that night the Clog Shop resounded with the noise of argumentative battle, and on the very Sunday when Jabe and Long Ben were luxuriating in the clover of grand preaching and grander singing, the church they had left behind was agitated with conflict.

All through the following week the battle had continued, and consequently, on their return, the Clogger and his friend found the society divided into two compact and fiercely belligerent parties, Sam Speck's being numerically and forensically the stronger, and Jethro's making up in obstinacy what it lacked in numbers and logic.

The return of the two excursionists meant, of course, a sudden accession of strength to the weaker party, and on the Sunday night after their arrival the Clog Shop parlour was the scene of one of the fiercest word-battles that even it had ever known.

Jabe had no great difficulty with his revolted lieutenant Sam. It was comparatively easy by characteristic torrents of raillery and satire to silence him. But there was a new combatant in the field on this particular night—no less a person, in fact, than Ben's son-in-law, Luke Yates. And the cool, adroit, and aggravatingly polite style of this young man's arguments provoked the irate Clogger almost beyond endurance. The fiercer and more boisterous Jabe became in argument, the quieter and more conciliatory were Luke's replies, so that the Clogger was angered, not only by the cogency of Luke's reasoning, but also by the consciousness that his own methods were clumsy in comparison, and that his favourite weapon of abuse was grossly unfair.

Every now and again during the debate Long Ben would interject some softening remark, which, though exactly what everybody expected of him, seemed on this occasion to be unusually irritating to his friend; the truth being that Jabe felt that the arguments which were steadily undermining his own position would be sure to be producing the same effect on Ben's mind, and he knew only too well that eventually Ben would go over to the other side if only in the interests of peace. Moreover, Luke was Ben's son-in-law, and Jabe felt that Ben's pride in the young man's debating power would lay him open to easy conviction.

Besides all this, Jabe, as the conflict continued, began to have an uneasy feeling that more was involved in the dispute than the question of the harmonium, and he found himself struggling with a consciousness that this was the first indication that the day of his absolute reign in the Beckside Church was over, and that in Luke Yates the Methodist people would before very long recognise a leader more suited to modern ideas, and, withal, altogether more capable than himself. The Clogger, therefore, rallied all his resources. Abuse, scorn, satire, and threatenings were all employed without measure or mercy; and when these failed, he fell back on inscrutable and obstinate silence, and pretended to regard the harmonium agitation as the offspring of feather-brained and utterly worthless individuals, of whom no serious notice need be taken.

But as time passed, Jabe gradually discovered that he was more alone in this matter than he had expected to be. The doctor and his wife were both in favour of the new instrument, the erstwhile schoolmistress, in fact, having gone so far as to promise to play it when it was introduced into the chapel. The young people of the Society were all enthusiastic about it, and even such staunch supporters of old-established ways as Aunt Judy and Long Ben wavered most disgracefully.

On Thursday, Lige returned, and though, as a rule, the Clogger had no great respect for the old road-mender's judgment, yet in his present circumstances he was glad of the slightest support, and looked quite eagerly for Lige's arrival.

Alas! alas! Before he had even seen Lige, or had had the least opportunity of sounding him on the question, he received the disheartening intelligence that his old friend was an enthusiastic supporter of the popular proposal.

Jabe had one hope left. The "super" would, of course, support him in his defence of established institutions, and as that gentleman was to preach at Beckside on the following Sunday, and was appointed to be entertained at the Clog Shop, the Clogger comforted himself with the hope that help was at hand, and that the representative of law and authority would stand firmly by him.

But, somehow, when the super came, Jabe could not for the life of him introduce the subject, and the minister, who, unknown to our old friend, had been fully enlightened as to the state of affairs, was almost as anxious to hear as Jabe was to speak. But although during the day they discussed every possible subject concerning the chapel, and the super deftly led up to musical matters several times, Jabe always avoided them, and the evening service was over and the minister was finishing his supper in the Clog Shop parlour before the subject he had been waiting for all day was introduced.

The other occupants of the parlour were Long Ben, Lige, and Jethro, but even now the Clogger seemed to have no intention of introducing the subject which was uppermost in everybody's mind.

"Han yo' yerd abaat th' bother as we han here, Mestur Shuper," asked Ben hesitantly, tilting back his chair, and puffing out a huge mouthful of smoke.

"Bother? Bother at Beckside! I hope not," replied the minister evasively, but with a sufficiently passable show of surprise to hoodwink the listeners.

"Ay!" cried the Clogger contemptuously, but with a nervous little laugh; "a storm in a tay-pot, sure*li*."

"A bother? A storm? What is the matter?" asked the super, putting on an even greater look of astonishment.

"Dunna meyther," replied Jabe, with an impatient jerk of the head, whilst his demonstrative leg began to rock excitedly over the other, "it's nobbut childer wark."

"Childer wark? It's *babby* wark," cried Jethro, leaning forward, and putting out his chin with a grim, pugnacious expression which looked very strange on his gentle old face.

"Ay! but wot Aw want to know is which *is* th' babbies?" retorted Lige doggedly.

"Gently, gentlemen, gently!" said the minister. "Someone tell me what is the matter, please."

"Matter?" cried Jabe, rising to his feet in his excitement, and holding his pipe away from him in one hand, whilst he gesticulated tragically with the other, "ther's a lot o' gawmliss young wastrils, just aat o' petticuts, an' they wanten ta rule th' church; that's wot's th' matter."

An exclamation of dissent escaped Long Ben, and Lige and Jethro both rose to their feet, and began to talk excitedly.

The super, putting out his hands, cried, "Sit down, gentlemen, please. Now, Mr. Jabez, what *is* the matter?"

"Matter?" shouted Jabe, rising to his feet again, in spite of the minister's injunction. "Mun Aw ax yo' wun queshten?"

"Well, what is it?"

"Han' yo' iver yerd better music i' ony chapil yo'n iver been in, nor wot yo' yer when yo' cum ta Beckside? Tell me that."

"It is very good; *very* good," answered the super diplomatically.

"Well, then, wot 'ud aar music be baat fiddles an' 'cellos?"

"Ah! indeed!" still more cautiously.

"Well!" and here he drew himself up to his full height, and stepping back to get more room for the sweep of his gesticulating arm, shouted more excitedly than ever, "they wanten awthem grand owd instruments turnin' aat, ta mak' room fur a yowling, squawking buzz-box as they cawn a H-A-R-M-O-N-I-O-N," and putting all the scorn that was in him into his pronunciation of the name of the object of his indignation, Jabe sank into his seat exhausted by his effort.

It was fully five minutes before the super could get a word in again, for Lige, roused by the Clogger's attack, began pouring out his wrath upon "owd-fashioned stick-i'-th'-muds" until Jethro was provoked to make an unusually fierce reply for him, and Long Ben felt constrained to get up and stand between them for fear of worse happening.

At last, however, the combatants paused for breath, and the super said conciliatorily—

"But harmoniums are very useful instruments, you know, Mr. Jabez, and quite fashionable nowadays."

"Fashionable!" began Jabe, with curling lip but before he could get any further, Jethro stepped up to the super, and touching him challengingly on the shoulder, demanded—

"Is they' ony harmonions mentioned i' th' Bible? Tell me that."

"No; and, for that matter, fiddles are not"—

"No fiddles? Wot does stringed instriments meean, if it doesn't meean fiddles? Tell me that naa?"

Now, during the preceding week, the super had received a respectful and courteously-worded note from Luke Yates, informing him that some of the friends at Beckside wished to present a harmonium to the chapel, and asking to be informed if the trustees would accept of such a gift; and, with this in his pocket, and the evidences of strong feeling before his eyes, he scarcely knew what to do.

At last, however, seeing no chance of rational discussion, he suggested—

"Well, this is a matter for the trustees, you know; shall I call a meeting of the Trust?"

Long Ben shook his head, and sighed. Lige eagerly approved, and Jethro as eagerly opposed. In this dilemma the super turned to Jabe, who was sitting back in his chair, sulkily nursing his short leg.

"Yo' can caw as mony as yo'n a moind," he replied, "an' we can pleease aarsel's whether we goa or not."

"Well, perhaps, it will be better to have one, and thresh the matter out," and with that the super rose to go, and Jabe, who had of late fallen into the habit of seeing the minister a little way on his journey, sat obstinately in his chair and stared hard at the joists above his head.

It was nearly three weeks before the meeting could be held, and during that time the relationships existing between the chief actors in this little drama were somewhat severely strained, and many and long were the word-battles that were fought.

The night of the meeting proved to be soaking wet, and consequently no trustees from a distance attended, and this terrible question was therefore left to be settled by the men on the spot.

For two or three days previously Sam Speck had been "drawin' in his horns," as Jethro termed it, and had made great efforts to come to an understanding with his deserted leader, but all to no purpose. On any other subject Jabe would talk with something approaching his old familiarity, but immediately the harmonium was mentioned he closed up like an oyster, put on a look of impenetrable mystery, and would not utter a single word.

Long Ben, too, had tried to bring about some sort of a compromise, but as he had not given his friend that whole-hearted support which

Jabe thought he had a right to expect, the Clogger kept him resolutely at arm's-length.

All the local trustees except one were present in the vestry some minutes before the meeting began, and when the super arrived and looked round the room he saw at a glance how the matter was likely to be settled.

Jabe and Jethro represented the full strength of the "Noes"; Sam Speck and Nathan the "Ayes"; whilst Long Ben and Jonas, sitting close together, represented the "cross-bench mind," but with strong leanings towards Sam's party.

"Now, Mr. Speck," said the minister, after the meeting had been formally opened, "you have this matter in hand, I suppose; let us hear what you have to propose."

Sam, with many a halt and many a bungle, and many nervous glances at his great opponent, expounded his scheme in detail, and finished by informing the meeting that the money to purchase the instrument was ready as soon as the trustees would accept it.

Then Long Ben gently suggested that the matter be deferred until after "th' next Sarmons," but, though Jabe neither moved nor spoke, the rest signified that they preferred an immediate settlement of the question.

Then as Jabe, in spite of nods and winks from Jonas opposite, and hard nudges from the knocker-up at his side, would not speak, Jethro, who was boiling over with excitement, made a long, rambling, but fairly complete statement of the case for the opposition, and was just finishing with an appeal that threatened to become pathetic, to "stick to th' good owd ways," when the door opened, and in walked Lige.

Somehow the road-mender's appearance just at this stage of the proceedings brought a sudden check to the discussion. There was no use in further argument. The case was settled, for Lige was more unswerving in his advocacy of the new instrument than Sam himself.

"Aar clock's slow," he said, in answer to the pulling out of two or three big verge watches.

And then there was a short pause, and, after waiting a moment or two, the super turned round in his chair, and looking at the Clogger, said—

"Now, Mr. Jabez, what do you think about the matter?"

Jabe, whose active leg was the only thing that moved about him, sat with his head tilted back against the wall and his eyes on the ceiling, and, as the super's question reached him, he jerked out—"Yo' known," and then was dumb again.

Every attempt on the part of the minister to provoke discussion failed, and a most uncomfortable feeling pervaded the whole meeting.

"Well, gentlemen," said the minister at last, "we must get on. Will somebody move a resolution?"

After another long pause, Lige jerked out—

"Ay! Aw'll pro-poase it."

"But what will you propose?"

"As we han a harmonion."

"That is, that we accept the offer of Mr. Speck and others to present a harmonium to the chapel."

"Ay!"

"Anyone second this?"

A pause longer than ever followed, but at last Nathan said timidly—

"Aw'll second it."

"Has anyone anything to say before the resolution is put?"

Still nobody spoke, and the super was just proceeding to take the fateful vote when Long Ben jumped excitedly to his feet, and looking across at Jabe, cried, with a pathetic break in his voice—

"Speik, mon, wilta?"

But the Clogger sat like a statue—silent, sphinx-like, inexorable.

Just then a new thought seemed to strike the perplexed super, and looking round, he asked—

"Why shouldn't you have both kinds of instruments, gentlemen? It doesn't follow that because you have a harmonium you can't have the others too, if you like."

Light seemed to break across the faces of the two waverers, Ben and Jonas, and after looking at the super to make sure that they had heard aright, Ben asked—

"Whey, will they goa togather?"

"Of course they will; and one will help and improve the other," was the reply.

This seemed to have a decisive effect on Ben and his companion, and Jonas said somewhat eagerly—

"Tak' th' vooate then."

The super hesitated, and turned once more to look at Jabe, but his face was as relentless as ever. And so the resolution was put. Everybody voted for it except Jabe and Jethro, and when the super announced the result, Ben heaved a great sigh, glanced wistfully at Jabe, and sighed again.

Some arrangements having been made for the immediate introduction of the new instrument, the meeting broke up, and a group of very serious-looking men made their way along the side of the chapel to the road in front. Jabe was leading the procession, and as he reached the road he suddenly turned round, and looking earnestly at the chapel, said in a dry, choking voice

"Th' day as a harmonion goas inta that chapil, Jabez Longworth comes aat on it for iver."

Without waiting for a reply, he limped rapidly off home; and although he had ordered Isaac to have the fire lighted before he came back in preparation for the usual evening's conversation, nobody joined him, and for almost the only occasion of its kind in his life Jabe sat the evening out in the inglenook absolutely alone.

III.

THE ANGELS' SONG.

NOW that they had gained their victory, the advocates of the new harmonium seemed strangely slow in accomplishing their purpose; and those who had voted at the memorable Trustees' Meeting not only rebuked all attempts at congratulation, but showed a most remarkable testiness on the subject, and could only be induced to discuss it when absolutely necessary.

Several earnest attempts were also made to bring the Clogger to a better mind, and the date of the introduction of the new instrument was deferred again and again.

Meanwhile Jabe maintained a dignified silence on the matter, and when compelled to allude to it he did so in the fewest possible words; and it was noted as an ominous sign that instead of being explosive and vehement, his remarks sounded sad and resigned.

But when, in their desire to win him over, anyone actually compelled him to show his mind, it was found that he remained solidly and stubbornly obstinate.

After several postponements, therefore, it was felt that the matter could no longer be delayed, and Long Ben reluctantly consented to go and examine the singing-pew to see what would be required in the way of structural alterations in order to accommodate the coming instrument.

But although Sam Speck and Lige were both there next morning to assist him, the carpenter did not turn up, and when they went down to the shop in search of him, nobody knew where he was.

Another and yet another appointment had to be made, and it was only on the third occasion that Ben presented himself.

And when he did come, he seemed very half-hearted about the matter, and but for Sam's persistence he would have gone away again without settling anything.

By dint of much pressure and prompting, however, they at length got him to work, but even then he was provokingly absent-minded. He measured the place that would have to be cleared to make room for the harmonium three times, and then if Sam had not taken down the measurements they would have been no further on with their business. After looking abstractedly around, and vainly trying to start discussions on other matters, Ben began absently to measure again.

"Wot th' ferrups arta doin'?" cried Sam, in vexed surprise.

Ben stopped, looked inquiringly at Sam for a moment, discovered what he had done, and then, turning round with an impatient gesture, cried—

"Confaand th' harmonion! Aw wuish Owd Scratch hed it."

And as Sam stared at him in indignant astonishment, he cried—

"Yo'll ha' ta dew this job baat me. My hert aches. Aw th' harmonions as iver wur made isna as mitch ta me as yond' owd chap i' th' Clug Shop," and choking back a sob, he gave another gesture of repudiation, and walked hurriedly out of the chapel.

Lige also showed great uneasiness. In one of the earlier discussions on the now painful subject Jabe had dropped a remark which showed that he regarded all this trouble as the result of their "gallivantin' at th' sayside," and, as the road-mender knew that he was primarily responsible for this, it gave him great unrest.

Jonas Tatlock went even further, and openly recanted, and would have had the subject dropped; and one or two others gradually lost all interest in the affair, only Sam and Luke Yates keeping up even a show of enthusiasm.

Then the conscience-smitten conspirators discovered, or thought they discovered, that Jabe was not looking well, and it was confidently stated that he was fretting. As if to confirm this, it was made known in the village one Saturday that Jabe was in bed with a bad cold. And everybody knew it must be a bad cold indeed to have kept the Clogger in his room.

Then the cold developed into a sore throat, and the sore throat into a quinsy, and Aunt Judy, on guard, refused to allow even his closest friends to see him, lest he should talk and thus make matters worse.

This illness spread dismay in the ranks of Jabe's opponents. Even some of the younger folk seemed anxious to disown any desire for the unfortunate harmonium, and Jethro went about declaring—

"If yond' owd chap dees, Aw'll smash th' harmonion wi' my knockin'-up stick," whilst others prophesied that the instrument would never get into the chapel after all.

Sam Speck, however, still held out, and so, apparently, did Luke Yates, the latter, in fact, being strengthened in his persistence by the support of his gentle young wife, who was passionately fond of music. The contract for the necessary alterations in the singing-pew had been given, on Ben's defection, to Tommy o' th' Top, a Clough End carpenter; and one evening when Luke went home to Beckbottom, and was sitting over his "baggin'," Leah, who had taken her chair near the door, and was sewing something she seemed afraid of being seen by her teasing husband, said—

"Aw seed 'Tommy o' th' Top' goa past taday. Wur he goin' to th' chapel, dust think?"

"Aw noather knaaw nor cur," answered Luke rather gruffly.

"Luke, wotiver's ta dew wi' thi? Dustna want th' harmonion?"

"Aw wuish th' harmonion wur smashed ta flinders."

"Luke!"

"Aw dew; it's makkin' me fair badly, an' if owt happens ta yond' owd chap"— But Luke got up hastily, and hurried into the back kitchen, and Leah heard a great deal of mysterious coughing and throat-clearing before he came back again.

A day or two later, however, it was known that Jabe's quinsy had burst, and that all immediate danger was over. Three days later Aunt Judy called at Ben's shop, and announced that Jabe wanted to see the carpenter, and in a moment or two Ben was striding away as fast as his long legs would carry him towards the Clog Shop. Passing through the shop, he paused at the parlour door, and gently opened it.

"Is that thee, Ben?" came in feeble tones from the parlour.

"Ay, lad. Mun Aw come in?"

"Ay."

And Ben found his old friend propped up in the bed with a huge comforter round his neck, a Paisley shawl upon his shoulders, and a red-tasselled nightcap on his head.

As he caught sight of the carpenter, he put out his hand, and gripping Ben's big palm tightly, he cried, whilst a big tear stood in the corner of his eye—

"Hay, lad! Aw'm *fain* ta see thi."

"An' Aw'm fain to see *thee*, owd lad; God b-l-e-s-s thi!" and the two shook hands, with a long clinging clasp, and gazed eagerly into each other's eyes.

After a while Ben began to tell his friend all the news he could think of, carefully avoiding, of course, the forbidden subject.

But Jabe seemed very apathetic about matters, and had an absent, far-away look that alarmed Ben most seriously.

"Sit thi daan, lad," he said at length; "Aw've summat to tell thi."

Ben did as he was bidden, and then Jabe wiped his face with his big red pocket-handkerchief, and began in tones so serious as to greatly distress his friend.

"Ben, lad, Aw've hed a dreeam."

"A dreeam?"

"Ay! an' Aw'st ne'er forget it as lung as Aw'm wik. Ben, Aw've been i' heaven."

Ben didn't like this at all; people who dreamed of heaven— But Jabe was proceeding—

"Hay, lad! but it wur a graand place! Ther' wur gardins and flaars an' hangils, and aw mak' o' graand things. An', Ben," —and here Jabe dropped his voice into a solemn whisper,—"Aw seed Him. Aw did! Aw seed Him. Hay, it wur glorious;" and, overcome with the memory, Jabe sat looking before him with a rapt face, as if the grand vision were still before his eyes. After a moment's pause, he wiped his pale face again, and went on—

"An' when aw th' angils seed HIM they began a-singin'—an' singin'—an' singin'. Hay, Ben, *thaa* ne'er yerd nowt loike it. An' sum o' th' angils were playin' herps, and sum wur blowin' trumpits. Hay, it wur graand, Aw con tell thi," and once more the sick man paused and wiped his face. Then he went on—

"An' aw o' th' wunce aw th' angils wi' herps an' trumpits geet togather, an' flew away aat o' my seet. But wot capt me, th' music didna stop! Soa Aw went a bit narer, an' then Aw seed just a tooathre singin' an' playin' by theersel's. But they hedna ony herps thaa knows, an' still Aw could yer th' music. Soa Aw went a bit narer, an' then a bit narer, and then Aw seed as they hed summat i' th' middle on 'em, an' wun o' th' noicest o' th' angils wur playin' on it. An' just then they seed me, an' they aw smilt at me, an' flew up an' cum towart me, an' when they flew up Aw seed th' music, an' wot dust think it wur?"

"Aw dunno knaaw," muttered Ben, divided between wonder at Jabe's story and fear lest it should be a warning of his speedy departure.

"Ben," said Jabe, in husky tones, leaning forward and grasping his friend's hand again, "it wur a *harmonion*."

But just at this point there was an interruption. Aunt Judy came back, and, glancing critically at her brother's face, announced that he'd been "meytherin' hissel'," and somewhat summarily sent Ben out. As he was going out, however, Jabe called him back, and, looking at him with a gleam of the old spirit in his eye that did Ben good to see, he said—

"Naa, then! Not a chirp o' this till Aw con cum aat mysel'."

During the days that followed first one and then another of Jabe's friends came to see him, and both they and the Clogger were greatly puzzled to know how it was that nobody ever mentioned the harmonium.

Jabe, lying in bed and castigating himself for his sinful obstinacy, was also trying to prepare himself to endure the hateful instrument on his first appearance at chapel. For the silence of his friends on the subject left him no room for doubting that the change had been made whilst he had been in bed. Whilst they, knowing nothing of his altered mind, had already abandoned all idea of getting the instrument.

The Sunday week after Jabe's relation of his wonderful dream to Ben, the Clogger received permission to go out, and, of course, going out meant to him going to chapel. His official duties had been for the time relegated to Ben and Nathan, and so he walked straight to his seat, nerving himself as he did so to endure the sight of the offensive harmonium.

For some time he knelt in his place in silent praise to God for his recovery. Then he groped under his little green cushion for his hymn-book and Bible, and, placing these in front of him, lifted his head and took his first steady look towards the singing-pew.

What was the matter? Nothing seemed changed. No! Everything was just as it was when last he took part in worship.

Ah! what next? Instead of at most two instruments at the morning service there were six or seven—'cellos, fiddles, a trombone, and even Long Ben with the double bass. Whatever did it all mean?

But just then the preacher came into the pulpit and gave out the number of the hymn. It sounded familiar, and whilst he was trying to remember what hymn it was, the instruments began to play the tune over. There was no doubt about that, it was Cranbrook, and as

Jabe sat in perplexity with his unopened hymn-book in his hand, the choir arose and sang out—

> "And are we yet alive
> And see each other's face."

And Jabe, lifting his head, caught Sam Speck staring hard at him over the singing-pew curtain and singing with all his might.

Then it appeared to the old Clogger that everybody was looking at him, and singing at him in pure joy at his recovery. What a sinner he had been to quarrel with friends like these!

How he got through that service Jabe never knew, but when it did conclude, before anybody could move from their seats he had opened his pew door, and was limping excitedly down the aisle.

When he reached the front he stood on tiptoes looking over the singing-pew curtain in vain search for the terrible instrument.

Then he suddenly lifted his head, and staring wonderingly at Sam Speck, he cried—

"Wheer is it?"

"Wheer's wot?"

"Th' harmonion."

"We hanna getten wun."

"Haa's that?"

And then there was a pause, and Sam Speck turned and looked at Long Ben, and Ben looked at Lige, and they both looked back at Sam, and so that worthy leaned over the curtain and cried—

"We wanten th' harmonion, bud we wanten yo' *mooar*."

Jabe suddenly went very pale, his hand shook, his face began to quiver painfully, and dropping his head upon his chest, he turned round and walked straight towards the chapel door.

Before passing out, however, he stopped, and turning round and lifting his head, he looked the smiling congregation in the face, and shouted—

"Aw said ther' shouldna be a harmonion i' this chapil, an' ther' shanna."

This was a bolt from the blue indeed. Surprise, perplexity, and keen disappointment appeared on many a face; and as Jabe limped off home, the rest, standing in little groups outside, were asking each other what this harsh and unnecessary outbreak might mean, and the prevailing opinion as they parted was that the old man's brain had been affected by his recent illness.

A few days later mysterious things began to be whispered about. The super, Long Ben, Jabe, and a strange gentleman had been seen going one forenoon to the chapel, and it was known that they had spent over an hour there.

And then several mysterious marks appeared on the chapel walls in the singers' corner, and one Sunday it was discovered that all the seats and fixtures had been removed from that particular part of the edifice, whilst an announcement was made from the pulpit that for the next two Sundays the services would be held in the schoolroom.

It was evident by this time that something very strange was going on, and also that several people were already in the secret. And when the third Sunday came, and the people gathered in the chapel, they found the singers' corner occupied by a beautiful little pipe-organ—

"THE GIFT OF JABEZ LONGWORTH."

THE HAUNTED MAN.

I.

THE MAUVAIS SUJET.

SOME two or three weeks after the opening of the new organ, and whilst Beckside was still in the first flush of its pride as the only country chapel in the Duxbury Circuit that could boast of such a luxury, Jabe caught cold again, and was threatened with a return of his old throat complaint. He was compelled therefore to stay indoors on the Sunday. This of course went badly against the grain; and in order to keep the old man "ony bit loike," Ben and two or three others called after each service and gave a full and particular account of all that had taken place at the chapel, dwelling at length on the achievements of the new organ, and the wonderful way in which Mrs. Dr. Walmsley played it.

As the time for the close of the evening service drew near, Jabe limped about in his parlour with his throat muffled up, fidgeting and talking impatiently to himself, and peeping every minute or two out of the corner of the window to see if the chapel was "loosing." For the life of him he could not sit still. One moment he was consulting the long-cased clock standing near the door that led into the shop, and comparing it carefully with his double-cased watch, and the next he was taking a sip at a jug of "balm tay" which stood on the oven-top. Then he limped to the window again, and after getting as close to the wall as he could in order to see as far round the corner as possible, he stood there peeping slantwise up the hill to see if anyone were coming down it. Every now and again he imagined he could hear the organ, and stood still in the middle of the floor to listen, although he knew, in spite of Jimmy Juddy's solemn declaration that he had heard it in their kitchen, that the chapel was too far away to allow of any such thing. Then he began to snarl under his breath at the preacher, and went twice to examine the "plan" hanging behind the parlour door to make sure that the man appointed was not one of those longwinded ones.

All at once, however, the front door was noisily burst open, and in rushed Sam Speck, almost out of breath in his haste to tell his somewhat remarkable tidings.

"Wot dust think? Whoa dust think's bin at chapil?" he cried excitedly.

"Haa dew Aw knaaw? *Aw* hevna, Aw knaaw that," and the Clogger looked and spoke as if Sam were responsible for his enforced absence, and had done him a grievous injury.

But just then Lige came hurrying in almost as much out of breath as his forerunner, and as he stepped towards the hearthstone, he turned to Sam, and addressing him, said, just as if Jabe were not bursting with impatience and curiosity—

"Well, wot dust think, naa? Wot's he up tew, think's ta?"

"Whoa? Wot? Wot are yo' meytherin' abaat?" demanded Jabe in fierce impatience.

But before either Sam or Lige could answer, Nathan and Jethro stepped in, followed immediately by Long Ben.

Jethro was the first to speak. Ranging himself alongside Sam, and turning his head towards him whilst he warmed his hands at the fire behind him, he asked—

"Well, wot's th' meeanin' on it, dust think?"

And Sam, turning to face his interrogator, knit his brows sternly, and, tapping Jethro on the second button of his seedy Sunday coat, replied emphatically—

"It meeans lumber; that wot it meeans. If he isna efther some nowtiness, Aw'll—Aw'll eit my yed," and, giving the knocker-up a little push as if to add additional emphasis to a statement already overladen with that commodity, he stepped back, and, putting his hand under his coat tails, stared doggedly at Nathan.

Jabe was "on tenter-hooks."

"Wot's up?" he shouted huskily. "Arr yo' aw gone dateliss? Whoa arr yo' talkin' abaat?"

"We're talkin' abaat Jooab, skinny Jooab," cried Sam.

"Well, wot abaat him?"

"He's bin ta th' chapel ta-neet; that's wot abaat him," and Sam glared at the sick Clogger as if defying him to contradict his statement.

Now Job Sharples, the pig-dealer, had never been to chapel since that memorable meeting at which Jabe had so scornfully returned his niggardly sovereign for the renovation fund. For years before this Job appeared to have been gradually losing first one and then another bond that bound him to better things, and this seemed to have been the last one, for though the renovated chapel had now been reopened some eighteen months, he had never put his head inside the doors, and had come to be regarded by the chapel-goers as entirely lost to them.

Of late years, too, Job seemed to have come so entirely under the dominion of the vice of greed, and was so constantly engaged in deep, tortuous schemes for his own enrichment, that his neighbours had ceased to give him credit for disinterestedness even in the smallest things, and his most innocent actions were suspiciously scrutinised, under the conviction that, when properly understood, they would be seen to be parts of some deep design for accomplishing a selfish end.

When Jabe, therefore, received the intelligence recorded above, it struck him exactly as it had struck the others; and so, after standing in the middle of the floor and gazing thoughtfully at Sam for a minute or more, he quietly dropped into a seat, and, setting his eloquent, short leg in rapid motion, stared first at Sam and then at Long Ben, as if in search of something in their faces that would give him a clue to this great mystery.

"He's happen come ta yer th' horgin," remarked Nathan at last.

Now, there was not a person in the company but believed that the new instrument was capable of even this miracle of attractiveness, especially as Job was an old bandsman, but after looking at the others for a while, Jabe shook his head, and the rest wagged theirs in reluctant rejection of the suggestion.

"Aw'll tell yo' wot it is," cried Lige after another pause, "he's cumin' efther Phebe Green; that's wot he's efther."

Several pairs of eyebrows were immediately raised, and Sam Speck was just about to make a remark evidently confirmatory of this view of the case, when Jabe, with his short leg moving at a frantic rate, interjected—

"Talk sense, Liger. Does a dog goa courtin' an owd cat efther he's worried wun of her kittlins?"

The elevated eyebrows dropped as Jabe began to speak, and were knitted into momentary frowns of perplexity as he proceeded, but when he had done every face was clear again, and it was evident that Lige's suggestion was held to be an impossibility, for Job had, many years before, badly jilted Mrs. Green's younger sister Lydia, and almost broken her heart, and since then Phebe, who was more like Lydia's mother than her sister, had regarded Job with feelings of intensest dislike.

From this point it became clear that Job's real reason for visiting the chapel would have to be given up, and so, as the cronies filled their pipes, and settled themselves round the parlour fire, the conversation turned upon the pig-dealer's character and life.

After two or three unimportant remarks, Sam Speck ventured to say, solemnly nodding his head—

"Ther's sum foak as is lost afoor they arr lost. An' Jooab's wun on 'em."

"Ther' worn't a dacenter young felley i' th' Clough when he wur a lad," said Ben gently.

"An' naa ther' isn't a *wur*," added Lige with grim conviction.

"Jooab," cried Jabe, rising from his seat and taking a "swig" at his "balm tay," "Jooab's tew men. Ther's a sawft-herted, common-sense, music-luvin' and welly religious Jooab, an' ther's a snakin', grindin', splitfardin' Jooab. An' wi' them tew—a—a—sperits feightin' togather i' wun skin, Jooab mun hev a ter'ble toime on it."

Now there was a gradual change in Jabe's tone as he delivered this summary of the pig-dealer's character. It went from sternness to apology, and from apology to sympathy as he proceeded, and so encouraged by the manifestation of a feeling something like his own, Long Ben broke in here.

Leaning forward in his chair and waving his pipe by way of emphasis, he said—

"If iver ther' wur an' owd hangil i' this wurld it wur that mon's muther."

"It wur that," murmured two or three together, and then there was an impressive pause, and each seemed busy with his own thoughts.

"Naa," said Lige at length, cocking his head at an argumentative angle, and evidently about to propound some abstruse problem, "has dun yo' mak' it aat, as owd saints loike Betsy hez sick childer as Jooab—an' he wur aw as hoo hed, tew? Besoide," he went on, as the position opened out before him, "his fayther wur a gradely good chap, tew."

Two or three sighed deeply, as if to show that they had often wrestled with the problem, but so far had reached no satisfactory solution.

"It's horidginal sin; that's wot it is," said Jabe sententiously. "Didn't Christ say as faythers 'ud be tewk fro' childer an' childer fro' payrunts at th' last day! An' it is soa."

"Thaa talks as if th' poor lad wur lost awready," said Long Ben, looking protestingly at his friend.

"Lost?" cried Jabe excitedly; "when a mon gets to fifty-five—an's gooin' wur ivery day—if he isna awtert he ne'er will be."

Ben turned and looked at the Clogger steadily with mingled reproach and indignation in his face, and then glancing away and leaning back in his chair, he said, in tones of slow, solemn conviction—

"Jooab Sharples 'ull dee a converted mon."

Every eye turned for a moment on this venturesome prophet, and then as quickly turned away from him, and as nobody spoke, Ben went on—

"Owd Betsy pruyed thaasands o' pruyers for her son, an' deed afoor her toime wi' meytherin' abaat him, an' as shure as there's a God aboon, them pruyers 'ull be answert."

One or two seemed impressed by the solemnity of Ben's manner, and appeared half inclined to believe his prophecy. Jabe himself shook his head, and of course Sam Speck did the same.

From this point, however, the conversation took a less interesting direction, stories of Job's meanness and hardness being related by one and another, and all seemed dubious about one or two instances of an opposite character related by Long Ben. Presently they worked themselves back to the starting-point, and once more speculated, but without success, on the reasons for Job's unexpected presence at the chapel.

On the following afternoon, as Jabe, not yet quite convalescent, sat musing and smoking in the inglenook, who should step into the shop but Job himself.

He had not been inside the Clog Shop for over twelve months, and Jabe thought as he glanced up at him that his visitor did not look quite as well as usual. There was a softness, somehow, about the red, sore eyes, and the face looked a trifle more pinched than usual.

He came into the shop somewhat timidly, but that was characteristic, and so the Clogger eyed him askance and waited for him to speak.

Job was evidently ill at ease. He took his snuff in a decidedly nervous manner, glanced uneasily round the shop, stole a sly look at Jabe as if doubtful of his reception, and then moving towards the inglenook, and hesitating at the edge of a seat, he said—

"Well, Aw yerd yond' horgin last neet."

So that after all was Job's reason for going to chapel. Jabe was a little disappointed, and answered gruffly—

"Th' horgin's reet enuff."

"Ay, an' hoo plays it weel," replied Job, with a little show of enthusiasm, and then he turned and glanced at a seat near him, as if waiting to be asked to occupy it.

The erstwhile schoolmistress's musical ability requiring no defence, Jabe leaned back against the chimney-jamb and stared steadily into vacancy.

Job made a movement as though he would sit down; but, changing his mind, he took another pinch of snuff and a sidelong glance at the owner of the shop. Would Jabe never ask him to sit? Evidently not.

The Clogger could not, or would not, see what his visitor wanted. But Job had come for a serious talk, and felt he could not open his mind until he got comfortably seated. So he turned and looked round again very significantly, but the Clogger would not respond.

Then he propped himself awkwardly against the inglenook and blew his snuffy nose. Then he resumed an upright attitude, took a step forward, picked up and began effusively to admire a pair of new clogs standing on the counter. But even this did not move the stolid Clogger, and at last Job, dropping his voice, as became the nature of his question, asked—

"Jabe, hast iver seen a boggart?"

The Clogger laughed a hard, contemptuous laugh. "Ay!" he cried, "Aw sees 'em ivery day."

"Ay, bur gradely boggarts—sperits, thaa knaaws."

"Aw knaaw nowt abaat 'em. It's tew-legged boggarts, wi' clugs on, as Aw'm bothert wi'."

Job took another cautious look round the shop, sighed a little, blew his nose again, picked up the short poker and tried to balance it on his finger, put it down carefully in the corner again, and then, leaning across and touching Jabe on the knee, he said, awesomely—

"Jabe, Aw sees 'em reglar."

The Clogger laughed again; but a gleam of curiosity shot into his eye, and turning his head the least bit round towards his visitor, he cried—

"Ay, ivery toime thaa leuks i' th' leukingglass, Aw reason."

"Jabe," replied Job solemnly, and ignoring his friend's mocking tone, "Aw sees 'em ivery wik, owd lad. Aw'm bewitched, an' it's killin' me."

By this time it was evident that Job was very much in earnest, and the Clogger, in spite of himself, was compelled to turn and look at his companion.

The man's face was drawn and white. His eyes had a frightened, appealing look in them, and dank moisture was beginning to gather on his forehead.

"Ger aat, thaa sawftyed! Whoa dust see?" answered the Clogger, with an odd blending of impatience and curiosity.

"Jabe, Aw sees—my—my—muther," and a choking sound like a smothered sob escaped the distressed man, and falling into a seat, he dropped his head into his hands and groaned.

"Thi muther! Well, tha'rt noa feart of her sure*li*?"

"Jabe, thaa knaaws wot a bonny sweet face hoo uset have."

"Well?"

"It's noa loike that naa; it's dark an' fearsome, an' it sets me aw of a whacker. An' Aw sweeats till th' bed swims."

Jabe felt almost tempted to tell his visitor that it served him right, but the poor fellow's face told such a tale of anguish that he could not find in his heart to do so, and so he sat looking thoughtfully before him without speaking,

"An,' Jabe," went on Job, in a pathetic voice little louder than a whisper, "Aw sees sumbry wur nor my muther."

Jabe looked up with a large note of interrogation on his face, but he never spoke.

"Whoa dust think Aw see, lad?"

"Th' owd lad?"

"Neaw; wur nor him, Jabe."

"Wur nor him? Thaa conna see nowt wur nor th' divil!"

"Aw dew, Jabe! Aw dew!" and Job shook his head with a weary, heartbroken moan.

"Whey! whoa th' ferrups const see wur nor him?" cried Jabe in amazement.

"Jabe,"—and here the speaker's voice became husky and thick with agitation,—"Aw sees Liddy."

Jabe felt a cold chill run down his spine, and he was bound to admit to himself that if he had acted as Job had acted towards Lydia Scholes, the appearance of her spirit to him would be more terrible than a visit from his satanic majesty, and so he sat staring before him with an amazed and dumbfounded look.

"Wot mun Aw dew, Jabe—wot mun Aw dew?"

Oh, what a sermon Jabe could have preached just then on the expensiveness of sin and the certainty of retribution. But for the life of him he could not compel himself to speak, and his long-pent-up anger with his hard, niggardly visitor was fast giving place to a feeling of deep pity. But Job was speaking again.

"My muther uset pray fur me, an' talk to me, an' coax me—hoo'd a laid daan her loife for me, an' naa hoo's turnt inta a fearsome boggart as freetens me loife aat, an' drives me maddlet. An' Liddy!—they'll kill me, Jabe, they'll kill me."

But Jabe could hold in no longer.

"It's thi conscience, mon; it's thi bad loife. Thaa mun repent, an' start o'doin' reet and give o'er scrattin' for brass, an' then th' boggarts 'ull leeav' thi. Nay, they winna leeav' thi; bud th' boggarts 'ull be turnt inta guardian angils, an', insteead o' scarrin' thi, they'll tak' cur on thi an' comfort thi."

Jabe having thus thawed at last, conversation became easy, and Job poured out the whole tale of his troubles to his companion, manifesting at one moment a desire to justify, or, at least, excuse himself, and the next accusing and condemning himself in unsparing terms as the author of much misery both to himself and others.

Presently, relieved and comforted by the conversation, he rose to go. When he reached the door he stood looking at and toying with the sneck for some time, and then turning back, he came to the fireplace again, and standing over the Clogger with fist clenched, and a face aflame with shame and bitter self-reproach, he cried—

"Dust knaaw wot hell is, Jabe? When a chap's badniss turns his blessed owd muther into a tormenting boggart, an' brings her aat o' heaven ta pester an' freeten him; an' when his sweetheart, as luved ivery hur o' his yed is driven aat of her restin'-place ta be a skriking ghooast tew him, that's hell. An' that's wheer Aw am."

And with a wild despairing gesture he fled from the shop.

II.

HOW THE BOGGARTS WERE LAID.

JOB SHARPLES lived in the first house in Beckside, on the same side of the road as the chapel, and about a hundred yards higher up the "broo." It was rather a large house for a solitary bachelor, being a good four-roomed structure, but old, and covered at both ends with ivy. It had narrow windows, a quaint porch, and a forlorn and neglected garden. The house had fallen into Job's hands some years before at a very low price, in consequence of the fact that old Tim Lindley, the original owner, had committed suicide in it, and a rumour, carefully encouraged after a while by the wily pig-dealer, had got afloat that Tim's ghost had been seen in it. At the sale nobody would bid, and so it fell into Job's hands at less than half its value. And as Jabe sat musing by the fire on all he had just heard, he could not but see in Job's recent experiences a strong confirmation of the doctrine of retribution in which he was so firm a believer.

It was well known in the village, too, that old Betsy Sharples had done her very best to wean her son from his grasping tendencies, and that when she failed she had solemnly declared to Job that his money would not only never bring him happiness, but would eventually work him earthly shame and suffering and eternal misery. And Jabe saw in Job's present condition a literal fulfilment of the old woman's prediction.

The heartless way, also, in which, after several years' courtship, he had jilted one of the sweetest girls in the neighbourhood could never be forgotten by any Becksider, especially as everyone knew that he gave poor Lydia up because he thought he saw a chance of marrying money, a chance that, after all, he missed. Poor broken-hearted Lydia, it was said, had, when goaded by Job's cold sneers, told him in a passion of tears that he had given her her death-blow, and that if she did die she would come back to him and spoil every pleasure he should ever have. And it was told, too, that after he had left her, Lydia had repented and gone after him to ask his pardon, and to tell him as long as she lived she would pray for him, and that after her death she would watch over him, for, living or dying, she could never do anything but love him.

Then Lydia, after wearing away almost to a skeleton, had left Beckside for a change of air, and since then, with the exception of her sister, Phebe Green, nobody knew what had become of her, and if Phebe knew, she never told. This was now nearly twenty years ago, and beyond a rumour that she had died in the Manchester Infirmary, nobody knew anything about her.

But, of course, as Jabe sat musing on these things by the fire, he realised that there could now be no doubt as to Lydia's whereabouts. If her ghost had appeared to the hardened Job, she must be dead, and that settled the matter. As he reflected on these things, his blood boiled with indignation at the pig-dealer's harshness towards his gentle sweetheart. But then, as he recalled Job's haggard face and wild, despairing looks, he melted again, and felt deeply sorry for the man.

That night he paid a visit to Job, and after trying to comfort the unhappy man, he preached him a very earnest and plain-spoken little sermon, exhorting him to mend his ways and return to chapel, and then perhaps the "boggarts" would trouble him no more. At the same time Jabe took care not to stay too long, for though he greatly honoured the two dead women, he had no desire to meet them again, especially in Job's company.

And Job seemed disposed to listen to his friend's counsel, and became most regular in his attendance at the chapel.

Then he took a pew—a whole pew—though there was nobody to occupy it but himself. His contributions to the collections were noticeably generous, and he began to put out feelers in the direction of returning to the band. At the same time he improved visibly in health, and appeared passably cheerful, spending at least one night a week at the Clog Shop fire. But after a little time less satisfactory signs began to show themselves. He sub-let part of the pew he had taken, began to give coppers again at the collections, and was commonly reported to have dealt in the old harsh fashion with a tenant who was behind with her rent.

Two or three times Jabe attacked him about these signs of lapsing, and told him again and again that half-measures would not do, and that a man like him must be everything or nothing. But Job apparently took no notice, and was evidently fast returning to his old hard ways, when one morning, before the Clogger was up, he presented himself at the Clog Shop, and with wild eyes and pallid cheeks, and hands that shook when he tried to use them, he cried as he met the Clogger at the foot of the stairs—

"Jabe, Jabe, they've bin ageean!"

"Didn't Aw tell thi!" cried the Clogger. "They're sewer ta come; tha'll ha' noa peace till thaa turns o'er gradely."

"Bud Aw hev turnt o'er! Aw come ta th' chapil reglar, an' Aw gees i' th' c'llection, an"' —

"Wot's that?" shouted Jabe with disdainful impatience. "Tha'll ha' ta turn o'er gradely, an' goa ta th' penitent form, an' jine th' class, an' give o'er money-grubbin', an' mak' it up ta them as tha's chizelled, an' be a gradely Christian."

"Chizelled! Aw hevna— Aw shanna ha' ta pay back, shall Aw?" And Job opened his mouth, and gazed at the Clogger with surprise and terror in his eyes.

"If thaa wants peace wi' God an' th' boggarts, tha'll ha' ta undew aw th' herm tha's done, as fur as thaa con," reiterated Jabe emphatically, for he realised that no half-measures would suffice with the pig-dealer.

Job sat for a long time after this, moaning and groaning, and evidently hard hit indeed. Nobody ever charged him with real dishonesty, but he himself knew how much there was in his life that would require to be undone, if this was the only condition on which he could have rest; and as his memory brought back to him case after case of hard dealing and mean trickery, he writhed on his seat in remorse and fear.

Presently he rose to his feet.

"Aw darr na sleep i' yond' haase anuther neet! Aw darr na! Hay, dear! Wot *mun* Aw dew?"

Then he left, and during the day Jabe obtained temporary lodgings for the miserable man. The following Sunday there were two large pieces of silver in the collection-box, and Job even stayed to the Sunday night prayer-meeting.

Then he took to frequenting the Clog Shop nearly every day, and adopted such a humble and conciliatory tone towards those who usually gathered there, that they soon made him feel at home amongst them, and missed him when he was absent. He began also to recover his health and lightness of spirit.

And so two months passed on, and though Jabe still held stoutly to his contention that Job would never get peace until he "gan in gradely," yet he was fain to acknowledge that there was an immense improvement in his pupil all round.

Amongst other things, Job had tried to get upon good terms with Phebe Green, the mangle-woman, and elder sister of his old-time sweetheart, Lydia. But though he was very persistent and patient, Phebe would have nothing to do with him, and repelled all his advances with cold and undisguised suspicion.

By this time it had got well on into autumn, and the Clog Shop fire had a large circle of visitors round it every night.

One evening Job was missing, and though it was known that he had gone to Lamb Fold to "stick a pig" early in the afternoon, no one knew whether he had returned or not.

Two or three of the early birds had departed, and Jabe, Sam, and Long Ben were seated deep in the inglenook, the flickering chip fire fitfully lighting up their faces as they discussed the approaching Christmas festivities.

Suddenly there was a dull, heavy thud at the door, and then, as they looked alarmedly at each other, all was still again. It was too late for boyish tricks. What could it be?

"Wot th' ferrups is that?" cried Sam in startled tones. But though they all held their breath, and listened, nobody answered. Presently Jabe rose to his feet, and limped cautiously towards the door. He stood a moment to look at it. It was still fast, and nothing unusual could be seen.

Then he jerked the door open and stepped back, partly to avoid any sudden attack, and partly to get the advantage of the light. Nothing could be seen, but, as he was about to take a step forward, a heavy groan came from somewhere near the door, and Jabe jumped back in a fright.

Sam and Ben came gingerly up to his side, and stood looking in the direction of Jabe's gaze.

Another groan! and evidently very near. Then Jabe, whose scepticism on the subject of boggarts was being severely shaken, thought he saw something dark on the ground inside the outer door.

He drew a deep sigh, glanced awesomely around, assured himself that his companions were still by his side, and was just putting forward his short leg, when a woeful voice wailed out piteously—

"Aw've seen 'em ageean, Jabe. Ageean! Ageean!"

Now the Clogger had kept Job's secret perfectly, and neither Sam nor Ben knew anything of what had happened. So with frightened starts they stepped back, and looked with scared faces at Jabe.

That worthy returned their look with interest, and then, snatching at the only candle that was burning, he brought it forward, and, stooping down, peered earnestly at the heap behind the door. There, all huddled together, lay the unhappy Job.

"Save me, Jabe! Save me, fur God's sake!" he cried. "Aw've seen 'em ageean."

Jabe turned round, put the candle on the little counter, laid down his expired pipe, and then going forward, gripped the miserable Job by the back of his coat-collar, raised him slowly to his feet, and led him into the dim light.

Job had a bruise on his forehead, and his nose was bleeding a little, whilst his face was white and haggard.

"Wotiver's to dew wi' thi, lad?" cried the Clogger.

But Job's head dropped upon his chest, and staggering towards the fire, he fell heavily into a seat. Then bending forward and propping his head upon his hands, he burst into a cry and sobbed as if his heart would break.

It eventually transpired that he had been to Lamb Fold, and was returning home after dark, thinking of anything except his recent troubles, when suddenly, just as he got down the Clough "bonk," and stepped upon the cinder path along the Beckside, there—right before him—stood the two ghostly forms he had learned to fear so much.

Maddened and desperate, Job went from fear to frenzy, and darted recklessly at the spectres, and as they vanished before him, he fell headlong into the Beck, bruising his face on a stone, and getting his clothes soaked with muddy water.

How he scrambled out and got into Shaving Lane he was never able to tell, and he had not much more idea as to how he had reached the Clog Shop.

As he sat there, wet and bruised, and almost ghastly, he would have been a heartless man who had not pitied him. Everything that could be done to soothe and relieve him was done. Jabe found him some old clothes, and insisted on his changing his wet garments. Long Ben slipped off to fetch some of his wife's famous coltsfoot wine, to which was added a few drops of a mysterious mixture of magical power, concocted by little Eli—rumour said in the dead of night—and called by him "Number Seven," which had never been known to fail in casting off the effects of a chill if taken in time. Sam, with a little rag and warm water, carefully washed the unfortunate man's wound, preparatory to applying a green wax plaster—also the invention of the aforesaid little Eli.

But even when these things were accomplished, Job seemed ill at ease. His eyes wandered wildly about the room; he started violently at every sound; and when it was mildly suggested that he should go to his lodgings and sleep, he became terribly alarmed, and utterly refused to go anywhere by himself.

Ultimately it was decided that he should sleep with the Clogger, but as he was still too excited to rest, he sat cowering by the fire, whilst Jabe related to Ben and Sam all that was necessary to enable them to understand the case. The two stayed until a very late hour, and when they had departed, and Jabe had administered another dose of coltsfoot wine and "Number Seven," he put the still excited man to bed, and lay down by his side.

Next morning there was a solemn consultation at the Clog Shop. Sam Speck, having seen Ben going into that establishment, came hurrying across the road from his own cottage, with the remains of his breakfast in his hand, and a great idea struggling for an opportunity of expressing itself in his mind.

As Sam entered, Jabe was just finishing his account of the weary night he had spent with Job, who had at last dropped off into sleep and must not on any account be awakened.

"An' Aw'll tell thy, summat," said the Clogger in conclusion, and looking with earnest conviction at Long Ben; "if they' isna a hawteration afoor lung, they'll be anuther mon fur th' 'sylum."

"Poor felley," said Ben softly; "hedn't thaa better send fur th' doctor?"

"It's a soul-doctor an' not a body-doctor as *he* wants," replied Jabe.

This was Sam's opportunity. Crowding the last piece of buttered oatcake hastily into his mouth, and thrusting his head in between his two friends, he swallowed the food, and said at last—

"If yo' tew han owt abaat yo', yo'll cure him yorsel's."

But Jabe was in no mood for trifling.

"Wot's th' lumpyed meytherin' abaat naa," he cried, casting a withering look at Sam, and limping off into the parlour to listen at the foot of the stairs, and ascertain whether Job were still sleeping.

Sam waited, secure in his confidence in his great idea, until Jabe came back, and then putting on a look of greatest gravity, and using his forefinger to emphasise what he was saying, he asked—

"Yo' tew's th' yeds o' th' church, arna yo'?"

"Well, wot bi that?"

"Well, doesn't th' owd Beuk say as th' elders is ta cast aat divils?"

"Thaa doesn't caw Liddy an' Owd Betsy divils, sure*li?*"

"Neaw; bud they're boggarts, an' that's th' same thing?"

"Well, o' aw th' bletherin' leatheryeds—Sithi'! Aw wodna cast 'em aat if Aw could! They're dewin' him good, mon! Mooar good nor they iver did woll they wur wik. They're savin' his sowl, mon."

"Well, they're takkin' a rough wey o' dewin' it, that's aw as Aw hev' ta say."

"We met hev' a bit of a pruyer-meetin' fur him, at ony rate," suggested Ben quietly; but just then Job began to stir about upstairs, and Jabe hurried off to attend to him, and the other two departed, Sam still confident that his plan for Job's recovery was the only likely one.

A day or two later the suggested prayer-meeting was held, Job himself being present, and responding very loudly to every petition at all applicable to his particular case. And whether it was the prayer-meeting, or the influence of his own fears, or both combined, sure enough Job was at the penitent form on the following Sunday night.

It was a long and desperate struggle, and when the after-meeting broke up about half-past nine at night, though Job declared that he felt a "foine soight leeter," the professional judges of this kind of thing could scarcely be said to be satisfied, and Jabe voiced the feelings of more than one when he said—

"He'll tak' noa harm fur being i' pickle a bit."

From that time, however, there was a very marked change in the poor pig-dealer. He joined Jabe's class, bought a new fiddle, and assisted the band at the Christmas tea-party, reduced the rents of several of his poorer tenants, and gratified the housewives living on his property so thoroughly in the matter of repairs and fresh wall-paper, that they became loud in his praises, and declared that he was "gradely convarted."

Then he had the cheap little tombstone on his mother's grave replaced by a marble one with gold lettering, the only one of its kind in the chapel-yard, and Jabe and his friends were divided between intense pride and delight in the new stone, and misgivings as to whether Job was not "showing off."

Then he gave up what remained to him of his original business, and made it over to a former assistant who was poor and struggling. So great, in fact, was the change in him that the very children noticed it, and the harsh, unsympathetic old pig-dealer and landlord became a popular favourite with them.

But perhaps the most remarkable of all his achievements was his success with Phebe Green. He not only got on speaking terms with her, but, by obtaining a situation for little Jacky in Duxbury, he seemed quite to have won the mother over, and became so intimate with her that he was once caught by Sam Speck actually turning the mangle; and as Job's amorous disposition was well known, it was confidently predicted that it would "end up in a weddin'."

Early in the following spring Job ventured to go back and live in his own cottage; and as he was growing visibly stouter and younger-looking, it was concluded that he had effectually got rid of his gruesome visitors.

Then he began to "fettle up" his house. He had large new windows put in the front. The outhouses were repaired, and Lige, who seemed to have taken the pig-dealer under his special protection, spent much of his time assisting him to weed and restore the long-neglected garden. And, of course, no stronger confirmation could be given of the idea that Job was going to marry the mangle-woman.

And Phebe's conduct seemed to give further support to this view. She certainly no longer shunned her old-time enemy; and when quizzed about him, she laughed in a very significant sort of way, and said in her own peculiar manner that "them as lives th' lungest 'ull see th' mooast."

Of course Job himself did not escape chaff on the subject, and those who treated him to it were encouraged by the discovery that he rather seemed to like it. For years he had been hankering after a wife, but hitherto his preference had always been given to women "wi' an owd stockin'," and in those days he probably never even thought of Phebe. She was poor, and had four children, one of whom was an invalid, but more than all he knew that the motherly sister of his old sweetheart, Lydia, would have scorned him in spite of his money.

But now everything was changed. He could help a brave woman who was making an heroic struggle. Her children with his money behind them would make something out; and, helping her, Job would be helping himself to popular appreciation, a thing he greatly coveted in these latter days. And, besides all this, to help Phebe was about the only means left to him of making atonement for his conduct to the gentle Lydia.

Job did not conceal from himself, either, that Phebe, though proud and close, was a clever, managing woman, and would be a great help to him in the plans he had formed for the future.

All these things, therefore, made the village talk very pleasant to Job, and he redoubled his efforts to ingratiate himself into Phebe's favour.

For four months now he had seen no "boggarts," and declared almost every day at the Clog Shop that he had never known what life was until now.

One evening in the early summer, after a hard day's work in his garden, he had seated himself on the little side-seat in the porch at the front of his house, and with a pot of nettle-beer at one side of him and his snuff-box in his hand was musing on his future, and his possible chances of winning Phebe. The look on his face told plainly how pleasant were his thoughts. The air was laden with the scent of wallflowers and early roses, and musical with the songs of the birds. All nature seemed to smile upon him, and as he looked around at the bright flowers and white-blossomed hedges, he heaved a great sigh of contentedness, and murmured softly—

"Hay! God's good! God's varry good!"

As Job sat musing thus, a woman stole out of the mangle-house at the bottom of the village, and, turning into Shaving Lane, crossed the stile, and began climbing slowly up the hill towards the Duxbury Road. She was of about medium height, with small regular features, soft dark eyes, and a clear white skin. Evidently she was about thirty-seven years of age, and a fair example of that type of Lancashire woman who is fairer at forty than at twenty.

She looked a little nervous and preoccupied, and every now and again a soft warm light rose into her eyes and made her face look tender and sweet.

When she got over the stile into the road, a little above Job's house, she paused and glanced rather anxiously about her. Then she sought the shelter of the high hedge, and stole quietly down towards the cottage with her heart beating almost into her mouth.

When she got close to the house she stopped, and after looking cautiously around again, she bent her head, and peeping through the hedge, caught sight of Job sitting in the porch.

Her eyes suddenly filled with tears, tears all shining with the light of a joy that was almost holy.

She put her hand on her beating heart, and sighed, and then bent down and peeped again—a good, careful look this time.

Then she took a step nearer, and touched the gate with a hand that trembled so that it shook.

"Job!"

The musing pig-dealer started with a terrified cry. The colour left his face. He rose to his feet hastily, and opened his mouth to shriek, but just then the gate clanked, and in another moment two soft plump arms were thrown around him, a hot tearful face was laid against his, and a low eager voice cried-

"Bless thi, lad! Aw knowed tha'd cum reet! God *does* answer pruyer! Bless thi! Bless thi, lad!"

"Liddy! Liddy!!" cried Job, almost beside himself. "It's no' thee! Tha'rt no' wik! Hay, wench! W-e-n-c-h." And Job folded his arms around his long-lost love, and hugged her to his heart.

Yes, it was Lydia. She had not died after all, but had been in service in London, and kept up secret communication with her sister Phebe. She had waited in prayerful faith and hope all these years, and at last, at her sister's instigation, had come home to her heart's only love.

And there they sat in the little porch, laughing and crying together, and making mutual confessions and vows for a happier future, and as the sun dropped behind Wardle Hill and the birds ceased their songs, poor Job at last found peace and all the wealth of a woman's unwearying love.

Lightning Source UK Ltd.
Milton Keynes UK
25 November 2009

146716UK00002B/125/P